AZURI FAE

INDIA
DRUMMOND

Azuri Fae

Editing by LJ Sellers

Second edition published in the United Kingdom 2013 by India Drummond

ISBN-13: 978-1492226680
ISBN-10: 1492226688

Author contact:
http://www.indiadrummond.com/

Acknowledgements

First and foremost, thank you to Bear: my son, my friend, and always my first choice of brainstorming and storytelling companions. He kept me on track and sparked my imagination, all the while not letting me stray and demanding that I be true to my inner voice.

Thanks also to my beta readers: Marsha, Patti, and Colin. You help me catch those little errors that elude me when I'm wrapped up in my faerie world.

Once again, I owe a huge debt to Inspector Dorian Marshall of the Tayside Police. His red pen kept me true, and I so appreciate the time he devoted to correcting any factual mistakes, not to mention my unintentional abuse of the Queen's English. Any errors in police policy or procedure are completely my own.

Fae Name Pronunciation Guide

In order of appearance:

Eilidh: AY-lee
Saor: SAY-or
Imire: em-IRE
Teasair: TES-air
Cadhla: KY-lah
Eithne: AE-nyuh
Griogair: Gree-GAIR
Tràth: TRATH
Riddich: RID-ick
Qwe: KWAY
Flùranach: FLOO-ran-ak
Reine: RAH-nay
Sennera: seh-NAYR-ah
Mira: MEE-rah
Zdanye: ZDAH-nie
Dalyna: dah-LEE-nuh
Juliesse: ZHU-lee-ESS
Conwrey: KON-ray
Cane: KAYN
Frene: FREN
Vinye: VEN-yay
Setir: SEHT-eer

CHAPTER 1

SARAH MCBRIDE DUG HER ELBOW into her husband's side. "There's someone outside, Hamish."

"It's just a cat. Go back to sleep." He started snoring again almost immediately.

"That wasn't a cat I heard. Go see who it is." She lay still in bed, hands shaking, afraid to breathe. Someone prowling around outside, and that great oaf of a husband was sleeping through it. Probably a pack of teenagers come to steal their telly for drug money. They might even come in and tie them both up.

Sarah swallowed and squeezed her eyes tight together. Hamish might not care, but she wasn't about to lie there and let a roving band of hooded teens catch her unawares. They'd probably try to do unspeakable things to her. It had been twenty years since she'd been attacked in a pub in Dundee, and she had been young and stupid then, out drinking...alone. She wasn't some vulnerable girl now. This time she would fight back.

"Hamish!" she hissed one last time with a sharp jab to his middle.

He sat up in the darkness, his tone barely civil. "It was just a dream. Now leave me to sleep. I have to get up in the morning." Hamish rolled over, heaving his bulk onto his side, bouncing the mattress. "You'll be the death of me, woman," he mumbled into his pillow.

"Fine. I'll do it." Sarah got up and wrapped her dressing gown around her, tying it at the front. A crash in the side yard halted her progress. She glanced toward the front room, where the house phone sat in its charger. She wanted to call 999, get the police out to look. But if they came, they'd wake Hamish. If it did turn out to be nothing, she'd never hear the end of it. Best to make sure, then call.

She crept down the hall in the pitch black. Her heart pounded so loudly she almost couldn't hear the intruders. She cursed her fear. She'd never wanted to feel this way again. Hamish couldn't understand that. He was a hulking man who'd never felt intimidated by someone else's size. Pausing in the hallway to collect herself, she caught sight of the gun cabinet in the spare room. It tempted her, but she decided against getting out one of Hamish's shotguns. Until, that is, she heard the rattle of the side gate, followed by footsteps on the path. Sarah rushed to the drawer where Hamish kept the cabinet keys. So what if his shotgun certificate was expired? If it saved their lives, she didn't care.

Anyway, she only wanted to scare them. After she retrieved the gun, she slipped a couple of shells into her dressing gown pocket. Just in case.

It took all her courage to tiptoe down the hall, the open shotgun folded over her left arm, ready to receive the shells. How Hamish could sleep through this, she didn't know, but anger burned inside her.

By the time she made it to the kitchen window and peeled back the blinds, her fear and anger had combined into a pulsing rush of adrenaline. Nobody would hurt her again.

A faint blue light came from the back garden, and shadowy figures stole around in the darkness. With trembling hands, Sarah slipped two shells into the back of the double barrel and snapped the gun closed. She knew better than to rush out with a gun that wasn't ready to go. They'd only take it away and turn it on her.

She noticed her mobile on the kitchen counter. The phone went into her pocket. Again, just in case. She turned the deadbolt, unlocked the back door, and walked onto the steps. The cold winter air made her shiver. "I…" Sarah cleared her throat and spoke louder. "I know you're out there. Clear off, you lot." She heard her voice as though it was someone else's.

The motion at the back of the garden stopped. "Come out where I can see you," she shouted, "Before I start shooting."

She held the stock of the gun in her left hand and with her right, reached into her pocket to get her mobile. Three figures slowly emerged. It was hard to make out their faces, but one might have been a girl. They looked young, but Sarah knew teenagers were the worst. She'd heard about an old man that was killed by a gang of them, just because he'd complained about their loud music. They'd kicked him to death on his own doorstep.

Sarah tapped the nine button on her mobile three times, hands shaking from the cold and adrenaline.

"Emergency Services. Which service do you require? Police, Fire, Ambulance?"

"I've got burglars," Sarah said. "Three of 'em."

She heard a brief pause, then another voice came on the line. The smooth voice of a young woman. "Tayside Police. This is Alison. What's your address?"

Sarah had to think. Why could she suddenly not think? "Eighty-two...

Suddenly, a man rushed her from the side. She hadn't realised there were more. She spun and pointed the shotgun at him, dropping her mobile. Fumbling to put her finger on the trigger, she looked at her hand for just a moment.

The man moved fast, like a neon blur in the night. Her vision went funny, and she had difficulty focusing her eyes. How many were there? She couldn't tell anymore. Four? Even more? Blood rushed through her veins.

"What in the name of hell is going on out here?" Hamish shouted from the doorway, startling her.

"Sarah?" He sounded shocked, then serious. "Sarah, come into the house. Just step back to me, love."

A distant and monotonously calm voice came from the phone, which had nestled in the Barberry bush. "What is your location, madam?"

Sarah didn't turn to look at her husband. It was cold and wet, and fear kept her frozen to the spot. She kept her eye on the man who stood mere feet from her now. She couldn't look away. He had the strangest eyes. They shone in the dark.

She tensed and her hands started to shake. Yet, despite the strange commotion around her, the young man held her attention. She felt peculiar, as though moving in slow motion.

Sarah stepped back toward Hamish, but her husband didn't speak nor move. She glanced around wildly, realising everything had stopped dead. Everything but her and this man. Her breaths sounded loud in the stillness. She could see the other faces in the garden clearly now, as well as a bright glow that had suddenly appeared.

"You," she said, doing her best to steady the shotgun as she raised it to point at his chest. "You get on out of here and take your friends with you. Hurry now. I don't want to shoot you." Her voice raised to a hysterical pitch. "Eighty-two Fordyce Way," she yelled at the Barberry bush. "See?" she said. "The police are on their way. Just go. I don't want trouble. You've got time to get out." She couldn't shake the strange feeling. The other burglars had frozen in place, and Hamish stood unnaturally still in the doorway.

"Time?" he said with a sad laugh. His accent sounded so strange. Probably some immigrant. "That's *all* I've got."

With a pop, a blue flash blinded her, and the last thing she felt was her finger squeezing the trigger.

∞

One week earlier...

"Ah, child, you look tired," Imire said, holding the gate open for his daughter Eilidh.

She stepped into his garden and sank into an oak chair he'd carved with his own hands. In addition to being a scholar, Imire was a true artisan. The canopy of green overhead revealed the glow of starlight. "Life has become complicated." She sighed. "I never understood humans before, thinking they were silly little ants, running around, rushing and using words like *complicated*." A wry smile curled her lips.

"I'm so glad you're back." Imire had aged greatly over the twenty-five years Eilidh had been exiled. Her crime had been simply to be what had come to be called an *azuri fae*, named after the Father of the Azure, who granted a few of her people the ability to cast the Path of Stars. The talent had been forbidden in the kingdom for a millennium. Like all other azuri fae, Eilidh had been sentenced to death. Her father risked everything and used his position as a priest to help her escape. A twist of fate allowed her to return to her homeland six months earlier, but her homecoming didn't yet feel real. She shied away from those who would treat her as a hero, preferring to visit her father privately in the quiet of his home, rather than seek the attention of those who wanted to make a fuss.

Eilidh inhaled deeply, drinking in the scent of the Otherworld. She spent most of her time in the human realm on the Isle of Skye, studying, practising, learning what she should have mastered a hundred years ago when she was a little girl. But she made the point to see her father when she could. If she let them, the azuri fae on Skye would have her learning incantations day and night. She looked around, watching fireflies appear and then vanish in the darkness. "It feels strange to me now. Everything is so familiar, and yet..."

"Give it time. Within a year, it will be as though you never left. Maybe if you spent a few months or even a few weeks here with me. Rest. Heal. You've gone through so much."

Eilidh smiled at her father. He was too wise a faerie to believe she was not changed forever by her experience, but she could feel him willing her to be happy. "I can't stay," she said. "Not yet."

With a sigh, Imire nodded. "I wish I had known about the azuri colony a hundred years ago. If I had sent you there as a child, so much grief could have been avoided."

"Wasn't it you who used to say there was no good done by dwelling on the past?"

Imire chuckled. For a moment he looked younger, his face less haggard and drawn. "I did indeed. However, the older I get, the more difficult it is to take my own advice. I have more memories than I once did, you know." He brushed a speck off his long green robes. "But let us talk and eat and enjoy the hours we have left before sunrise. Then stay the day, sleep under the sun in the tallest bough like you did as a little girl."

She opened her mouth to answer when a uniformed faerie strode through the gate. The fae did not observe the same rules of privacy humans did, and Eilidh noticed even the fae of Skye had adopted more human ways. They still kept to the night and slept during the day, but they had box-like houses and doors that locked. So it startled her to see an unannounced visitor invading their private conversation. She was doubly surprised by the uniform that identified him as a royal servant.

The young and handsome faerie had gleaming golden hair braided down his back. He addressed Imire with a slight incline of his head. "I am Teasair. I have a message for Eilidh, daughter of Imire and Eithne."

Imire nodded. "Welcome. May I offer you refreshment?"

The messenger slipped his hand inside his cornflower-blue doublet and produced a small coin-like token, carved into complex scrollwork around an ancient rune. He held it out to Eilidh, who stared.

"A summons?" she said in disbelief.

The messenger inclined his head politely. "Queen Cadhla requests your presence."

Eilidh stood and accepted the small disc, which fit into the palm of her hand. The queen's sigil thrummed with earth magic.

Imire raised an eyebrow. "In all my years, I've never met the queen. I've only caught glimpses of her from a distance. This is quite an honour."

Eilidh paused in worried silence. The queen was notoriously reclusive, but that seemed to be what people expected. She was a distant, almost symbolic figure in Eilidh's mind, more of an emblem than a person. "Of course," she finally managed to say. "I will attend. At what hour?" She glanced at the stars above, gauging the time before sunrise.

"Now," Teasair said, gesturing toward the door.

"I need time to prepare. I am not suitably dressed." Eilidh's mind whirled. She had no idea what to wear. She had little fae clothing left after her long exile, only what she'd left behind a quarter century ago. Most of it suitable for a child, not a woman past the century mark of adulthood. At the moment, she wore the human clothing she'd worn during her exile: jeans and a hooded sweatshirt. All the fae on Skye dressed similarly and even cast illusions to disguise any distinctively fae features, such as twisted ears, so they would blend into the human realm. They lived apart from the humans, in a small village populated only by their own kind. Away from the Otherworld, though, they were ever cautious.

"Queen Cadhla realises the suddenness of the summons, and along with the entire kingdom, celebrates the sacrifices you made on behalf of our people. Her Majesty will no doubt be most forgiving of any slight lapse in protocol that might, on any other day, cause offense." He said it with mild disdain, as though Eilidh should be grateful the queen extended such understanding.

Eilidh glanced at her father, who nodded. She had no choice. One did not refuse a summons from the faerie queen or delay when ordered to appear immediately. "The Halls of Mist?"

"No," Teasair said, leading Eilidh through the gate. "Her Majesty is in residence at Eirlioc Falls in the North." Once out of earshot of Imire, he lowered his voice. "She will be well protected. One whiff of the Path of Stars, and you will be cut down where you stand." His tone held menacing promise.

Eilidh bristled. "I am no threat to anyone, least of all the queen." She held the messenger's gaze, refusing to look away as he stared into her eyes.

He blinked slowly, a subtle gesture of acknowledgement, one so slight, a human would not have understood the exchange. Eilidh's thoughts went to Quinton Munro as she and the messenger set off on a slow lope north through the Otherworld. She wanted to show her bonded druid this place, but not until she could promise him safety. She didn't know if a human had ever set foot in the fae realm and lived to tell of it. But it was home, as much a part of her as Perth, Scotland was of him.

Although the time of exile had led to a sense of alienation from her kinsmen, when she breathed in the magic of the kingdom, she felt whole again. The pair jogged through mighty trees that reached hundreds of feet into the air. In many ways, the forests of the Otherworld were similar to the forests of the Scottish highlands, with towering pines and a soft floor of moss and fallen evergreen needles. The differences, although subtle, meant no faerie could wander outside the Otherworld and not keenly feel the loss. The faerie realm had vibrancy and colour, a strength that made the human world seem dead by comparison.

Besides lacking the unpredictable and untameable weather that haunted the human realm, in the Otherworld, magic swirled like mist, touching every plant and creature. Humans were clever with their machines—held in disdain by the fae—but Eilidh had come to appreciate industry in her time among the humans. But even the smallest things had great beauty in the Otherworld, where raindrops shone like diamonds. The human world could feel grey, lifeless, and empty.

After a short, moderately paced run of a few hours, the messenger stopped atop a hill and gestured ahead to a gap in the trees. Eilidh stepped forward and looked into the valley. Just beyond a low, snow-blanketed landscape, Eirlioc Falls rose like a towering flow of ice, carved into granite mountains beyond. Although she'd seen many wonders in her lifetime, this astounded her. Tall white spires rose into the northern sky, reflecting luminous blue moonglow.

She smiled at Teasair. "Thank you for showing me this moment of great beauty."

He tilted his head, as though uneasy with her gratitude. "Come. Queen Cadhla does not wait easily." They trotted down the hill and joined a main road, where many fae walked slowly to and from Eirlioc Falls. Eilidh's human clothing and short-cropped hair caught a few glances, but otherwise, no one paid them any attention.

On close inspection, the falls were even larger than they had appeared from the hilltop. They were not true ice, but carved from brilliant white stone. Eilidh could detect no seams or a single tool mark on the surface. The entrance was wide and open, with no visible doors or barriers. Eilidh knew this to be a deception. The queen would be well protected, as Teasair had remarked so pointedly. Eilidh could not imagine any of the kingdom wishing harm to their queen. Loyalty to her was loyalty to the Caledonian kingdom itself. However, theirs was not the only kingdom in the world. In fact, it was a small one. Peace had been kept during Eilidh's lifetime, but her father had known wars in centuries past.

As they moved into a wide courtyard, Teasair motioned for Eilidh to follow him up pure white steps softened by an ice-blue tapestry. She hated to tread on something so beautiful. As they climbed several winding staircases and proceeded down long pathways through the high-walled but open-topped corridors, her thoughts returned, as they often did, to Quinton Munro. The human druid was part of her now, their minds joined through ancient magic, making him literally difficult to forget. Because of that bond, her magical powers had increased many times over. She could now learn the earth magic kingdom faeries knew naturally, but was difficult for azuri fae. His presence, heavy and pulsing, filled a corner of her mind. Along with his happiness, his pain, grief, or even flashes of jealousy that spiked from time to time, causing a distraction she had not yet learned to cope with since the bonding put them in touch with each other's emotions. Despite the difficulty, she also felt his love. He was so unlike the calculating fae. The intensity of his primal emotions shook her to the core.

Her thoughts had wandered, and she was startled when she realised they had arrived at an immense chamber. The arched entryway opened onto a curved promenade, which led to a dais raised twenty feet above.

As Eilidh and Teasair travelled, the darkest part of the night passed, but the canopy of stars still sparkled overhead. The blue-cast moon illuminated the room. On the dais sat a woman who could only be the queen. Dressed in a filmy gown of iridescent white, she watched the approaching pair with interest, then turned to whisper to a tall faerie who stood behind her. She glowed with power.

Eilidh walked beside Teasair half way up the promenade. He paused and bowed, and she dipped into a low curtsy. The movement felt awkward, but she could no longer bow or salute as she might have done in her days as a kingdom Watcher. They stayed that way, immobile, until the room grew silent and voices in the chamber stilled. The queen said, "Rise and come forward," her voice clear, with a soft, haunting tone.

The pair rose and Teasair spoke. "Queen Cadhla, may I present Eilidh, daughter of Imire and Eithne, born of the Caledonian kingdom and follower of the Path of Stars."

A murmur went up in the room at the mention of her forbidden talents. Eilidh fought the urge to cast a glare at Teasair, who had said it as a warning to all in the chamber, to brand her as dangerous before the court.

"Thank you, Teasair," the queen snapped. "You may go." She turned her brilliant blue eyes on Eilidh, taking in her appearance, as though evaluating every nuance. "Eilidh, come forward. We wish to speak with you."

"Yes, Your Majesty." Eilidh walked up the ovoid steps that led to the dais.

Something about the faerie queen would not let Eilidh look away as she approached. She was vaguely aware of the man dressed in black, who stood behind the queen, and the many others in the chamber: bodyguards, advisors, courtiers, attendants, servants, and those whose roles she could not guess. But even with the crowd of unfamiliar faeries, Eilidh's eyes were locked on this unbearably beautiful creature, seated on a swing that appeared to be carved out of glass. It hung in the air, supported by nothing, swaying slightly, as though a breeze blew through the room even though the air remained still.

Finally, when she ascended the last step and stood only feet from the queen, the heavy compulsion to meet the queen's eyes lifted, and Eilidh dropped her gaze to the floor. "Your Majesty," she said.

"The decision to lift your sentence of death was that of the conclave," the queen said. "I, on the other hand, am unconvinced. Your past actions have been both devious and violent."

Eilidh stayed motionless, eyes down. She could think of no response, so she kept her silence.

"However, let it not be said that I am without mercy. Of your own accord, you dispatched a menace who, by all accounts, fancied himself worthy of this throne." The queen laughed sharply, sending an echo through the immense room. "For ten thousand years, my family has ruled this kingdom. I wonder why this blood faerie of yours considered he had the power to break that trend." When Eilidh did not immediately reply, the queen added, "You may speak."

Eilidh took her time formulating an answer. It would not do to insult every faerie present with an idea they would consider unthinkable. Yet she had little choice but to offer the truth. "Although it pains me to say it, it became clear to me that the one of which you speak suffered greatly in his ability to reason."

"Insane? Are the fae so weak of mind that they could succumb to this human malady?" The queen scoffed, and an uncomfortable titter of laughter went up around the chamber.

Eilidh looked up. “It is difficult to contemplate, but the ritual this dark faerie sought to perform, of which the conclave has implored me to say little, exacted a terrible price. I saw this with my own eyes. He killed for pleasure, even murdering his own father. He spoke with phantoms from his past and said little that was rational.”

“And would this…impaired faerie, do you think, have been a threat to the royal house?” The queen smirked, twisting her glossy red lips with disdain.

“Yes,” Eilidh said, silencing all onlookers.

Fury flashed in the queen’s brilliant blue eyes. “You believe a deficient faerie could challenge the throne, Eilidh, daughter of Imire and Eithne?”

A thrum of magic swirled around the queen. Eilidh had to summon every ounce of her courage to continue. “Your Majesty, the blood faerie was deficient in reason, but not in power. With little effort, he dispatched four strong kingdom Watchers and another of the azure, an elder and master of astral powers. The dark ritual could have increased his power ten-fold, had he succeeded in his efforts.”

The queen leaned forward. “And yet *you* defeated him.” The unspoken question hung in the air: If he had been powerful enough to challenge the throne, did Eilidh think she could do the same?

“I was fortunate to survive.”

“And modest too, it seems. I understand this elder deemed you to have considerable power.”

How had she learned that? Beniss, the elder faerie, would not have said that to anyone she did not trust. "I am young and barely trained, Your Majesty. I believe she sought to bolster my confidence, considering what we faced."

The queen sat in silence for a long time, making Eilidh nervous under the scrutiny. Finally, Queen Cadhla spoke, her voice low. "Show me an illusion."

Eilidh hesitated. Her astral talents were, at best, unrefined.

"Now!" the queen shouted. Thunder boomed overhead, and Eilidh jumped. The unexpected volatility unsettled her.

"Forgive me. As I said, I am unpractised." Eilidh put her mind to a simple illusion she had learned as a part of a meditative exercise. She held out her hand and opened her mind. The power of the Path of Stars swept over her like an ocean wave. She focused on the space above her palm. A pinpoint of pure blue light appeared in her hand. It flickered at first, then grew until it was larger than a fist. She sent it floating upward to the ceiling. A few gasps scattered throughout the chamber. Eilidh blinked and the glow disappeared.

"I have heard you disguise yourself as human using illusion."

Eilidh hadn't dared show the court that trick, even though she practised it the most often, turning her brilliant white hair a duller shade of yellow, rounding her twisted ears, adding flaws to her skin. The queen might have been insulted, as the kingdom fae would no doubt consider it demeaning to appear human.

Eilidh looked down at her human clothing and focused her thoughts. She altered the shape and colour, until her attire matched that of Teasair, the royal messenger who'd brought her here.

The queen frowned and glanced up at the handsome faerie behind her, who squeezed her shoulder reassuringly.

"You can alter yourself further if you choose? Your face?" she asked.

"An astral faerie such as myself cannot make a true alteration, Your Majesty, only an illusion that fools the eye. Only one of blood talents could truly alter their features."

"What of the other talents? The temporal or spirit magic also offered by the Path of Stars?"

"Those lines are long extinct. None living are known to possess those powers, and we have lost even memory of that lore."

The queen nodded, then knitted her eyebrows as she considered Eilidh's response. "You and your kind possess dangerous magic. How can we trust anyone, even our own mates, when they might be a spy in disguise?"

The question lingered for a moment before Eilidh offered, "Much magic has dangerous potential. But as you have suggested, the fae are a noble race. To use these abilities for an ill purpose is as alien to those of the azure as it would be to one gifted with earth talents."

"Do these azuri fae not bear a grudge for their exile from our kingdoms? Do you?"

"My exile was a source of sadness and pain, but I am glad to be home."

"Tell me. Can you read my thoughts? Send words into my head without my consent? It is said the most talented of your kind have such abilities."

"No. Mind-speaking is beyond my knowledge, and I know of none who can read thoughts."

The queen questioned Eilidh for some time, asking her to repeat the events of the most recent summer, and also to divulge information about the azuri colony on the Isle of Skye. The group had begun as three exiles a thousand years ago, but their number had grown over the centuries. They took in others as they found them, and the Great Mother blessed them with many children over the centuries, many more than Eilidh would have imagined possible, considering how rare fae children were in the kingdoms.

When Eilidh first met Oron, the head of the azuri conclave, he warned her against betraying their weaknesses and number to the kingdom. But now, she'd been invited to be part of the kingdom once more. To whom did she owe her loyalty? To a kingdom that cast her out, but was ultimately her home and that of her father? Or to the exiles who'd invited her to learn from them?

Rather than answer directly, Eilidh said, "Your Majesty, since the conclave has determined I am no threat to the kingdom, perhaps it is only a matter of time before all on Skye are brought home."

"That is why I summoned you, Eilidh. I will enter into talks with this azuri colony. If they are willing to dissolve their conclave and submit to the crown, we will consider them each for entry into the kingdoms. You will relay this message and report their response. Any action taken by the kingdom will be made slowly, as we must be assured they are as noble as you claim them to be, and not…corrupted, as this blood faerie had become."

Eilidh wasn't sure Oron and the others would be so easily brought into line, but it was the answer she hoped for. The unification of the azuri and the earth fae would right a grievous wrong.

"I will serve however I can," Eilidh said, bowing slightly. It was only then she realised she still appeared to be wearing the clothing of the royal messenger, and she dropped the illusion.

The queen stood and towered over everyone on the dais. Her power shone. She glanced around the room briefly, then flicked her eyes to the faerie who had touched her hand. Without another word, she turned and walked through a small archway behind the throne. At her departure, a murmur went up in the room, and chattering in small groups grew louder.

The faerie behind the throne stepped toward Eilidh. He was slightly taller than she, with straight black hair and the most remarkable violet eyes. He wore a fur-collared black wool cloak draped over his shoulders and fastened slightly off-centre by a golden chain. His clothing, from the black tunic and trousers to his high leather boots, must have been hand-made by the finest craftsmen. Even Eilidh could see the beauty in the details. He stopped in front of her and gave a quirk of a smile. "I am Prince Griogair, consort to Queen Cadhla," he said. "You have had a long day. Please accept the hospitality of the kingdom."

Eilidh curtsied without grace. "Your Highness. Thank you."

"A room has been prepared for you. I will show you the way." He led her to a door beyond the dais, and she followed him through. She wasn't eager to stay any longer than necessary in this forbidding white maze. Being in Queen Cadhla's presence had tired her, and Eilidh wanted to speak with her father again before travelling to Skye. Yet it would be unwise to refuse the offer.

When they came to a nearly deserted corridor, the prince-consort spoke in a low tone. "There is a matter of some urgency about which we must speak."

"Of course," Eilidh said, watching him closely.

He stopped in front of a large red door inset into a white wall. Like most of the palace, it had an open roof, but the walls loomed high above, showing only the stars. "But before I confide in you, I must know where your loyalties lie."

She felt his power swell. Tightness built in her chest. He used air flows, wrapping them around her. Six months ago, she might not have detected it. But thanks to having a bonded druid in Munro, she could see the earth forces as easily as any kingdom faerie. She did not resist, but let the prince hold her. He stepped closer, searching her eyes. He would have no power to delve into her thoughts. Kingdom fae could not touch the astral plane, where powers over the mind lay. He seemed intent on trying anyway.

Frustration rippled over his features. "Faith," he swore. "I have no choice. I must trust you." The pressure in her body released. He opened the door and motioned her inside.

The chamber was large and luxurious, with an immense swing bed, in the style favoured by the fae. A table had been set with delicate fresh foods, as though it had been prepared in the moments before her arrival. Lighting orbs glowed with earth magic. Despite the room's size, it felt small. The prince-consort stepped close to Eilidh, his violet eyes swirling. She fought not to step back. The fae were conservative in their displays, and yet both he and the queen seemed on edge, showing more emotion than Eilidh would have expected. Perhaps the royals indulged their emotions, she thought, since few would dare criticise them.

Eilidh's skin prickled with goose bumps at the intensity of his presence.

"Eilidh," he said, "I need your help. If you will aid me, I will owe you a great debt. One I'm not sure I could repay."

"Your Highness," she said, flushing. "Just tell me what I can do."

"Before I do, I need you to swear you will tell no one." He turned from her for a moment and breathing became easier. He stepped toward the table and took a fig from a golden platter. "Not even the queen." He put the fig in his mouth and chewed.

Eilidh stared at him. "Your Highness—"

"Griogair," he interrupted. "If I'm going to involve you in a conspiracy, you should call me by my name, at least when we are alone."

A rush of thoughts overwhelmed Eilidh, and she couldn't sort them out. Only one summer ago, she was an exile, living among humans, perhaps even falling in love with one. Today she'd met the faerie queen and was now standing alone with the queen's mate. Her heart thumped at his powerful presence. "What are you doing?" she asked sharply, suddenly suspicious. "What magic is this?"

The prince shrugged, but the air cooled and his presence dimmed. "I will do what I must to secure your help." He lowered himself into a chair and ate another fig.

"You do not have to seduce me. Only ask." If it had been anyone else, she might have been insulted. After seeing the worry so plainly etched on his features, though, she couldn't muster the indignation.

"Will you keep my secret?" he asked.

"If I am caught lying to the queen, I could be convicted of treason. At best, I would be exiled again. Is it likely she will question me about this secret you wish to keep?"

"Not if you are careful, no. It would not occur to her I would come to you." He paused. "Not about this anyway." A smile flitted across his lips.

Although the fae did not practise monogamy the way many humans aspired to do, it surprised her he would even allude to infidelity, since the royal family by tradition took mates for life. She suddenly felt very much a naïve child.

Eilidh considered her words carefully. "I will keep this conversation private, but I will fulfil no treasonous request. I was exiled, but I am no traitor to the fae."

Griogair smiled. "I would expect no less." He walked toward one of the hanging light-globes and tapped it with his finger, causing it to flicker.

Realising she was hungry, Eilidh sat at the table and waited. It seemed as though he would take his time getting his story out, and she thought she may as well eat. She doubted it would fit with the rules of decorum, but after all, she was the guest, and he the host.

With his back still to her, Griogair asked, "Do you know of my son? He's barely older than you. He recently marked a hundred and seventy-five years."

"I know little about Prince Tràth."

Griogair turned. "You are being diplomatic," he said, but waved his hand. "You will not offend me. The Great Mother blessed us with a child, but even the royals do not get to choose."

Eilidh concentrated on her food and chewed. She did not want to have to recount to the prince-consort the things she'd heard about his son. That as a boy Tràth had little talent in magic or craft, that he was undisciplined and lazy, rarely showed his face in public, and when he did, it didn't reflect well on the queen. He was hardly a model faerie. But then, seeing his parents close-up, the rumours surprised her less. The queen appeared angry and volatile and her mate equally expressive, even though it was a different emotion he showed.

"But I love my son. Should the Mother bless you with a child of your own, you will understand." Griogair sat across from Eilidh at the table. "A child will move even the most dispassionate of the fae to extremes. Look at your own father. It is said he broke his vows as a priest, lied to the conclave, travelled the kingdoms...all for you."

Eilidh tilted her head in acknowledgement. It surprised her how much the queen and prince-consort knew about her.

"I would do no less for Tràth. In fact, I would go further. I will commit treason and risk death or exile."

"And why would you need to take such risks for your son?"

Griogair smoothed a non-existent wrinkle on the tablecloth. “He is missing.”

“Missing, Your Highness? How can he be…missing?”

“We have already searched our kingdom, and discreetly done the same for friendly kingdoms beyond the Halls of Mist. In as much as was possible, without alerting the Watchers as to the truth, we have searched the borderlands as well. It has taken time, but both Cadhla and I are satisfied he is not anywhere we can reach him. He simply vanished.”

“How long ago?”

“Four new moons. It is growing increasingly problematic to cover his absence. For now, we have spread the rumour that he is in a meditative retreat. Somewhat difficult to believe, but Cadhla would not agree to anything that might cast a questionable light. As weeks go by, more questions are asked, and the lies become more challenging.”

Eilidh put down her food and looked at Griogair. “And why do you think I can help you? I assure you, my astral talents will be of little use. Do you wish me to speak with the azuri conclave? See if one of their number has some power that would locate him?”

“No!” Griogair said sharply. “No one must know. No one but you.”

“I’m sorry, Your Highness, but I don’t know what I can do.”

A silence hung between them for a while as Griogair seemed lost in thought. "It is said you have bonded with a human. Is that true?"

Eilidh met his eyes. "Yes." So many of the fae seemed to find it somehow disgraceful, but these were only the ignorant among the kingdom fae. Only one who followed the Path of Stars could bond with a true druid, and Munro had magic of his own. He was no ordinary human, and she wouldn't be shamed at their connection. It saddened Eilidh that centuries of ignorance caused the kingdoms to lose such a powerful magic as the druid-fae bond.

"And he is a Watcher?"

"In a manner of speaking, yes. He is what they call a policeman."

"And is he powerful among his kind? He has rank and influence?"

Eilidh considered. She didn't understand so much of human society. "He is what they call a Police Constable. He has been honoured among his people."

"I see." Griogair scratched his chin, pondering, but sounding impressed.

"And does your bond ensure his loyalty?"

Without thinking, Eilidh looked away, probing her mind, feeling for Munro's presence. When she reached for it, it responded like rippling water, and its warmth came over her. She nearly told the prince Munro's love ensured his loyalty, not any magical bond, but she wasn't certain Griogair would understand. Love was not a word the fae used often, especially not in the romantic sense. Once again, she was reminded how different the two races were, and how much she had been wedged between two worlds. She simply replied, "Yes," then added, "but as I've already said, I don't see what I can do that your own trusted advisors can't do better. My powers are untrained and untested."

"There is one place we have not been able to search for him. Although Queen Cadhla denies the logic of my reasoning, there is one place I believe the most likely for him to be. There, you and your druid are more suited than any to find his trail."

Eilidh glanced up sharply. "You think Prince Tràth has gone to the human realm?" The idea shocked her. Even journeying to the borderlands, the place where the two worlds overlapped, was rare for any other than fae Watchers. Before her exile, like most fae, she stayed on her own side of the boundaries.

"Left, perhaps, or was taken. We do have enemies who would think nothing of harming us…or our family. On the other hand, it's the one place he could get away from all this." Griogair gestured around her. "Away from the guards, the court, the advisors, the politics…the rumours." He frowned, his violet eyes growing dark. "From his mother."

There was so much Griogair wasn't saying that Eilidh hardly knew what to ask first. "And the queen would not want me to search for Prince Tràth?"

"She does not even want *me* to continue looking for our son. She has begun to thwart me at every turn, now even forbidding me from speaking to our advisors on the subject." The prince-consort took Eilidh's hand, a shockingly intimate gesture. "Find my son. Please."

His plea was moving, but she felt certain he had not told her everything. "I must think on it. I believe you are sincere, but you are asking me to subvert the queen's will, to risk *another* death sentence. I was fortunate to escape the first one."

Griogair nodded and released her hand. He stood. "I understand. If you cannot do this, I'll find another way. I will..." His voice trailed off.

"Give me a few days. I must travel to Skye. The queen expects me to deliver her message to the azuri conclave. I can promise you this much. I will think on what you've said, and I will speak to my bonded druid."

The prince went to the door. "I'm sure you are eager to be on your way. I will keep the queen occupied until morning, and she will make her excuses for not asking you to dine as our guest."

Eilidh tilted her head in acknowledgement. "Thank you."

Griogair put his hand on the door, then turned, his brow furrowed. "I will give you anything you ask if you bring my son back to me. I swear it." With that, he left her alone.

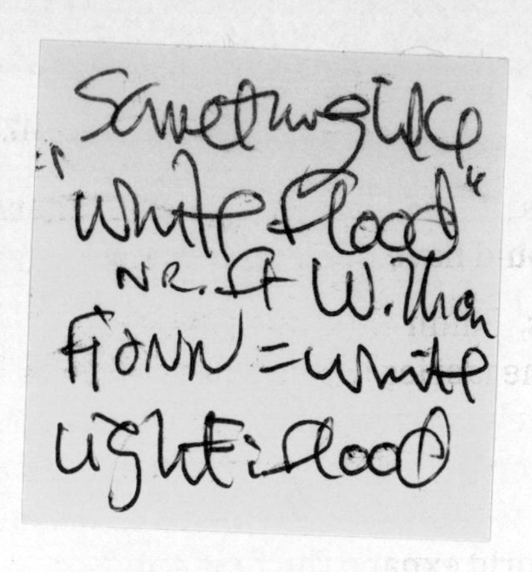

CHAPTER 2

SOON AFTER PRINCE GRIOGAIR left Eilidh's room, an attendant arrived and conveyed the queen's regrets. Eilidh was welcome to stay as long as she liked, but she instructed the attendant to thank Queen Cadhla for her generous hospitality and to let the queen know Eilidh would be leaving immediately for Skye.

She could move much faster in the Otherworld than in the human world. Only a scant three hours later, Eilidh arrived at the Otherworld gate parallel to her borderlands' destination. The closest she could get to the Isle of Skye was Fionn Lighe. Winter had set in, and the highland forest air held a crisp chill. Here, in the woods and in the dark, the scent of the Otherworld still lingered, but she knew she would keenly feel the loss soon. The azuri fae of Skye had blocked the one Otherworld gate on the island and lived completely outside the kingdom's influence. All but a few had been born after the rebellion a thousand years ago. They never knew the world that should have been their home.

Perhaps, Eilidh thought, she could help set things right. The faeries of this colony were safe, protected for years by secrecy and now in part by fear of their mind powers, but they could never leave this small island without danger. The borders to the Otherworld expanded at night, leaving little beyond the holes burned into it by the encroaching human society. To avoid the kingdom that would have ordered their deaths, the Skye fae had to stay in their secure little corner of the human world.

Only one faerie had agreed to help Eilidh when she faced the blood faerie that killed so many this past summer: Beniss, an elder, had earned Eilidh's respect. Now Beniss was dead, and Eilidh had delivered the news to her sister, her children and her grandchildren. It was a terrible moment, one from which the community hadn't fully recovered. They took Eilidh in and began training her in the Path of Stars, but she did not feel entirely trusted or at home.

As she moved through the forest, she called on earth magic, which had been alien to her before joining with Munro. Through him, in addition to her astral talents, she had access to air, water, stone and fire, spheres of power that kingdom fae could touch naturally, although most could only master one. Although she was not yet adept, the lessons of her childhood, forced upon her because her father and teachers could not acknowledge, much less encourage, her real abilities, came back with clarity.

The stones trembled with the slightest touches as animals passed around her. She felt the life of the river nearby and could sense the flows of magic pulsing cold within it. The air carried sounds to her ears, buzzing, whistling, chirping forest noises. In the distance, she detected the hum of a heavy farm vehicle. After she crossed the sound that separated Skye from the rest of Scotland, skating across the water on a gust of air power, she used a lick of fire to dry her leather shoes in an instant. She singed them slightly, not being accustomed to wielding the force. Before she'd bonded with Munro, fire had been her weakest element. She could not help but revel in her new competencies.

As she made her way toward the centre of the island, her earth powers drained away. An enchantment cast by the azuri fae rendered the powers of the kingdom useless. She hadn't been affected on her first visit, because her abilities had been so insignificant then that the loss didn't affect her deeply. But this time, it was as though a dark cloud passed between her and the sun.

Eilidh headed for the community centre building the faeries had taken over. She assumed they would be wrapping up the conclave meeting around this time. Even though the Skye fae had taken to disguising themselves as humans, even dressing like them and eating what human food their systems could tolerate, they kept to the night. It didn't take long for Eilidh to revert to her natural nocturnal rhythm after coming here to train.

Hesitating only a few moments at the door, Eilidh walked in. The notice boards were filled with papers advertising local events, and the small kitchen just off the entry held a kettle, a coffee pot, and polystyrene cups. The only clue that this place was anything other than what it pretended to be was the faint smell of kliesh, a strong drink brewed from a plant that grew only in the Otherworld.

As Eilidh approached the back of the building, she saw a familiar face.

"We have been expecting you," Oron said.

∞

Quinton Munro sat on the floor of his spare bedroom, the walls covered with shelf after shelf of small stone and metal talismans, crafted over the months by his emerging druidic powers. The earlier works rested on higher shelves, more crude than his recent efforts.

His current project had properties that still eluded him. The material was once a plain, brass house key. Now, it stretched into filament-thin wings, which he delicately shaped onto the back of a shimmering dragonfly. He could feel the earth power thrum within it, vibrating hard enough to send a tremor through the wings. Even he could appreciate its beauty and craftsmanship, for which he took no credit. But somehow, it frustrated him.

He and the other druids he knew felt something close to a compulsion to create. Since his primary element of power was stone, metal and rocks responded to his touch easily. The others were all water druids, so their talismans were wooden or sometimes made of reed. Phillip had tried to make one of cloth, but failed. Rory found cotton responded to him, while silk didn't. They wondered if perhaps it had to do with Rory being able to touch air flows, where Phillip's talents leaned toward the stone end of the spectrum. There was so much they didn't understand about their own abilities, none of them having more than a year or two of experience.

But neither they or the other two druids they knew had constructed anything with life in it, and therein lay Munro's frustration. He could feel something missing, but couldn't draw out whatever was locked inside his creations. With a sigh, he put the tiny brass dragonfly on one of the shelves.

The craft provided such a contrast to his other life, his *real* life, where he worked as a beat cop in his hometown of Perth, Scotland. In that life, he found order, even in the chaos of dragging drunks off the street, breaking up fights, or the simple activity of giving directions to a lost tourist. Those things made sense. That world was simple in comparison to the elusive and foreign realm of magic he'd discovered quite by accident last summer.

He stood and stretched his back from the long hours sitting in one position. Time passed strangely when he worked on his talismans. He would go into a trance-like state, and everything else faded away. Even if he couldn't unlock the secrets within the things he made, the activity helped focus his mind, something he and Eilidh had been working on. A smile stole across his lips as he thought of her, and he felt a tug in his chest in response. She was thinking of him too. With every week that passed, their bond grew stronger, her emotions a little more clearly defined.

This weekend, he'd planned to stay home and potter about with his trinkets, to see if this time he could finally manage to find the missing element. Eilidh planned to spend a few days in the Otherworld with her father, and he wasn't comfortable on Skye without her. The faeries were friendly enough, but like with his talismans, something was missing.

But when he felt Eilidh touch their bond, he knew she had returned to Skye. His mind pointed northwest. He didn't know if it was their bond, or simply that he had fallen in love with her, but he couldn't resist her pull. Before he realised what he was doing, he'd grabbed a bag and headed for his car.

CHAPTER 3

EILIDH STOOD BEFORE THE HIGHER Conclave, the twelve faeries who ruled the azuri fae on Skye. At first, she found it difficult to treat the back room of a village community centre as a seat of power, but the faeries were each more than five hundred years old, most closer to seven or eight, two had passed a thousand, and all immensely powerful. She concentrated on keeping her voice clear and her thoughts uncluttered. "While in the Otherworld visiting my father, I was summoned before the queen."

Oron leaned forward. "Is that so?" He was the eldest among them and the conclave leader, in addition to being Eilidh's main tutor in the astral arts. He looked at the others, and they exchanged glances she could not interpret. "And what was the nature of your conversation?"

Eilidh outlined the queen's offer, couching it in as friendly terms as possible, but careful not to distort the intent behind the message. She very much wanted them to accept and reunite the kingdom, but she knew it would not be as easy as saying yes and reopening the Skye gate. Centuries of distrust would take time to heal.

"Have they lifted the death orders?" one member asked. He'd been quiet throughout much of her questioning, but now he turned his dark, penetrating eyes on Eilidh and held her gaze intently. "Is it not still a crime to even be *able* to touch the azure?"

Eilidh offered a small shrug. "Queen Cadhla said each would be considered, and I took her at her word. She did not strike me as deceptive, although she was not telling me everything. One thing that seemed odd; she asked for a demonstration of my abilities. As you know, I'm unpractised, but I did what I could. I showed her a ball of light, and when pressed, altered my clothing. She seemed shocked, even horrified. I wondered if she was not also considering what it would mean to have hundreds of azuri fae, all more practised than I, at her disposal. If I were queen, the thought would have crossed my mind."

"Would it now?" The elder seemed amused, and Eilidh quickly assumed a delicate illusion to hide her reddening cheeks.

"I don't mean to presume, of course," she said. "It seemed an obvious thought. Prince Griogair mentioned that they have enemies. I admit I don't know everything that goes on in the royal gatherings in the Halls of Mist, but the fae have been known to employ machinations." The Halls of Mist formed the intersection of magical worlds. Each kingdom joined there, no matter where in the human world that kingdom had its borders. Any faerie of any kingdom could walk the stronghold without fear, and many spent as much time as they could there. Within it was the source of fae power, the quality of magic that spread throughout the kingdoms, even seeping into the edges of the human world through open Otherworld gates.

The conclave sat in silence for a time, as though each was lost in his or her thoughts. Eilidh's shoulders sagged with exhaustion. She had not eaten, except for a few bites when she spoke with Prince Griogair. She'd spent hours without respite and endured two gruelling sessions of questioning.

She had become aware of Munro's approach an hour into her questioning. At first, she attributed the feeling to the renewed intensity of his presence, which came over her when she crossed into the human realm. As time passed, she realised he was moving toward her, and at enough of a pace that he had to be in a car.

Although Munro visited most weeks, she missed him. She didn't know if their bond was responsible for her need to be close to him, but she also enjoyed his company, his odd, human sense of humour, his insight and talent. He hadn't told her he would come that day, but it made her heart lighter to feel his approaching presence. Not to mention that even though her magical capacity had grown because of the bond, it would gain her little from people like the queen or from the conclave. She appreciated having an ally.

Her thoughts turned to Griogair. As promised, she didn't mention their conversation to the conclave, but she had considered it. He'd tried to manipulate her. On the other hand, she believed he'd told her the truth. She looked forward to consulting with Munro. He would know what to do.

Eilidh felt her strength wilting. Oron stood and came to her. "My dear child, you are about to collapse. You must be exhausted."

"I'm sorry," she said, embarrassed at the weakness. "I haven't been sleeping well since..." Her voice trailed off. She didn't want to mention the deaths that still haunted her: Saor's, Beniss', the druids—the other fae who died last summer. Beniss had been an elder and a member of this conclave. Beniss' sister Galen, still held Eilidh responsible.

"Come," Oron said. "Let's go home." While she was in training, she stayed with Oron. She should have accepted it as a great honour, but instead it reminded Eilidh that many of the others might have refused to work with her. Oron put a hand on either side of her face, and warmth flooded into her. The ache in her bones subsided. "There. You need rest, but this will soothe your mind."

She slumped onto his shoulder. Not yet asleep, but not far from it. It surprised her, she thought distantly, that one as ancient as Oron had such physical strength. He was an oak, and not nearly as frail as he appeared.

He guided her to his house, a short walk from the centre. Her eyes were heavy, and she could barely fight to keep them open. Once inside, she heard voices, but couldn't even muster the energy to be polite. A soft hand took hers and led her to her room in the back, where she sank into her swing bed. She fell asleep before the hands finished pulling a blanket over her.

∞

Eilidh awoke to find Munro on the floor between her bed and the door. He lay with his back to her, as though guarding her. His presence filled the room and her heart. She felt certain now that the bonding magic was responsible for her responses to him. It swirled around the room, knitting their minds even more tightly. How long, she wondered, before their thoughts flowed into each other as though coming from one mind? Eventually, they would not even have to speak.

She watched him breathe, taking in his sleep-tousled hair and the curve of a rounded ear. It had freckles on it, and for no reason she could explain, the sight made her smile. Turbulence filled his mind, and she realised he was dreaming. This bond held so many unexpected twists. She couldn't help but wonder if the faerie who developed or discovered this magic millennia ago had understood what the consequences would be. Of course, in those days, the relationship between humans and the fae was quite different. Time, technology, religion, fear—all had eroded the path from both sides.

Eilidh was tempted to touch Munro's mind even deeper, to see if she could somehow access his dream, to know what visions made his mind tumble. Did he fight a battle? Argue with someone? Or did his heart race because he dreamt of more pleasant things, perhaps even of her? She had felt his desire surge many times when they were alone together, and she found its primitive strength enthralling.

His mind, heart and body seemed locked in perpetual battle. It gave her newfound respect for him, and all humans. The fae kept their emotions tightly controlled; it seemed second nature. Humans, on the other hand, made continuous choices.

His mind rushed toward wakefulness, and he sat up suddenly, whispering "Eilidh" into the darkened room. Knowing he could not see well in the dim early morning, she created a pale glow over her hand and sent it to rest in a corner. As his eyes adjusted, she increased the luminance.

He turned to her, and she could feel the fog of sleep lift from his thoughts. He gave her a smile, and she could not help but return it. "Good morning," he said with a stretch that turned into a full-body shudder.

She couldn't help but notice how tired he looked. He must have driven through the night.

"You're doing it again," he said. "Reading my mind."

"I constantly explore our bond," she replied and stood. "I am glad you are here, Quinton."

He stood and folded his blanket. "I felt... Did something happen in the Otherworld?"

She felt a twinge in his question. "Yes, several things. While visiting with my father, I was called before the queen and then had to report to the Higher Conclave. There is something else, but before we speak, I must have your word that nothing I say to you will be repeated, ever, to anyone."

He cocked an eyebrow, but nodded. "Of course."

Suddenly aware of where they were, she said, "Not here. We must have absolute privacy."

"Is everything all right?"

She gave a brief shake of her head and focused a thought toward him. *Trust me.* Not being trained with mind-speaking, she doubted he would hear her, but she hoped he would at least feel the emotions behind it.

"Come," she said. "I will check in with Oron, then we can find a quiet place to talk."

Eilidh led Munro to the front of the house. It was, in structure and layout, much like a human home, enclosed and squared-off, but with high ceilings. Its interior walls and floors were stone. Fae tapestries covered the walls, and the furnishings were hand-crafted and of fae design. A mural of crystals had been fashioned into one wall in the main room. She could see the magic resonance moving around it in a beautiful harmony she doubted Munro would be able to sense.

An adolescent faerie, who couldn't have been much more than fifty years old, came in from a side room. She was a lovely girl with eyes the colour of rich earth and long hair twisted down her back. "Grandfather is in his meditation chamber. I'll tell him you're awake." Eilidh had never met her before. Oron had the largest family of any faerie she'd ever encountered. This girl could be a granddaughter, or even the granddaughter of one of his grandchildren. In the six months Eilidh had spent on the Isle of Skye, Oron kept her busy and practically locked away with her studies.

"No need to disturb him," Eilidh said.

The girl smiled shyly, not yet having mastered the art of polite disagreement, and without another word went up the winding stone stair on the opposite side of the room.

"Hello," came a small squeak from the side room. Eilidh turned, shocked to see a faerie child inching toward them. Children were so rare among the kingdom fae, that babies under ten years old were closely guarded. She stepped back. Somehow the Skye azuri had been blessed many times, growing their numbers to a proportion no kingdom faerie would believe.

Munro, on the other hand, reacted quite differently. "Hello, Princess," he said with a grin. "Come on in. Don't be shy."

"Quinton," Eilidh whispered, wanting to warn him to stay back. If any fae thought their baby was in danger, they might become terrible indeed. The last thing she wanted was to draw Oron's ire. Even after months in his household, she never forgot her place. As a student, she was lower than any servant. Oron tried to tell her the azuri colony's way was different, and besides, she was no longer a child, as most students would be. He tried to treat her as a guest, but the habits of her kingdom life were too deeply ingrained.

Munro went down to one knee and hunched a little, so the child could look him in the eye. She skipped up to him fearlessly. He held out a hand, and she took it. "I'm Quinton Munro," he said. "What's your name?"

"Flùranach," she said. "You're not supposed to cast illusions in the house. Grandfather says so."

Munro grinned. "You mean these?" He flicked one rounded, freckled ear.

The child nodded.

"Feel," he said.

She reached up and grabbed the top of his ears with her small hands. "That's pretty good," she said. "I can usually tell when Alyssa does it."

"How old are you?" he asked.

"I'm seven. How old are you?"

"Thirty-four."

"You don't look like a little boy," she said, obviously not believing him.

"I'm not. I'm human. We age up fast. And you don't sound like a little girl."

"I'm little, but I'm clever. Everyone says so."

"That doesn't surprise me."

"So you don't have any magic at all?" she asked.

"I'm a druid. I suppose technically I have some magic, but I'm just learning. I don't really know what it does or how to use it. So far all I can do is make pretty rocks."

"Can I see?"

"Sure. I'll need a regular rock to start with."

"I'll get one!" she squealed and thundered through the front door into the garden, completely ignoring Eilidh.

Munro stood and turned back to Eilidh with a smile. "She's cute," he said.

"Quinton, you mustn't."

"Mustn't what? What's wrong?" A shadow passed over his face, but he quickly brightened again when the girl returned.

She handed him a rock, which was small, flat, and half-covered in mud. "This felt like a good one."

Munro sat cross-legged on the ground, and the faerie child did the same. They faced each other with serious expressions. Eilidh stepped forward, her mind spinning with warnings, but unable to speak.

Oron's voice came from behind her. "Let's just see what happens," he said. When Eilidh started to protest, he shushed her. "Flùranach is a talented child. I'm curious to see what she makes of your druid. He certainly has no ill intention. I can see that much."

Eilidh relaxed. She could see it too, but she couldn't help but worry. Even though the azuri fae seemed to be more fertile than their kingdom counterparts, she couldn't shake the deep-seated instinct to protect the girl. Fae children were so valuable to their race.

Munro was busy scraping mud off the rock, careless of where the bits fell. He polished the last of it off with the bottom edge of his shirt. "There we go. That works." He turned the rock in his hand, looking at it from all angles.

"What're you going to do?" the child asked.

"Patience, my little flower." He frowned as he contemplated the rock. "Maybe it would help if you held my hand."

"Okay," she said, looking serious. She put her tiny hand in his large powerful one. "Ooh!" she exclaimed.

Eilidh stepped forward, but Oron stopped her with a touch of his hand on her shoulder. "Wait."

A blue ribbon of light formed around Munro and Flùranach's hands, flowing between them and into his other hand. He closed the fist that held the rock and shut his eyes. The pair sat like that for almost an hour, neither flagging, as though unaware of the passing time or that they were closely watched. When Munro opened his eyes, he opened his hand as well.

Eilidh and Oron stepped forward to peer into Munro's palm. In it nestled a stone rose, petals so delicate they looked like paper. The flat grey had taken on the faintest blush. Flùranach's large eyes grew wide with wonder. "It's so pretty," she said.

Munro handed it to her. "For you."

She glanced up and saw her grandfather, and her eyes lit up.

"Look, Grandfather! Look! Isn't it beautiful? My new friend Quinton Munro made it for me. He's a druid, you know. He has special magic." She turned and looked up at Munro, who had risen. "Where did you come from anyway?"

"Perth," he said.

"I mean why are you in Grandfather's house?"

Oron answered, "He is our honoured guest, Flùranach."

She nodded, then asked, "May I keep it?"

Oron looked at the rose without touching it. "It is an object of power, Flùranach. It should be treated reverently. You may meditate with it during your third-hour contemplations."

"Yes, Grandfather."

"And you should thank your new friend for sharing his magic with you." Oron smiled at Munro, giving his own subtle nod of thanks.

Flùranach grinned and took Munro's hand, tugging it to encourage him to bend down. When he complied, she whispered in his ear, "Thank you."

He leaned over and whispered back, "You're very welcome."

"Now off to your studies, child, before your elder sister discovers that you've wandered off when you should be practising your runes."

She clambered off with a wave for Munro.

"When I was her age," Munro said to Eilidh, "I was chasing frogs."

Oron chuckled. "When I was *your* age, I was chasing frogs. Come. We have things to discuss."

CHAPTER 4

THE THREE OF THEM WENT OUTSIDE to chat in a garden. The cold air bit, and Munro wished he'd brought more than just a jacket. He would have liked gloves, a scarf, maybe a woolly hat. Neither faerie seemed aware of the hard chill on the wind. He listened as Eilidh and Oron spoke. She hadn't yet filled Munro in on what happened in the Otherworld, but he could piece some things together based on what the two of them said. Besides, they talked about royalty and politics, and although he was vaguely interested, it reminded him of the feeling he got when hearing about the latest South American coup or protests on some distant continent. Interesting, but only to a point.

What he really wanted to know was how Eilidh felt. Their bond let him sense some things, flashes of emotion from time to time, but it didn't tell him what he wanted, and it never reassured him. In the past six months, she'd lived here, studying and working, and he came when his schedule would allow. They'd grown closer, but they also spent a lot of their time working. Oron was so eager to probe and test the bonding magic that it left him and Eilidh with little time to do normal things. Of course, how normal could they be?

One thing he'd noticed the last time they studied their bond was that he could sense her magic. He didn't know how to put words to it beyond that it felt ancient. It spoke to a part of him he wasn't aware of before. If he was honest, it scared him a little, seeming like an endless black ocean full of unknown perils, of monsters and storms. He hadn't told her, because he wanted some time to chew on his thoughts.

Munro shook himself, focusing on Eilidh and Oron. He'd missed a bit of their conversation, but then realised they hadn't gotten far. They were talking about someone called Queen Cadhla wanting Eilidh to act as an ambassador and Oron not wanting her to.

"Oron," Eilidh said. "I can't refuse."

The older faerie replied with a snort. "Of course you can."

"Why would I? Is the Higher Conclave not willing to speak with the kingdom?"

"Many are distrustful, especially those who have never been to the Halls of Mist. My children and grandchildren were born on this island."

"Will there be no going home for any of you?"

"Home," Oron said. "I can smell the Otherworld on you." He did that thing Munro noticed faeries did a lot: sat without saying much. Munro couldn't tell if they were thinking, or just sitting. He didn't mind. His dad had been a quiet thinker too, and silence never bothered Munro. But it was cold out, and eventually he'd have to go get warm, or he'd freeze his arse off on this stone bench. "We had always believed the source of our power was in the Halls of Mist," Oron finally said.

"Isn't it?" Eilidh asked, surprised.

Instead of responding to her question, Oron went on, "If we submit, we would always be kept on a leash. Centuries of suspicion are not easily overcome. It certainly won't happen quickly. The azuri conclave has wondered if there is any reason to subject ourselves to the queen's will."

"Why not be independent?" Munro interrupted. "If that's what most of you want. Who needs the queen anyway? She sounds like a pain in the arse, making all these demands that you bend a knee." Both faeries stopped and stared at him. "You told me yourself that you lot are pretty powerful. There's loads of you here too. It's not like she could *make* you do anything."

"The kingdom should be healed, not cleaved even further. What you are suggesting is unthinkable."

Munro could sense the tension in Eilidh's voice with more than just his ears. "Doesn't sound to me like you azuri could be any more *cleaved* than you already are. Look, they kicked you out. I'm not saying start a war. But you told me all the kingdoms join up at this Halls of Mist place, right?"

Oron nodded but didn't speak. He seemed fascinated, but Munro couldn't tell if it was in a "this is a good idea" sort of way, or more like, "wow, who knew humans could talk."

"Build your own gateway," Munro said. "Make an azuri kingdom. You seem like you'd make a decent enough king, Oron. Or you could be president or something. Let people vote on things rather than bowing and obeying and crap."

The old faerie stood and smiled, not even acknowledging the suggestion. "This afternoon I'm going to examine the talisman you created for Flùranach. I'd like to observe another creation ritual, should you perform one."

Eilidh spoke up, "Of course he will. Any time you wish."

Oron glanced at her, his face unreadable, but then went on in a different vein, "Eilidh, we are half way through your first year of training. It's time to consider your house." Eilidh looked puzzled, but Oron said, "It will wait until your druid returns to his city, but it's time to think about it."

Munro glanced at Eilidh. He couldn't help but wonder again what kind of plans she had. He supposed it wasn't too bad, her being in Skye with him in Perth. It wasn't the easiest drive, but he couldn't ask her *not* to move here. It would mean spending a lot of time apart, but they needed to take their time, and cities made her uneasy, even a small and sedate city like Perth.

Oron said, “If I’m not mistaken, my granddaughter Alyssa has prepared a meal. I suggest you eat while the food is hot and before your druid freezes.” He nodded to them both and walked toward the house.

As soon as he was out of earshot, Munro said, “So what do you need to talk about?”

“There is much I need to tell you,” she said. “But not here. Let’s go into the human settlements.”

In all the trips he’d made to Skye, they’d spent their time in the company of faeries, never venturing outside the colony’s village. “Sure, we can head over to Portree after we eat. See what there is to see. Or we can go now. I can tell you have a lot on your mind.”

“We’ll eat, then go,” she said. “It would be rude to refuse the meal. You should have told me you were cold.”

Munro grinned and stood. “I thought you could read my mind.”

∞

Eilidh wandered into one of the shops in Portree. She needed new clothes, and she didn’t like using illusions to hide the wear in the ones she had. Especially when she never knew what lessons Oron would have her do that would require her to drop all illusions and focus her mind on something else. Her visit to the queen made her realise how ragged her human clothing had become. When she’d lived in exile on the streets of Perth, she hadn't worried about what she wore. Now she missed proper fae clothing and felt discontent with having to make do with rags. With a sigh, she chose a pair of jeans, a t-shirt, and a baggy, hooded sweatshirt. She planned to steal the clothes, especially since she'd gotten better at making herself nearly invisible, or invisible enough to humans. It wasn't so much that they couldn't see her, as they didn't *notice* her.

When she told Munro what she intended, he whispered, "Jesus, Eilidh. I'm a cop. I'm not letting you steal things."

"Don't be ridiculous. I'll be in and out before they know something is missing. I've done it a hundred times." Granted, it had never been this easy. Before, she'd relied on her speed and natural abilities. Now that she had a little training, it was simple to fool the human eye.

"Well, you aren't doing it again." His voice grew hard, and she realised he wasn't playing. She felt his thoughts grow rigid.

She understood and felt suddenly guilty because of all the things she'd taken during her quarter century of exile. She'd lived on the streets of Perth, stealing and killing rabbits or sheep in the countryside to eat, sleeping in abandoned buildings or sometimes isolated corners of city parks. Gaining human employment wasn't an option, and she didn't entirely understand the monetary system humans used. In the fae kingdoms, they traded precious metals, gems, talismans and supplies. She suddenly wondered how the faeries here on Skye paid for things. Did they engage in commerce? It would be difficult to feed and clothe several hundred faeries without working out some kind of trade, but she didn't know how they managed.

Humans counted hours, sold time, and exchanged paper to tally what was owed. It seemed a cruel, distrustful system. She would never have considered stealing from one of the fae, but when taking from humans what she needed to live, she hadn't counted it as theft, only survival. But seeing the look in Munro's eyes as he waited for her to promise she would not take anything without paying, shame burned within her.

"I don't have money," she said.

"I've got it," he told her. She watched with fascination as Munro produced a piece of plastic, which he called "a credit card," and took it to the merchant.

He came back with her new clothing in a plastic bag and handed it to her. As they walked outside, she said, "You show him your card, and he gives you items in exchange?"

"It's like a promise to pay later."

"Can I have one? So I will not have to steal?"

Munro chuckled. "We'll see. For now, let me help you with anything you need." He touched her lightly on the cheek, the harshness of their earlier exchange gone. She still had difficulty accepting the help of a human, even him, but she didn't argue. He leaned in and kissed her lips softly. It flustered her, because they were standing in the middle of the street, people milling, going in and out of shops. She had not yet grown accustomed to allowing herself be seen by humans. She glanced around, but no one noticed. Her reaction made Munro chuckle again.

"Why are you laughing, Quinton?"

He ran his hand up her cheek and over a twisted ear, hidden by the illusion that made her look human. She hadn't bothered to make it *feel* round, and she wasn't very good at that anyway. "You are so powerful," he said quietly. "And yet, something like a public kiss scares you."

She shuddered at his touch. "I should tell you," she said, biting her lip, "that touching a faerie's ears is very…intimate." Glancing down, she suddenly didn't want to meet his intense blue eyes.

"Is it now?" He leaned close and whispered, "I'll have to remember that." He took her earlobe into his mouth for just an instant before backing away. He grinned and reached for her hand. "Let's find someplace quiet to talk."

She allowed him to lead her, wondering if he could tell how her stomach fluttered at the exchange. They hadn't discussed or explored their relationship much over the months. He knew the kiss scared her, so he could at least glimpse into her emotions. She could only assume he knew the same things about her she could see in him. The idea left her feeling vulnerable.

They walked east, toward the sea and away from the small town of Portree, making their way up a small hillside. Below them were boats, tied in their harbour. Eilidh and Munro sat on the grass. She funnelled a bit of earth magic through him and warmed the air around them. It took more effort than usual, because of the enchantments on Skye, but oddly, being near the human settlement helped. After just a moment, he relaxed. He rarely complained about the weather, or about anything, she realised. She watched him looking out over the water. He seemed fascinated with it, but she could sense a knot of fear as well.

"You do not like the ocean?" she asked.

"I like the sound of it." He didn't elaborate on what he didn't like. She was about to ask when he said, "So, what don't you want Oron to know?" He took her hand, but he did it as though touching her comforted him.

She recounted her meeting with the queen, filling in pieces of what he'd not managed to gather from her conversation with Oron, this time including her thoughts and fears. She described Eirlioc Falls and recalled details. He let her talk without interrupting or asking questions, and she loved that. She could almost forget he was human at moments like these.

Then she explained how Prince Griogair took her aside to a guest chamber afterwards. Munro tensed inwardly, but he made no outward sign, which she found interesting. She would not have considered he would be so accomplished at deception. He did his best to hold his jealousy in check, but she could detect it as she described the magic the prince used to try to persuade her. She also felt a flash of annoyance directed at her.

But when she came to the story about Prince Tràth, Munro's focus shifted, and she felt his mind grow very ordered. His emotions almost completely disappeared.

"I told Prince Griogair I would bring the matter to you. I assured him you are respected among your people."

Munro didn't answer, but his thoughts moved like the mechanical ticking of a clock. His eyes flitted back and forth, as though reading. Finally, he said, "I need more information. I have to talk to this Griogair."

"Quinton," she said, "There is no way the prince-consort will come here. There is only one time the queen and her mate would ever leave the Otherworld."

He looked up and met her eyes, his face serious. "When?"

She flushed. She did not want to explain the mating rituals of her people, how they came to the fringes of the human world to make a sacrifice to the Great Mother to ask for her blessing of fertility. "That time, I believe, has likely passed for the queen." Of course, the queen was only four or five hundred years old, perhaps six at most, and *could* have more children, but considering what Griogair had told Eilidh, she didn't expect the royal couple to make that journey again. "However," she said thoughtfully, "I must return to the Otherworld to see the queen. I can question Griogair further, if you need me to, and I'll tell him we'll do what we can for him and his son."

She smiled. "I'm glad you're willing to help. I wasn't sure you would consider it."

"No," Munro said, shaking his head. "I need to speak with him myself. It isn't the answers to the questions as much as the *way* he gives them. I won't know if he's lying unless I see him with my own eyes."

Eilidh felt the blood drain from her face. "I can't risk bringing you to the Otherworld, Quinton, and even if we could travel to the fringes, I certainly can't take you to the Falls."

"He asked for my help, Eilidh," Munro said. "This is what my help looks like. I have to talk to him face to face."

"Very well," she said, her mind turning. "I'll relay the message. We should get back. I must speak to Oron again. I know he will want to talk about the gift you gave his granddaughter." She paused. "That was very reckless of you. If your actions had been misconstrued as hostile..."

Munro looked up with a half-grin. "You're jealous."

Eilidh blinked. "Jealous?"

"That I made a stone with someone else before I tried it with you."

"That's absurd," she said, but slowly and without conviction. Had she been jealous? She'd thought she'd been trying to protect the girl, but perhaps there was a kernel of truth in his words. All of their attention in the short time Munro spent in the colony had been used to test the magic of the bond.

They'd devoted no time to Munro's talismans, although she knew he crafted many on his own.

"Let me see your face," he said, tracing his finger along her chin, tapping it upward so she would meet his eyes.

Even though they were alone, Eilidh cautiously glanced around before dropping the human illusion, revealing the curl of her ears and turning her hair brilliant white. She watched his smile grow as she revealed her true face. Although she didn't alter her appearance much, just enough to pass for one of the younger race, it pleased her that he liked her real self better than the illusion.

He pulled her close, and his musky human scent mixed with the salty breeze blowing off the ocean. He kissed her again, this time fiercely and without reservation. She felt his love for her as though the sun had appeared from behind a cloud. He took his time, tasting, exploring, enjoying the sensations they shared. "You and I will make things together, Eilidh, my love. All kinds of things."

Then as quickly as he had revealed himself, the light dimmed, and he reined his passions back. She had no idea how he did it, but he seemed well-practised. In all these months, he'd touched her tenderly, kissed her, and held her, but he'd never suggested they become lovers, not since that time soon after they'd first met, when she'd turned him down because of his race. So much had changed since then, yet he did not pursue it, even though she could sense his attraction for her. She couldn't help but wonder why.

"Come on," he said, standing and extending his hand to help her rise. "It's getting late. We'd better get back."

CHAPTER 5

"YOU'RE OUT OF YOUR FUCKING MINDS," Munro said. At first, he'd been intimidated by all these old faeries. Eilidh had told him the youngest of the bunch was likely around six hundred years old. And this, apparently, was an "open conclave" meeting, so there were more in attendance besides the eleven members. Naturally, he'd always been nervous around them. He could sense Eilidh was too, and that made it worse. He'd gotten to know Oron and had run into others, but this was his first time before the whole conclave. As soon as he sat down that night, he saw they had an agenda beyond the queen's offer of reconciliation. No, what they really wanted was more druids, and they expected him to deliver.

"Quinton!" Eilidh hissed between her teeth.

He turned and saw the warning on her face, but he held firm. "No, Eilidh. I'm calling a spade a shovel. These people expect me to go back to Perth, round up my human druid *friends*, and deliver them, so this lot can pass them around to see who can bond with whom."

"Quinton," she repeated, but softer this time.

The conclave sat there, staring smugly at him, as though he were an errant child who didn't know any better than to piss in the potted plants. He met their eyes, one by one. "Surely you remember the last faerie who tried to bond with one of them also planned to kill them all."

One of the conclave sat forward, his eyes flashing with anger. Obviously, they were used to getting their way. "The last faerie who tried to bond with one of them was Eilidh. They know of your bond, do they not?"

"Yeah," he relented.

"It has given you fast healing, long life, power. Your speed and endurance will increase to match Eilidh's. Your eyes will grow sharper, your senses will heighten."

"All of this good stuff I've been promised will happen, hasn't," he argued. "Yeah, the healing happened fast, but after six months, I've seen no other physical changes."

"Eilidh has gained access to earth power, something the azuri are usually denied, and not just one branch, but all four. Even you can understand what that means to her."

"But that isn't all. I'm in her head all the time. I know where she is. I feel her dreams, her fears, her anger right this minute." He glanced her way and gave an apologetic smile. If he hadn't thought it would embarrass her, he'd have taken her hand. He couldn't explain why, but touching her comforted him. It quieted his mind. She didn't smile back.

Munro went on. "When I met Eilidh, I thought faeries didn't feel anything. But now I know better. I don't suspect, I know. I know because I feel every inward flinch, every memory that floats by. Even if she is so familiar with an old pain that she doesn't suffer with it, I do." He lowered his voice, not wanting to say it, but knowing he had to. "When she went to her friend's death rites last summer, her grief nearly killed me. You don't know what you're asking."

Oron looked to the others in the conclave. They didn't seem moved by what Munro said. The elder turned to Eilidh. "And do you similarly experience Munro's mind?"

Her silver-green eyes swirled, but she looked only at Oron. "He… he is turbulent, sometimes angry and jealous. Wild, like an animal. His mind is unfocused. It never stops. There are good things, of course, but I can't choose. I sense it all."

Oron leaned back in his chair. "And what if you could learn to quiet his voice? You will have a long time together. Your bond is new, and you are both exceedingly young. You will grow more disciplined and discover ways to wall off things you wish to."

"There is…a sexual attraction," Eilidh said, blushing slightly and still refusing to look at Munro.

The conclave members looked at one another. Munro realised they couldn't imagine being sexually attracted to a human.

"The bonding magic fuels it, I'm certain," Eilidh continued. "You might be able to resist it, but from what Munro tells me he learned from the other true druids, the blood faerie and his bonded druid indulged their bond in many ways."

Munro felt slightly sick. He remembered vividly the way she'd told him months ago that a faerie and a human could never be together. He knew she cared for him, he could sense that, but he'd determined never to push, to wait for her to make the first move, even though keeping his distance had proven difficult. His heart ached, and she must have known. He did everything he could to harden himself against the pain of thinking her feelings for him weren't real and focused on the present moment.

"I've been physically weak," he said, "ever since we bonded. When Eilidh fought the blood faerie, she made a choice to sacrifice my life to kill him. She drew out my life force, using it to fuel her earth magic. She didn't channel earth magic through me, she took it *from* me. She could kill me with a thought."

Eilidh whipped her head around and met Munro's eyes. He sensed her anguish, but he ignored it, looking instead at each of the conclave members. "If you think I'm going to deliver a bunch of humans into virtual slavery, so you can invade their minds and suck their lives away, you're off your trolleys, every one of you." As soon as the words left his mouth, he regretted saying them. He was angry with Eilidh for what she said, and he'd lashed out. He had understood what he was getting into when he bonded with her. He knew she might never return his feelings and he'd told her he could handle it. He'd said the bonding words first, practically insisting she finish the ritual, swearing up and down that saving all those lives was worth the price. And it had been, but it cost them both.

The room grew heavy with silence, and all eyes centred on Munro. He hung his head. No matter what happened, he didn't regret the connection he had with Eilidh. "I'll talk to them," he said finally. "I'll *invite* them to come meet with you. But you have to swear to me that if they want, they leave unmolested."

Oron smiled. "That's all we ask, Quinton Munro. No one will be forced to bond."

A high-pitched trill sounded, startling Munro. "Sorry," he said, taking his mobile out of his jacket pocket. He looked at the display screen. Sergeant Hallward. "I have to take this." He stood and went to the corridor, shutting the door behind him. Without another thought for the faerie conclave, he pushed the answer button and said, "Munro."

The call only lasted a couple of minutes, but he lingered in the hall after it finished. Why had he said all that? He trusted Eilidh. He just didn't trust all those other faeries and their plans for the druids.

Just as he was about to open the door to go back in, Eilidh came out. She only had to tilt her head slightly to look him in the eye. She was magnificently tall and so beautiful. Why was he such an idiot?

"I didn't intend to hurt you, Quinton."

"If you hadn't done it, he would have killed us both." He remembered that day in the woods like it was yesterday. Sometimes, on a bad night, he still dreamed about it.

One corner of her mouth quirked into a half-smile. "I meant by saying our attraction was part of the bond."

"Ah, that." He shrugged. "I suppose it's only fair they know. Most of the boys aren't bad looking, but Rory's a bit of a minger."

Eilidh's grin turned into a small laugh. It melted his anger to see her smile. He held up his phone. "I have to go home. There's a police Professional Standards Department inquiry. My boss doesn't seem to think it's a big deal, but I need to be there."

She nodded as though listening, but not quite understanding. They still had a bit of a language and culture barrier to contend with. "And I have to return to the Otherworld to speak with the queen, as soon as the conclave decides what they want me to tell her." She lowered her voice. "I will speak to Prince Griogair about your request. I'll find you when I have word."

"Too bad you can't just *think* it to me."

"You must be tired of having me in your thoughts." She said it lightly but couldn't disguise her emotions. It was bad enough seeing the hurt on her face, but sensing its depth cut him to the core.

"No," he said. "I'm not."

Eilidh nodded, looking down at the ground, as though reluctant to meet his eyes. He'd noticed her doing that now and again, and it made him wonder what she saw in them. He didn't know what to say, so he muttered, "I'm sorry. I have to go. I'll see you when you get back."

Again, she nodded. Munro reached out to take her hand, but she'd already turned and slipped back into the conclave's meeting room. He sighed heavily. He'd never understood women. He'd always suspected if he could read their thoughts, it would make things clearer. Yet, at this moment, he knew exactly what Eilidh felt, and he was none the wiser. There was nothing more to do but go back home and wait.

∞

Eilidh felt no less a sense of wonder visiting Eirlioc Falls the second time. The remarkable monument to fae craftsmanship held unfathomable secrets from the foundation to the spires of ice-like stone that reached high into the air. She breathed in deeply as she approached, enjoying the rich air of the Otherworld. No matter that she spent a good portion of her life in the human world, the Otherworld felt more *real* to her. All fae constructions and settlements were crafted from the elements and magic, wrought with care and focus. Human structures were nailed together and pounded into submission.

When she climbed the steps and entered the small courtyard, one of the many stewards greeted her. She told him her name and her business, and he nodded as though he'd expected her and led her within.

This time she was taken to a much smaller area than the huge audience chamber where she'd met the queen and her consort. Queen Cadhla stood by a large balcony, speaking quietly with a faerie Eilidh recognised from her first visit. He had to be an advisor of some sort, but the queen did not introduce him.

When Eilidh approached, she curtsied deeply. The queen looked her up and down with distaste, obviously not approving of the simple dress Eilidh chose for her illusion. She resorted to illusion because she hadn't wanted to ask one of the azuri for a dress. Even if she hadn't promised Munro she wouldn't steal again, she couldn't have found something appropriate in Portree. Considering the kingdom attitudes toward any kind of astral or thought magic, she took a risk using illusion in front of a kingdom faerie, and even more so when meeting the queen.

Cadhla said to the faerie beside her, "Leave us," and he inclined his head and departed. She went to a side table and poured a drink from a clear crystal pitcher into a tall, thin glass. She drank deeply without looking at Eilidh. "So, what say the azuri to my offer?"

"Your Majesty, the head of the azuri conclave has agreed to meet with you himself, providing you lift the standing death order, of course."

The queen's eyes flashed. "Has he? He will condescend to come to me, will he?"

Eilidh furrowed her brow, confused. "I..."

"And all I have to do to be so privileged to speak with him is to change the law for the entire Caledonian kingdom, to allow this filthy azuri magic to spread unabated?"

"Did I misunderstand? Did you not offer to consider the azuri to be integrated into the kingdom again?"

"Will they submit to my rule?" The queen laughed sharply. "I already know what that fool Oron sent you here to say, and like a good little doggy, you have come to deliver the outcasts' insults in person. I should kill you where you stand."

Eilidh kept completely still. The queen's magic pulsed, thickening the air in the room. Her fury shone out of her eyes. Eilidh lowered her eyes and said nothing. She was unprepared for how unguarded the royals could be with their emotions.

It was true the azuri agreed to meet with Queen Cadhla, but it was also true they had sworn they would not dissolve their conclave or swear fealty before the talks even began. The queen obviously knew that, but how could she, unless it came from someone at that conclave meeting? After Munro left, the conclave had cleared out every non-member besides Eilidh to discuss their proposed message to the queen. Eilidh couldn't understand why any of them would betray the conclave, or even how they could communicate with her without being discovered.

It took several long minutes of silence before the queen calmed down. "When you go back to Skye," Cadhla said, "do tell them what you've seen here." She smiled pleasantly, as though she'd not had an outburst at all. "Remind them of the Otherworld. It can't be agreeable to live among humans, huddled in exile. I have visited the human realm with Griogair, of course. It was a strange and empty place. It must be so difficult for them. I'm not without sympathy. These people should be part of the kingdom under my rule. Would it not be a small price to pay to submit to the crown? Is it really better to have autonomy in a desolate and hostile land than to enjoy the light yoke of kingdom rule?"

Since the question didn't seem to be aimed at her, Eilidh didn't answer. Instead, she said, "Most of the azuri were born into exile, Your Majesty. I will remind the elders, of course, as you request, but even a temporary reprieve in the law would be required before they would dare set foot across a gate."

"They think I would invite them here and then kill them?" The queen narrowed her eyes, taking on a dangerous expression.

"Not you, of course. None would question your integrity." Eilidh didn't believe *that* to be true, especially considering the queen had just offered to kill her. "But some of the kingdom might see our existence as a crime in itself."

"Do *you* feel threatened here? Have we not been gracious?"

"Of course, Your Majesty." Eilidh had killed an enemy to the kingdom and been rewarded by the conclave. The fact that the other fae tolerated her did not mean they would take to an invasion by hundreds of azuri, many more powerful than they, all able to perform a type of magic the kingdom feared.

"You either think me a liar, or that the fae of my kingdom would not obey my word."

"The azuri have no doubt that if you lifted the exile or death orders on those with higher magic, they would be completely safe in kingdom lands."

"Higher magic? *Higher* magic?"

Eilidh fumbled over her words. "Forgive me. It is the ancient phrase. I didn't mean to imply..."

"Of course you didn't mean to *say* it, but you do *believe* it, don't you, child?" The queen cast a predatory look at Eilidh.

"No," she said. "I believe we are all one people and *should* be under one rule."

"Interesting," the queen muttered. "I wouldn't have thought it of you." She spoke quietly, as though thinking aloud. Then, in a clearer voice, she said, "Give Oron my assurances of safe passage. But tell him also that I know of his plans. Once the kingdom is united, there will be no azuri conclave. And, Eilidh?"

"Yes, Your Majesty?"

"If I wanted the azuri dead, I would simply send my ten thousand Watchers to Skye and wipe them out. That many should be able to handle your four hundred."

Eilidh blinked slowly, stunned at the queen's words. Ten thousand Watchers would be their entire number. They could indeed eradicate the entire colony on Skye with that kind of force. But more troubling than the queen's knowledge of the azuri's numbers, was that she had considered the force necessary to kill them all, and that she would have the Watchers abandon the kingdom borders to do it.

"I will deliver your message with all haste."

The queen waved her hand in dismissal, and Eilidh dipped into a curtsy and left as quickly as she could.

She had to find a way to see Griogair, but realised she had no way to get a message to him. She couldn't risk the queen finding out about their meetings, and any servant Eilidh questioned might report back. Her nerves frayed as she slowly progressed toward the castle entrance. She tried to walk with purpose, so as to not seem like she was skulking, but neither did she rush, in case Griogair hadn't yet heard she was here. All she could do was hope he'd have someone watching for her.

As she neared the exit to the castle, a voice came from across an arched entryway. "Mother above, that is an ugly dress."

Eilidh turned and met Griogair's violet eyes. "Her Majesty thought so as well," Eilidh said.

He slipped into the hallway and motioned for her to continue the way she'd been walking. "Of all the things I can say about Cadhla, I cannot say she has bad taste."

"In clothing," Eilidh added, then instantly regretted it. She had to remind herself she was speaking with the second most powerful faerie in the kingdom and mate to the queen. He couldn't be trusted, no matter how charming his tone or how sincere he was about finding his son. He had an agenda, she reminded herself.

Griogair laughed. "Indeed, she has atrocious taste in men." He lowered his voice as they walked. "Did you speak to your druid?"

"Yes. He says he needs to talk with you in person."

Griogair hesitated only briefly. "When?"

"He has travelled several hundred miles in the human realm, and I must go to Skye first. The queen has ordered me to deliver a message to the azuri conclave." She narrowly avoided saying "Higher Conclave" as she usually did. "I suspect she will know immediately if I don't do it today. However, I think it will take them several days to argue about what to do. I can slip through the gates and tell Munro you have agreed. I will try to arrange the meeting for tomorrow's nightfall. When the weaver crosses the four brothers."

The prince-consort nodded, coming to a stop as they approached the courtyard. "Which gate is nearest?"

"Ashdawn."

"I will be as close as I can. When you cross, I will find you."

"Your Highness," she said. "Is there any way you can come to us? It would be a great risk to bring Munro to the Otherworld. Sneaking past the Watchers in the borderlands would be difficult if I were alone, but with a human, I think it would be impossible."

"I cannot leave the realm without Cadhla. It's forbidden, and she would know immediately. Don't worry about the Watchers. I have enough influence to ensure they will let your druid pass."

She nodded, wondering how the queen would know if he left the Otherworld but not doubting the truth of it. "Very well." She started to curtsy, but he stopped her, reaching up and running his hand along her arm.

Griogair grinned. "Could you not smile at me, Eilidh? Everyone in the castle thinks I have seduced you, and it would not do to look so...formal."

"Faith," Eilidh swore, then coughed when she realised what she'd said, and blushed as Griogair chuckled. "Then they will just have to think we have had a lovers' argument." She turned on her heels and marched toward the castle gates, his now earnest laughter ringing in her ears. It wasn't too difficult to feign anger. *Presumptuous*... She stopped mid-thought because she couldn't think of a word that fit how she felt about the prince at that moment.

CHAPTER 6

"HOW DID IT GO?" Sergeant Hallward asked Munro, who sank into a chair next to the sergeant's desk. He'd driven straight over after his meeting with the Professional Standards Department in Dundee.

"Well enough, I suppose. I did what you said. Told the truth as far as it made sense, pled memory loss where things got weird. I didn't like it, but like you said earlier, it was the only thing to do."

"I don't like it either, son," Hallward said. "I will tell you this much, I don't envy them their job. Most hated men in the department. I know you didn't do anything wrong with the...incident last summer, but questions had to be asked. There's nothing worse than a bent copper. I'd just as soon someone rooted out the problems, and I'm glad it isn't me having to do it. Hard enough to keep the public trust without giving people reason *not* to trust us."

"Not that most of them need a reason." Munro paused. "The worst part was it felt disloyal, like I was pinning something on my dead cousin."

"I know you want to defend your family. It's natural. But the truth of it is, if Frankie had come to you about his suspicions sooner, he'd probably be alive today."

Munro wasn't so sure. He'd faced the blood faerie, whose actions were explained to the human public as those of a cult serial killer. Munro didn't think anything he could have done would have saved Frankie. If it hadn't been Frankie lying dead in that clearing, it would have been one of the others. Munro sighed, feeling guilty that part of him wished it had been one of the others. They had families too, he reminded himself.

"All right," Hallward finally said. "Get on out of here. Probably don't have time to get back to Skye, though."

Munro chuckled. "Aye, but my girlfriend is used to my odd hours." It felt weird calling Eilidh his girlfriend. The word didn't fit any part of their relationship, but he didn't know what other term he could possibly use. *Bonded faerie* sounded strange, even to his ears. He couldn't imagine what Hallward would think of that, even though the sarge had heard the rumours she wasn't human.

"You're still looking pale. I know the doc cleared you, but you aren't yourself. Go home. Get some sleep." Hallward turned his attention to a stack of papers on his desk.

"Aye, Sarge." Munro walked out to his car and went to run some errands. He wasn't ready to face the empty house quite yet. While he strolled the aisles at ASDA, putting stuff in a shopping trolley without paying attention to what it was or how much it cost, he thought about what he was going to say to the other druids about going to Skye. In some ways, he didn't know what his hesitation was. Long life, healing, magical power—most people would jump at the chance. Part of it was he felt like he was leaving Frankie behind. And he wasn't sure he trusted all the other druids. Some may have taken a passive role in the deaths that summer. Once he took them to Skye, they'd all be part of his life forever, or at least for the next several hundred years.

He shook himself out of his dazed train of thought. All he would do was introduce them to some people who might or might not want to know them. It wasn't his responsibility to decide who was and who wasn't worthy of power.

When he arrived at the till and took out his wallet, Munro stopped, staring at his credit card, thinking of Eilidh. With a smile, he inserted his card into the reader and punched in his PIN, remembering the way she'd blushed when he confronted her about stealing. The clothes at the tourist shop cost him sixty quid, but it was worth it to see the wonder on her face when he explained credit cards. He loved how she took delight in little things, like the light in the refrigerator.

By the time he pulled up to his house, he knew Eilidh was inside. Earlier, he'd felt her coming and going from the Otherworld. She must have word from this prince of hers. Munro couldn't put a finger on why the mention of the guy made him twitch, but he didn't trust him.

He found Eilidh in his bedroom, rummaging through his closet. "Hi," he said from the doorway. She didn't have a key to his house, but with her newly flourishing earth powers, she could manipulate metal, including simple locks. It never occurred to her to knock, but Munro didn't mind too much.

"Your clothes are all the same," she said, turning to him with a frown.

"Since when do you care what I wear?" Munro was puzzled. He'd never seen her in anything but jeans.

"You're meeting the prince-consort tonight." She went to his dresser and started digging through his underwear drawer.

"Do you mind?" he said, taking a pair of boxers out of her hands and folding them again. "What difference does it make what I wear?"

"You have a queen, do you not?" Eilidh said impatiently.

"Yeah."

"And she has a consort?"

"Prince Phillip. But it's not the same."

"Why not?"

"A guy like me isn't going to meet Prince Phillip."

"Ah!" she said with triumph in her voice. "But if you did, you wouldn't wear any of this, would you?"

"I'd probably wear a suit, I guess. You really expect me to wear a suit to meet this guy?"

"No, I've seen what you call business suits. They're ridiculous."

Munro sat on the bed and muttered, "At least we agree on something." Then he asked, "What are you going to wear?"

He watched as she shifted her clothing into a long, dress. It was a beautiful earth brown with a high, square neckline. It flowed to the ground, hugging her hips in a way he found alluring, even though very little flesh showed.

"You look great," he said.

Eilidh quirked her mouth into a grin. "The prince hates it."

Munro stuffed down the irritation as quickly as he could. Something in her smile told him she enjoyed the idea of annoying the prince, and that bordered on flirting in his book. He went to his closet and pulled out some black trousers and a plain black button-down shirt. "This will do," he said, trying to put finality in his tone.

"It's very human looking."

"I'm very human. He'll have to deal with it. Besides, isn't this a clandestine meeting?"

She nodded.

Munro rolled his eyes. "Then this'll do."

She looked outside, and he could feel her frustration and eagerness to be on their way. She made no motion to budge from the room, so he took the clothes into the *en suite* loo to change. He was just about to use the toilet when she opened the door and walked in. “We really should go now.”

He stood there, trousers undone, hand in his shorts arranging himself. “I’m takin’ a piss here.”

She shrugged. “Well, hurry.”

“Fine,” he muttered and went about his business. She just didn’t understand privacy. If they were going to be bonded for a few centuries, he’d have to get used to it, but she didn’t make it easy. He wasn’t raised to be so open and unselfconscious, but on some things, Eilidh refused to budge. She thought humans were strange and repressed about nudity, bodily functions, and sex. To hear her tell it, faeries had sex if they felt like it, and it was all good and healthy and open.

Except, of course, if it came to having sex with humans. It bothered him, and he couldn’t help but wonder if that meant Eilidh wanted to have sex with other men. Well, faeries. She seemed to care about him, and he would have known if she’d had sex with someone else since they’d been bonded, but that didn’t mean she wouldn’t eventually.

He washed his hands, and she said softly, “You’ve retreated into your thoughts.”

“Do you want him?” Munro asked. He liked that Eilidh didn’t mind a blunt question. He wasn’t quite used to asking them, but she never seemed bothered when he did.

“He’s mated to the queen. I told you, the royal family mates for life.”

“That isn’t what I asked you.”

“We should go,” Eilidh said, walking into the bedroom.

He followed, watching her closely. “Eilidh?”

“Quinton, you should know before we meet him. Prince Griogair has allowed the court to think he and I are lovers, so we would have an excuse to be seen talking alone. He may feel the need to keep up the pretence tonight. It depends who he has to bring with him.”

Munro’s gut clenched. “But it is pretence, right?” His anger boiled. “The royal family mates for life, you said.”

Eilidh looked embarrassed. “I was naïve, I suppose. He is mated to the queen, yes, stays by her side and always will. But it seems they both indulge their desires as any common faerie would.”

As annoyed as he was, knowing she wasn’t telling him everything, he said, “The idea upsets you. I can tell.”

“I suppose I believed a child’s dream, that the royals had a love that would make them special. There is a part of me,” Eilidh said, “that is jealous of human tradition, of taking one and no other.”

"It doesn't always work out." He gave up thinking she would leave him alone to change clothes, so he unbuttoned his shirt and hung it up.

"Did it *work out* for your parents?" she asked.

"Yeah." He thought about them as he changed into the clothes he'd chosen for the meeting. "They were together nearly thirty years when my mum died. That's a long time for us."

Eilidh smiled. "Yes, it would be. And they were not a political family? Not officials or royal?"

Munro laughed. "My father was a painter and my mother a bookkeeper. Not official and definitely not royal."

"Your father was an artist?"

"Houses, not canvases." Munro chuckled and shook his head. He couldn't help but think his father would have liked Eilidh. But then, seriousness overtook him. He hated the uncertainty hanging between them. "We need to talk." He hated that expression. It always sounded like a break-up phrase, but he didn't know what else to say.

"I know," she said. "But we have many years ahead of us. Some things sort themselves out with time."

He nodded, grabbing his wallet and keys and sticking them in the pockets of his black trousers. Some things *did* sort themselves out with time, he thought, but other things fell apart. "How far do we need to go?"

"Ashdawn." Seeing the confusion on his face, she added, "It's not far. We'll run it from here."

He hesitated, then sat down on the bed to put on his comfortable, rubber-soled black work shoes. "I'm not sure I can," he finally said. "I've been weak ever since that night." He knew he wouldn't have to explain which one.

With a frown, Eilidh knelt on the floor in front of him and looked up into his face. She put a hand on his chest, as though feeling for his heart, but she shook her head in frustration. "You feel too different to me. I cannot tell what is unbalanced and what is normal for your people."

"It's only been a few months. Maybe it'll take a little time. If it wasn't for our bond, I'd be dead right now."

"If it wasn't for me, none of this would have happened." Her silver-green eyes swam with emotion. "When you told the conclave I could kill you with a thought..."

"Eilidh," he began.

"You were right. I should never have taken from you that way."

"Look. I'm a cop. I get it. Some things are more important than my aches and pains." He ran his hand along her cheek, then tilted her chin so she would look into his eyes. "Some things are more important than me." He took her hand and helped her to her feet. "Come on. Let's go interrogate a prince." He gave her a mischievous grin. "This should be fun."

As they approached the front door, Eilidh formed the illusion that made her appear human. Although darkness was falling, she always took care when they went out together. Alone, she could flit through the streets, on rooftops and dance through traffic without anyone noticing. Munro slowed her down, and tonight, that fact weighed on him.

The place she'd called Ashdawn wasn't far from the grounds of Scone Palace, as far as Munro could tell. Normally, he wouldn't have any problem running that far, and Eilidh seemed surprised at just how slowly they had to move. Everyone told them their bonding would make him stronger, but instead, he still felt weak from the drawing she'd done six months earlier.

As they made their way through the woodlands, her eyes began to glow. He had to stay close, because he couldn't see well, and she wouldn't let him use the small torch he kept on his keychain.

A tingle passed over his skin. "There's someone here," he said.

Eilidh glanced back, her eyes shimmering green. "I know," she said. "A Watcher."

It felt almost like a ghost had passed, and fear tickled Munro's spine. His senses grew sharper, and gradually, as though the moon shone brighter, he could see the outline of the trees. He thought he caught a glimpse of someone nearby, but the shape faded into the surrounding forest, and he couldn't be certain anyone had been there at all.

The deeper they went, the more he noticed a rich, loamy smell. It triggered a memory he'd forgotten, his mother working in the garden when he was little, planting strawberries around a path border out back. He'd learned from Frankie that he must have inherited his magical abilities from his mother. According to Frankie, women carried it, but only boys manifested druidic talents. He wondered if his mother had any clue. Did the earth magic give her even the slightest affinity? It hurt him that the more time that passed, the more difficulty he had remembering much about her beyond flashes and glimpses that felt like dreams.

"We're close," Eilidh said, still holding Munro's hand.

"I know. I can see." He put his hand in front of his face and wiggled his fingers. It was pitch black out, but the darkness had receded. Colours had grown soft, and he could see his surroundings sharply now. It was like using night-vision goggles, but without the strange green tinge. Ahead, he could make out a glow. The pair walked forward together and came to an immense arching gate made of pale light. It stood nearly fifty feet tall and had intricate scrollwork, as though it was etched into invisible stone.

Munro reached out to touch one tall pillar, and when he did, it gave light resistance before his hand passed through. The gate stood open, but beyond it, Munro could see only darkness.

"We must hurry," Eilidh said. "Prince Griogair will be waiting on the other side. He assured me you would be safe, but we shouldn't linger longer than we have to."

"You're afraid," Munro said.

"Humans do not pass through these gates. I'm not sure what will happen."

Munro nodded in the darkness, knowing she could still see him better than he could see her. "Let's get it over with then."

Eilidh went first, and Munro followed. They hadn't gone four paces past the gate before he let go of her and dropped to his knees, hands flat on the earth in front of him.

She darted back, crouching beside him. "Quinton?" He looked up, smiled, and breathed in deeply. "Are you all right?" she asked, a puzzled expression on her face.

Munro touched the ground, fingering a tall blade of grass in front of him. The landscape on the fae side of this gate looked very much like it had in the borderlands, but there was no mistaking one world for another. The moon hung large and low and cast a blue light. Fireflies danced in the air, and plants glowed with vitality.

"You must get up," she said. "Can you stand?"

He nodded and she helped him to his feet. "I feel stronger. Lighter." He breathed in again. Every time he inhaled, he drank in life itself.

"Come. We can wait for Prince Griogair nearby." Eilidh seemed suddenly worried and wary, but Munro's mind surged with robust confidence. In fact, he'd never felt better in his life. He'd never done drugs, not even in his teens, but he couldn't help wondering if this was what it was like. He believed he could take over the world. "I thought he would be waiting for us."

Eilidh shook her head. "He said he'd come if he could, but if he ran into trouble, he probably won't come at all. We'll go wait. He'll find us when he arrives."

"I thought he was the top man. What sort of trouble could he run into?"

"I think," came a voice from the trees, "she means my mate, the queen."

A faerie that could only be Prince Griogair came walking into the clearing. He didn't wear a crown or any type of uniform or decoration, so Munro wasn't sure how he knew. Munro found all faeries haughty and full of themselves, and so it wasn't the prince's bearing that gave away his status. But the instant Munro laid eyes on him, he felt a pull, like it would be difficult *not* to stare at him.

The prince, on the other hand, looked only at Eilidh. She had changed into the illusion of that same brown dress she'd showed Munro. The prince seemed amused when he noticed it, but less so when Eilidh curtsied. "Didn't we talk about this?" he asked, taking her hand and bringing her to her feet.

"Your Highness," she began.

He rolled his eyes. "Griogair."

"Your Highness," she said firmly. "This is PC Munro." It amused Munro that she used his rank and last name, but he would be the first to admit he didn't know anything about faerie politics.

Only then did Griogair turn his attention to Munro. The prince had the strangest eyes, even more remarkable than Eilidh's, Munro thought. Perhaps it was the night that made them glow purple, but they locked on Munro and held his gaze for a good, long while, with neither man speaking.

"Quinton," Eilidh said, seeming quietly distressed, as though Munro were being frighteningly rude. "This is Prince Griogair, consort to the faerie queen."

Munro held out his hand. "Nice to meet you," he said, knowing faeries didn't shake hands, but wanting to see what the prince would do. He hadn't planned to be confrontational, but he suddenly felt as though he'd completely lost the upper hand. He had to get it back if he was going to get a read on this guy.

The prince looked at the outstretched hand, then met Munro's eyes. He knew what Munro was doing. He put his hand in Munro's, copying his grip and movement exactly. "So, you are Eilidh's druid. A human with earth magic. You'll have to forgive me for staring. I never thought I'd see such a thing."

Munro smiled briefly. "Neither did I." Then he switched into cop mode, approaching the prince as he would anyone who filed a missing persons report. "Eilidh tells me you want my help finding your son. Is there someplace we can sit and talk?" Munro didn't like to admit it, but the rich air of the Otherworld made him a little lightheaded. "You can invite your friends to join us." He gestured to the trees, beyond which he sensed at least four, possibly five others. He wasn't sure how he sensed them, but in the strange night air, he decided to go with it.

Griogair tilted his head. “They are fine where they are, thank you.” His tone revealed amusement. “Don’t worry. They are trusted companions.” To Eilidh, he said, “Can he run?”

Before she could answer, Munro said, “I can.”

Griogair became a blur, and he moved silently away. Munro watched as though in slow motion. He stepped after the prince, running easily behind him. He felt Eilidh follow, but he kept his eyes on the prince’s trail. The prince’s companions went with them, keeping just far enough away to stay hidden.

When they stopped, they were in a small glen next to a shimmering river. The moss became a rich, soft carpet under their feet. They stood beneath an enormous tree, whose roots formed perfect steps that led up into its boughs. Munro looked at the water, at the stones that made it sparkle. He stepped toward it and reached in. The water was icy, a cold that went down to his bones. He picked up a rock, but it was no ordinary rock. It was a solid piece of quartz, but it had a blue tint like he’d never seen. When the water passed over the stones, they sung.

Munro felt his earth magic surging and realised that was what was making him feel so strong. His magic fed on the air. His primary element of strength was stone, which was perhaps why these rocks called to him. The air and the water seemed rich and beautiful, but not alive.

The quartz melted in his hand like putty. He saw a shape forming within it, as though it was the rock's true form. No rock of his own world responded to him like this. For just a moment, his mission faded to the side, and he lost himself in the beauty of the stone. As he had when crafting the rose for Flùranach, he tried something a little different than when he made his talismans at home. He focused on the prince's powerful presence. Unlike when he worked with the child, here in the Otherworld, he didn't even have to touch the prince to feel his essence.

Neither Griogair or Eilidh said a word. They watched in silence as Munro teased the rock, pulling it like taffy. Its tips became sharp, and he guided the mass into the form of a star with razor-like edges. The crystal lost any clouded imperfections. When Munro finally finished, it was beautiful, with life shimmering within. It sparkled in the strange moonlight of the Otherworld, resting in the palm of his hand, perfect in its symmetry, lovely, and yet deadly.

He held it out to Griogair. "For your hearth," he said, suddenly remembering the faerie tradition of giving a gift when invited to another's home. It wasn't a tradition he understood the nuances of, but he remembered how Oron reacted when Munro crafted the rose with his granddaughter. He figured it would be a decent gift.

The faerie prince looked at Munro carefully and then inclined his head. "I misjudged you, PC Munro." He whispered a word and a gust of wind surrounded Munro's hand, lifting the blue star out.

"Wait," Eilidh said. Munro could feel her focusing her magic on the talisman as it hung in the air between the two men. She glanced at Munro. "This is like none of the other talismans I have seen you make. I can feel Prince Griogair's own essence much more strongly since he touched it with his power."

The fae always seemed entranced by the things he made, but Munro felt frustrated that he didn't understand the process better. He just hoped he wasn't passing out weapons of mass destruction, now that he thought about it.

"Fascinating." Griogair watched the star carefully as he used air flows to lower it into a leather pouch. Once the star was out of sight, Eilidh seemed to breathe easier.

"Come," Griogair said finally. "Let us sit upstream."

He led the pair up a mossy path to another clearing, where swing chairs fashioned out of roots and leaves swayed in the low boughs of a willowy tree. It took Munro a moment to get comfortable as the other two sat. He wasn't yet used to the strange furniture faeries favoured. For some reason, they didn't seem to like anything too stable, where he preferred to feel himself solidly on the ground.

"I don't know all the rules and protocols," Munro said. "And I don't want to offend you or anything. So if I say the words wrong, or speak out of turn, I'm sorry in advance. But your boy is missing, and I know what that does to a family. Tell me about him, and I'll do what I can to help. Let's start with when and where you saw him last, all right?"

Griogair leaned forward, his expression intent. "Very well."

CHAPTER 7

EILIDH HAD WATCHED MUNRO craft the star and present it to the prince. She felt proud of him and noticed how silent his mind became when he worked with the stone flows. The Otherworld agreed with him, but it still worried her, even more now that they had travelled away from the gate. She had to trust Griogair could protect them and ensure they hadn't been seen.

"The last time I saw Tràth was the night before the Glade Festival," Griogair said.

Munro looked at Eilidh expectantly. She felt flustered. Human clocks and calendars had never made much sense to her. "The Glade came to its peak one hundred and seventy-four nights ago."

"Jesus," Munro muttered and reached for his wallet.

Both faeries watched him with some curiosity. He pulled out a small white card with blocks of numbers on it and stared for a while, counting the lines. "So, mid-August." He glanced at Eilidh, as though expecting confirmation, but she could only shrug apologetically. She hated to confess her ignorance, especially on such a small matter. She realised their new relationship meant she had a lot more to learn than just astral magic. They were going to have a busy century ahead.

"What were the circumstances?" Munro asked.

Griogair leaned back in his seat. "He'd been talking with his mother. He came to me. He was not in the best of moods."

"What was their argument about?"

"Quinton," Eilidh hissed. Munro cast her a warning glance, but she ignored it and said, "You cannot ask such questions."

He turned to Griogair and repeated his question. "What was the argument between Tràth and your wife about?"

The prince shrugged slightly. "There was no argument."

Munro stood. "Okay then." He turned to Eilidh. "Let's go. There's nothing I can do here."

"What?" Eilidh didn't move. She was too stunned. She'd known he was jealous of the prince, and he hadn't been happy about the deliberate rumours that Eilidh was Griogair's lover. She hadn't expected Munro to allow those feelings to get in the way.

Munro shrugged. "Missing persons cases are hard anyway. Not to mention that the best chance of finding someone is within forty-eight hours of his disappearance. A trail several months cold? Nearly impossible. Add the secrecy involved, that I'm not allowed to talk to the boy's mother, that I have to do this with no support from other police, forensics, and no back-up. All of that I'd accepted. But when the one person I *can* talk to lies to me..." His words trailed off.

"Your Highness, I must apologise for my druid." Eilidh took her time with her words. "He meant no offense."

Griogair watched them closely, not saying a word.

"Actually," Munro said. "I don't care if you're offended."

Eilidh was surprised at his strength and confidence. She couldn't detect so much as a flutter of nervousness about him.

He went on, "In fact, *I* am offended. You're wasting my time, Griogair, and I don't have as much of it as you do."

Eilidh closed her eyes. Munro had no idea how powerful the prince was. If it made him nervous that she could have killed him with a thought, he should have been shaking in the presence of the prince-consort. She blamed herself for not explaining the situation better.

When she opened her eyes again, she was shocked to see the prince smiling. "Sit down," he said to Munro with a slight chuckle, waving at the empty seat. "I don't see what the argument has to do with my son's disappearance. Isn't it enough for you to know there was one?"

Munro sat down on the edge of the seat, not reclining fully or making himself comfortable. "I won't know until you tell me what it was about."

After a few moments, the prince said, "Cadhla has always found our son to be a disappointment. He isn't as strong as she thinks suitable for someone of his noble lineage, and he has little ambition to learn. She frequently expresses her opinions to him. Over the centuries, he has come to resent it. Their argument was the same one they often have. Our son is an adult, and he spends time at various homes throughout the Otherworld. But at the same time, he is young, and..." The prince paused, as though choosing his words carefully. "He is not as adept at handling royal society as we would like. He therefore spends much time alone."

"This might seem an odd question, but are you certain he's missing? Could he just be avoiding his mother?"

Griogair shook his head. "He is guarded constantly, and we have eyes and ears everywhere. It might have been possible for him to hide for a short time, but not half a year, and not with an active search, no matter how secretive. Every faerie in the kingdoms knows what it would mean to defy the queen. The Watchers have done their duty. That I can promise you."

"How did he slip away then, if he's guarded?" Munro asked. Eilidh felt his sudden concern and discomfort.

Griogair shrugged. "He has friends."

"So not *every* faerie is afraid of your wife," Munro said quietly. Before Griogair could comment, Munro asked, "What makes you think he's in the human world?"

"About a year ago, there was rumour of a child, one who practised the Path of the Azure, much like Eilidh, although this child was barely an adolescent, around forty, I believe. It has become more common for parents of such children to exile them before they are discovered."

Eilidh sat up and met Griogair's eyes. "There are more like me? Out on the streets?"

"Like most, this child was caught in the borderlands," he said softly. "I wouldn't hold such hopes."

Munro put his hand over hers. He must have felt her surge of emotion. He gave her fingers a squeeze, turned back to Griogair, and asked, "What does an exile have to do with your son?"

"One night, my son and I were talking, and he asked about the exiles. This was only weeks after your own deeds became known in the kingdom. He mentioned you," Griogair said, watching Eilidh's face. "He said he envied you. You made it. You survived, thrived even, in his eyes. I was shocked, of course. No matter how difficult his life may be, he is the crown prince. But he asked me…" Griogair shifted slightly. "He asked me if his mother and I have continued making sacrifices to the Mother of the Earth."

Munro turned to Eilidh, obviously confused. She hesitated only slightly before saying, "When a couple wish to conceive, they make a journey past the borderlands to make a sacrifice to the Mother of the Earth, our Goddess. Only She can grant the gift of fertility."

Munro nodded and waited patiently for the prince to continue.

"I told him we stopped thirty years ago," Griogair said. "It had become obvious the Goddess would not hear us." The prince sat back, looking tired. "My decision caused a rift. Cadhla was obsessed with having another child, but I could see what it was doing to her. To us. I thought with time she would accept the Mother's will."

"And you told your son this?"

"When he first asked, I thought he was concerned his mother still wanted a daughter to succeed her. Tràth would only take the throne if we had no female children," the prince explained to Munro. "I thought perhaps it would comfort him to learn that regardless of the difficulties between him and his mother, his place in line was secure. Instead, he began asking me about the human realm, the places I might have seen on our visits." To Eilidh he said, "We have gone to every altar in the kingdom at least once."

"And where are these altars?" Munro asked Eilidh.

"There are fourteen left in this kingdom,'" she said. "They are usually near gates, but far enough that when the gates close, the couple is outside the borderlands. Most in Caledonia are marked by what you call *standing stones*, but not all."

"Would he have gone to these altars?"

"I don't think so," Griogair said. "When we spoke, he was more interested in human dwellings, their habits. At first I thought it merely curious, but I occasionally heard rumours he had slipped away from his guards. It took a few months before I realised it was always near a gate. That's when I started to suspect he visited the human realm."

"Did you ever confront him about it?" Munro asked.

"When I asked, he denied having ever left the borderlands."

"But you didn't believe him," Munro said.

"No," Griogair replied. "I did not."

"Can you tell me anything that will give me a place to start? Even if he stayed in Scotland, it's a big place."

"His last five sojourns were all near Ashdawn."

"Perthshire?" Munro asked. "Why there?"

The prince shrugged. "I don't know. Perhaps because of Eilidh, or perhaps for some other purpose. But it's one of the reasons I sought your help, PC Munro."

"Do you have a photo of him?"

Griogair frowned at Munro, then glanced at Eilidh, who said, "He means a likeness, Your Highness. A painting or image of any kind?"

Griogair nodded, then touched the air, as though sketching with his fingers. Lights played in front of him, dancing and responding to softly muttered words.

Munro watched with wonder, staring intently at the weaving flows of air.

It took only a few minutes before the prince stopped. He blew on the lines with a puff of air, and the image turned toward Munro and Eilidh. The face was remarkable. The boy looked very like Griogair, but with startling blue eyes. His mouth was slightly softer, and his brow a little higher, but there was no mistaking the resemblance.

Munro reached into his pocket and took out his phone. Before Eilidh could protest that it would never work in the Otherworld, he'd tapped a button on the front and it made an odd clicking noise. He glanced at the screen, tapped a few times on it, then put the device back in his pocket.

"What about friends? Are there faeries who would have gone with him?"

Griogair shook his head. "They have all been questioned. Some had knowledge or at least suspicions of his trips to the human realm, but none admitted accompanying him."

"I'll need to speak with them," Munro said.

Surely he didn't expect Griogair would allow it, Eilidh thought.

"I'm afraid that's not possible. I cannot risk Cadhla learning of your investigation."

Munro nodded. "And money? Would he have access to bank accounts? Credit cards? Cash even?"

The prince glanced at Eilidh for explanation. She shook her head at Munro. "He would not have these things."

"What about jewellery or something he could have sold for money? We might be able to trace him that way."

Griogair frowned. "Tràth only ever wore one ring, a sign of his rank. He would never sell it."

"All the same, can you show me what it looked like? It might help us find him, if someone has seen or recognised it."

At first, Eilidh thought Griogair might refuse, but after a moment, the prince drew a picture of a plain white metal band with symbols etched into the surface. Munro repeated the process with his phone, and Eilidh could see he'd captured an image of the ring. Munro then asked, "How can we get in touch with you if we have more questions?"

Just then a tall female faerie swept up the mossy steps and moved in close to Griogair, whispering into his ear.

The prince's eyes widened with alarm. "You must go," Griogair said. "Now. Mira will guide you back to the gate. Quickly." He stood and without another word, went down the steps and into his tree-house.

"Come," Mira said. Her face was serious, and Eilidh acted quickly to obey. Munro also got to his feet and followed, and Eilidh was grateful the Otherworld had made him well enough to run.

When they stepped through the gate between the Otherworld and the borderlands, Eilidh and Munro kept running, but their guide stayed behind. The sky was still dark, and it would be several hours until the gates closed at dusk. Eilidh had said very little during the conversation with the prince, wanting to let Munro do his job, but she was shocked at the way he'd behaved. Interestingly, though, his techniques worked, and the prince opened up. It surprised her and gave her new respect for Munro.

Only when they'd reached the edge of the still-sleeping city did they slow down. Munro took Eilidh's hand, and again she sensed it comforted and calmed his mind, but she was surprised at how cold his hands were. She constantly had to remind herself it was winter. The grey skies and crunching snow seemed mere background to her, but the weather affected Munro in a way it didn't touch her.

She watched him as they walked. In the Otherworld, speaking to Griogair, Munro's mind seemed remarkably focused. Now, though, it spun with thoughts. As they walked over the bridge toward town, Munro stopped and looked over the water. The River Tay was remarkably calm, its surface almost glassy. It reflected the pale yellow glow of the human moonlight.

"How can we find out where he went?" Munro said. "How far apart are the gates? We can assume he would go someplace closer to this gate than to another one, at least. If he'd been in Perth itself during the past few months, you would know, right?"

Eilidh hesitated. "I think so." She'd been on Skye much of the time during the past six months, but journeyed back and forth several times to visit Munro. The astral training had proven difficult, and she often snuck away during the day, when Munro would be awake, but the Skye fae were sleeping. Using the Otherworld gates, if she timed things well, she could come and go easily. Distance in the Otherworld was more fluid than in the human world, and she could travel in a tiny fraction of the time it would take Munro to drive the distance.

"So we can rule out the city. And he'd stay away from the borderlands, right?"

Eilidh suddenly saw what he meant. "Yes. He must have had one or two friends among the Watchers. It would be difficult to pass through the gates without them knowing once, much less several times. But the Watchers move, and he couldn't always be certain the same ones would be around. If he truly did not want his mother to know he was in the human world, it would be too big a risk."

Munro nodded and pulled out his phone. "Let's look at a map." He laid it flat on the stone side of the bridge. "This is Perth," he said.

Eilidh peered at the shiny surface of his phone, and saw the green representation of the woodlands, the blue ribbon of the river, and a cluster of lines and boxes that Munro said indicated the city. She took the phone in her hand and stared at it.

He pinched his fingers together on the screen, and the city became smaller, the river longer, and the forests wider. "This is about where Ashdawn is. We can rule out all of Perth, Scone, and what about Crieff?"

She looked at the spot west of Perth that he indicated on the tiny map. "I think that would be closer to the Moonstone gate, which is near this body of water."

"Loch Earn," Munro muttered. "Okay, what about south?" Munro asked. "Toward Edinburgh?"

"To the Wastes? No, he would use the Kingsbrine gate if he wanted to go there."

"I think we must assume he's in a town or village, but the more isolated it is, the more the kingdom borders would encroach at night. He wouldn't want to risk that a Watcher would come close enough to detect him. If he was here," she tapped on the phone's screen, "here, or here, I think I would surely have felt him at one time or another, especially over recent months when I could move more freely. We can rule out the North between here and the closest gates, because I have run this path between Perth and Skye, and sensed only Watchers in the woods. I believe I would have noticed a faerie's presence in the human habitations nearby."

"So it makes sense he would have gone west then?"

Eilidh shrugged. "A faerie could theoretically mask his presence. So it's possible he could have hidden from me." Munro sighed. "But, remember," she continued, "Griogair said his son wasn't strong or well-trained. It would take a great deal of energy to keep up such an enchantment. When I was in exile, I decided to make it as easy for myself as possible. I stayed near the cities, where the kingdom influence is almost non-existent. I hid from humans, which is much easier than hiding from the fae."

"What about Dundee? It's a much bigger city than Perth. Is there a gate closer than Ashdawn?"

Eilidh shook her head. "No, we do not build gates too near the eastern sea. The waterfae are no friend to faeries of Caledonia. "

Munro looked at her. "There are faeries in the sea?"

Eilidh nodded. "Strange creatures. Powerful and ancient, but they look as much like fish as they do the fae."

Munro stared at her a moment, then looked back to the map. "Even narrowing it down to Dundee makes it difficult. It's a city of a hundred and fifty thousand, with even more in outlying areas." He tapped his phone screen and it went black. He slipped the device into his pocket and turned to look at Eilidh. "What kind of magic can we do? If we're relying on me alone, without anything to go on but a vague direction, I'm not sure what our chances are. I want to help Griogair, but if our plan is just to go out and start wandering around until we find the kid, the whole thing sounds like a waste of time."

Eilidh frowned. "I don't have to see him. Just be close to him."

"Eilidh, if I was approaching this situation as a cop would, I'd be talking to his friends, his mother, the Watchers who might have let him pass, checking bank details and phone records. A trail like this, especially one so long cold, isn't going to be made up of bent twigs and footprints. We need to talk to the people who know him best. We need to get Griogair to change his mind, otherwise..."

"That's not possible," Eilidh said. "He has already taken too great a risk, just by allowing you into the Otherworld."

Suddenly Munro's head whipped around. "Holy Christ!"

"What?" Eilidh asked.

"Didn't you see that?"

"See what?"

"Come on," he said.

"Quinton? Come where?" Eilidh could feel him almost quivering with excitement, but she couldn't understand the source.

"I don't know," he said, and he pointed his finger toward the road. "That way."

∞

Munro ran like his legs would carry him forever, heading southeast, generally following along the A9. He stayed away from the road, and Eilidh came close behind. It felt so good to run, he thought. He had no idea what had happened to him in the Otherworld, why he suddenly felt not only healed from his injuries, from the draining of his life-force, but better than he'd ever felt. He was stronger and more agile, like some kind of X-Man superhero.

The blue blaze he'd seen in the sky flashed so suddenly and lasted only a fraction of a second, so he couldn't judge how far away it was. When they reached the River Earn, about six miles away from the city, he stopped. He growled in frustration.

"What?" Eilidh asked, with more than a little impatience. "What are you chasing, Quinton?"

"A flash," he said. "It was this way, but now I don't know how far to go."

"What makes you think it has anything to do with Tràth?"

"I don't know that it does. But it wasn't natural." He just had a hunch. He couldn't explain to Eilidh. She knew about magic, but to her, it was like science, easy to explain. His hunches were just a feeling. He didn't know if it was Tràth at all, but it was something strange, magical, and *wrong*. He didn't like to admit he thought the whole thing with Tràth was going to come to nothing. Tràth sounded like a young man who hated his parents and had run away. People who didn't want to be found often weren't. Simple as that. And it wasn't like they could track his mobile GPS.

Suddenly, Munro got an idea. He pulled out his phone again, but grumbled when he got no bars. "We should keep going. I can get some reception in Aberuthven."

"Quinton, will you please tell me what you're doing?"

"Where's the nearest gate this way?" Munro asked and gestured further southeast.

Eilidh paused and considered. "The Moonstone gate is that way," she said. "But I'd say we're about half-way between it and Ashdawn."

"If you were trying to get here without being seen by kingdom faeries, would you take Moonstone?"

A smile crept across Eilidh's face as she understood what he was getting at. "No."

"No," Munro said. "Because there's nothing but forest. This way, you could come along the highway. Faeries hate the highways. And southeast?"

"Firearch, but it's near a place I believe you call Carron."

"So if you wanted to go this far, you'd come through Ashdawn. Anywhere between here and Dunblane."

Eilidh nodded. "All right. Let's go then."

"Pay attention," he said. "Tell me if you feel anything. He might be close—if we're right."

They started to run again, this time with more purpose, covering the next two miles in what felt like an instant, despite the rough terrain they had to negotiate to avoid being seen from the highway. His new strength made him want to laugh out loud with joy. It distracted him, and he had to focus to keep his mind off the exhilaration pumping through his body and on the task at hand.

They stopped close to the village of Aberuthven, and Munro scrolled down on his mobile's contact list to call his partner, Andrew Getty.

As usual, Getty didn't bother saying hello when he answered Munro's call. "Heard you went to Skye."

"Eilidh's got some friends up there," Munro said quickly, then added, "Need a favour." The pair didn't chit-chat, and they both liked it that way.

"Sure. What's up?"

"You know those thefts reported lately down the A9? What's the latest word on them?" He'd been briefed at the beginning of his shifts about the mad string of break-ins. It was unusual for the area, but like everyone else, Munro chalked it up to drug users breaking into cars and sheds. People reported broken windows and missing tellys when they'd gotten home from a night out.

"Aye, funny you should ask. Just a bit ago we got a treble-nine from someone claiming they were being robbed. The call went strange though. We've got people on the way now."

"Strange how?"

"Not sure. Anyway, the control room got cut off, and it might be nothing. But considering the recent problems, they're sending a unit to check it out."

"Where?"

"Auchterarder. Fordyce Way. Do you know something?"

"Nope," Munro said. "I'll give you a call if there's anything." The promise was vague, but the pair knew each other well enough to accept that Munro would tell Getty everything he could make sense of. They'd both come to appreciate that Munro often got hunches he couldn't explain and had a way of being at the right place at the right time. Or, in Munro's mind, the right place at the *wrong* time. "Cheers," he said.

"Yep," Getty replied, and they both hung up.

Munro looked at Eilidh. "A couple more miles." They took off again, slowing a few minutes later as they circled the village of Auchterarder. It was a small place, with only a few thousand residents, but with it being the home of the famous Gleneagles hotel and golf course, it had a certain shine to it some villages didn't.

Eilidh seemed put out, but Munro couldn't figure out why. "What's wrong?" he asked, as they picked their way through the last of the dense brush, heading to the main street.

She muttered the enchantment to create her human face and ears, then revealed her jeans and t-shirt, scowling the entire time. "You think all fae are thieves," she said.

"I think people off the grid do what they have to do." He shrugged. He didn't approve, but now wasn't the time to have this discussion. He understood why Eilidh had to steal to survive when she lived on the streets. He didn't *like* it, but he understood. "Getty said a call just came in on Fordyce Way. That might be where the flash came from. Let's check it out."

His body thrummed with the power of the Otherworld, so much that it jangled his nerves. He had no idea how Eilidh could stand this intense rush without jumping out of her skin, but she gave no sign that the Otherworld had done anything other than relax her. He needed to move.

It was still full dark, but Munro's eyesight stayed keen. He suddenly understood why the fae preferred the dark. It had a calm quiet about it. And because he could see as well now as he could at high noon, it took on a whole other feeling. Eilidh watched him closely, and her attention pressed into his mind. He knew she must be questioning the changes in him, but she didn't say a word. They walked toward Fordyce Way, but instead of having to move slowly and silently, they ran, knowing if a human happened to see them, he'd just rub bleary eyes and assume it was his imagination or the glow of the street lamps playing tricks on his eyes.

Munro calculated it wouldn't take long for the beat cops to turn up this time of night. Auchterarder had its own small police station that was part of the Tayside region. It didn't give them much time, considering they'd come all the way from Perth. He motioned Eilidh toward the end of the cul-de-sac. "Feel anything?" he whispered. He glanced at her in the darkness as they crept up to a house, hugging the wall of someone's garage.

Eilidh grumbled with frustration. "It's strange."

"What?" He had half-hoped that his newfound strengths would mean he too could sense whatever it was that told her if a faerie was nearby, but he noticed nothing out of the ordinary. But then his nerves were still hyped up on Otherworld air.

"I feel something, but it is unfamiliar." Her eyes shone as she peered around the various houses. He didn't know what she was looking for, but from the frustration he detected in her mind, she didn't either.

"Fae?"

"Yes, and it's no magic of the Ways of Earth."

"Astral?" he asked. He knew the only surviving magic of the Path of Stars was either blood magic or astral. He hoped they weren't dealing with another blood faerie. Not since the last one he'd met had broken his ribs in several places.

"No." She frowned. "This is like nothing I have ever touched before. It is completely alien to me."

They moved from their hiding place closer to the address the 999 call had come from. Munro felt it in his bones. Something had happened here. He understood Eilidh's uneasiness, though, because his hunch was taking on a different flavour than he'd ever experienced.

Glad that the ground was hard from the cold winter, they stepped to the side gate. With a gloved hand, he silently lifted the latch. Just as he swung the gate open, he heard a car approach. "Shit." Then to Eilidh, "They're here."

It was only then he noticed Eilidh's eyes were fixed near the back door, which stood open. "This was the source," she said quietly.

"We have to go," Munro insisted. Just as he turned, a movement caught his eye. He spun back, and a figure appeared in the garden. It didn't slip out of the shadows, it *appeared*. "What the...?"

He caught the sharp silhouette of a curved ear as the figure turned toward the sound of his voice and heard a faint mutter. As quickly as it had appeared, it vanished.

A car door shut in front of the house. Munro heard the familiar squawk of a police radio. They couldn't leave by the front now, and he couldn't get caught here. Eilidh seemed to sense his urgency. She pulled him into the back garden and left the gate banging in the breeze. With practised steps, she glided over the stone path toward the fence, vaulting over it with ease. Munro copied her movements, although he felt more awkward. He found his magically enhanced speed and strength made up for the lack of grace, and he landed easily on the other side.

They snuck through the other back garden and onto the street toward the town centre, moving quickly, but with Eilidh able to glide more silently than he. Something cold touched his cheek, and Munro looked up. Snowflakes like fat goose feathers floated from above. It was only then Munro realised that despite the wind and the wet, he wasn't cold at all.

CHAPTER 8

MUNRO WATCHED EILIDH GO THROUGH the Ashdawn gate, savouring the rich air coming through it. He hadn't realised how long he'd stared at it until rustling brush made him realise he wasn't alone. He turned warily, then stood stock still as one by one, Watchers filed past him, stepping into the Otherworld. As the sun rose, the last in line shut the gate behind him. It locked with a strange clanging echo, then shimmered out of sight.

He hoped Eilidh made it to the gate nearest Skye before it closed, but he knew she could travel quickly in the Otherworld. He hadn't understood it, but he also wasn't surprised to hear the normal laws of physics didn't quite apply.

With nothing more to do there, he turned and ran toward home. He and Eilidh had hardly spoken on the way back from Auchterarder. She said only that she needed to go to Skye, and he didn't argue. He had to be at work in the morning, well, in less than an hour, now that he thought about it, so there wasn't time for a talk. All he'd said was, "He lied to us."

"I know," she said. Her thoughts were far away though, and they didn't have time to make a plan. His plan would have been to tell *His Highness* to shove it up his arse. Oh, his kid might have run away all right, but Griogair had left out some critical details, that was for sure. It was difficult to tell if the faerie Munro saw in the back garden looked like the portrait of light the prince had shown them, considering how fast everything went and how strange and blurry he appeared. But Munro *knew* it was Griogair's kid. As much of a kid as a hundred and seventy-five-year-old faerie could be. With all the things Griogair did tell them, he'd left out the part about, oh, disappearing into thin air.

Half an hour later, Munro was at work. The strength and speed he'd acquired from his visit to the Otherworld had perks. It took all his willpower to get in his car and drive to work as usual.

Around lunchtime, he and Getty were back at the station filling in endless paperwork. Sergeant Hallward stormed into the room, his fury not settling until he cast an eye on Munro. "Police Constable Quinton Munro," he said evenly.

Getty glanced at his partner and muttered, "Shit. What have you done now?"

"I don't know," Munro said quietly, then called out, "Yes, Sarge?"

Hallward crooked his finger. "Come with me."

Munro stood and followed his boss down the beige corridor. It was a quiet day, but other officers strode here and there, giving the station a feeling of orchestrated urgency.

Hallward stopped in front of an ugly brown door. He opened it and pointed. "In there," he barked.

Inside was a table, a couple of chairs, and a television on a rolling black stand. Without another word, Hallward slipped a disk into the box under the telly. "You want to explain this?" he asked as the video started to play.

Munro watched slightly grainy CCTV footage flick onto the screen. It immediately showed him. And Eilidh. In Auchterarder the previous night. The clip looked like it came from a security camera mounted above an intersection. He watched as the silent footage played out. He recognised the moments after they'd left the house where they'd seen Tràth. "Sarge," he started, then stopped when he saw his own eyes shining in the darkness. It could have been a trick of the bad street lighting, but they both knew better.

"Wait," Hallward said, holding up his hand. "This isn't the best part."

After a few moments of watching him and Eilidh talk, Munro realised he'd been standing out in the snow in just a shirt. No jacket, no nothing. When had he taken his jacket off? He didn't even look like he'd noticed. But then he saw what caught Hallward's eye even more than him surfacing on CCTV footage near a potential crime scene. Suddenly, he and Eilidh nodded to one another, then stepped into a run. It looked so strange, especially considering how natural it felt to do. They moved like the video was on fast forward, but the snow continued to drift in front of the camera, adding further contrast to the now long-gone couple.

"Sarge," he repeated, then realised he wasn't sure what to say.

"You can explain?" Hallward raised an eyebrow.

"I could. Do you want the truth?" Munro couldn't see any point in acting like it was nothing. The digital recording spoke for itself. Kind of. Then again, the sarge had seen some pretty strange things back in the summer when a blood faerie turned out to be a serial killer, and like the hardened copper he was, he took them in stride.

"Let's sit down." Hallward pulled out a chair and sat, looking at Munro expectantly.

With only a moment of hesitation, Munro joined him. "The thing is, it's going to sound crazy."

"Tell me this. Can you do anything besides run fast?"

"It's all new, mind you, but I'm strong too. I heal quickly, and I can see in the dark. They said I will live longer, and my endurance is pretty unbelievable. I ran all the way to Auchterarder without even breathing hard."

"They?"

Munro lifted a shoulder ever so slightly, then realised it was a distinctly fae-like shrug. *Christ.* For a moment, he feared he might be turning into one of them.

"I'm ordering a drug test."

"What?"

Hallward said, "Look, I believe you, but I want to *know*."

Munro nodded. "I don't actually know what a blood test will show, but we'll find out."

Hallward didn't seem particularly happy with that reply, but he let it go. "Tell me what you know about Auchterarder."

"Not a lot, and that's the truth. A friend of Eilidh's asked me to look into a situation. One of their people is missing. And that led me to Auchterarder. I didn't find much of use."

Hallward leaned back in the chair, putting his hands behind his head and looking at the ceiling. He sat that way for a few minutes. "Damn, son, how long before everyone starts to notice you can run like The Flash?"

"I can tone it down in front of people."

"Yeah, and you will. But what I'm saying is there's weird shit going on, and you seem to know what it is. I'm not wasting you writing reports and kettling drunks when I have the only expert I've ever heard of on whatever the hell this is. There are ways we can use you, starting with Auchterarder."

"Why? What happened?" Munro couldn't help it. His curiosity about the case overrode his worry about his job or his uncertainty about what Hallward had in mind. They'd get to that.

"Your girlfriend isn't the only one with a missing persons situation. That house, you saw it?"

"Aye," Munro said.

"Did you see anyone else?"

"A copper pulled up just as we got to the back garden, so we legged it."

Hallward rolled his eyes. "Yeah, because identifying yourself would have been out of the question." He paused a beat. "Sarah McBride called treble nine at 5:03 AM, saying she had a burglar. I want you to listen to the playback, by the way. You'll understand why when you hear it. When PC Dorman arrived at 5:23 AM, he found an open door and an empty house."

Munro nodded, picturing it in his head.

"PC Dorman immediately radioed in what he found, and by 6:30 AM, the local night shift sergeant was on site, and house-to-house enquiries had begun. No one answered their door."

"No one?" Most people would be home that time of day. Sure, one or two might not answer no matter how they banged on the door, but someone should have been about.

Hallward nodded. "By 10:00 AM we established that every house within three hundred yards was empty, with one exception. Janice and Thomas Flemming disappeared from their house during the night, two streets over. They were reported missing by their children, thirteen-year-old Michael and eleven-year-old Sophie. The children's bedrooms were on the south side of the house."

Munro frowned. "Furthest away from the McBrides."

"We aren't going to be able to keep this completely quiet, not with so many people missing, and it won't be long before we're overrun with psychics and UFO spotters. I'll do what I can, but after seeing this," Hallward pointed toward the telly, "I'm fairly well convinced this is one of those cases where your *expertise* will come in handy."

"I need to talk to Eilidh," Munro said.

"You do what you have to do, but keep in touch. You'll be assigned to a special project for me. For right now, you report only to me, and I'll get the information you need from the DCI handling the official Auchterarder case." Hallward stood and looked down at Munro. "You don't know where they are?"

Munro shook his head. "No. And I can't promise results. Eilidh said the magic felt alien to her, so we don't know much more than you do." He paused. "I never thought I'd be talking about magic with you."

"Let's keep that to a minimum. You figure out who took those people and how we can get them back. I don't need to know the specifics." Hallward chuckled.

"Aye, Sarge. I hear you."

"Then get to work."

∞

Munro listened to the treble nine call, which definitely ended on a strange note. The last sentence sounded warped. He asked the dispatcher if something could have gone wrong with the phone or phone line, and she simply said, “Must've. What else could it be?”

Hallward gave him copies of the reports, then sent Munro home so he wouldn't have to deal with awkward questions from other cops. The sarge didn't want anyone to know Munro was working on this particular case.

He sat in his living room with the files spread out on a coffee table. The incident had only happened that morning, but they'd gathered as much information as possible. Munro had also asked for copies of all the CCTV recordings, and Hallward said Munro would have the full set as soon as possible. The sergeant gave him stills from the nearby speed cameras, but Munro knew they wouldn't be of any use. Even if Tràth was involved in these disappearances, he certainly didn't get there by car.

No, what Munro especially wanted to see was the rest of the camera angles from nearby shops or bank ATMs that might have caught an image of Tràth or who he might be with. The glimpse Munro caught of Tràth in the McBride's garden didn't tell him much.

Most of all, he needed to talk to Eilidh. He looked at his watch, then grabbed the duffle bag he never seemed to unpack, thanks to all the trips to Skye, and headed to his car. He'd just locked his front door when the phone in his front hall rang. It occurred to him to pretend he hadn't heard it, but it might be someone from work. "Ah, dammit." He unlocked the door and raced inside to catch the call before it went to voicemail.

"Yeah," he said sharply, almost dropping the phone as he yanked it off the cradle.

"Hey, Quinton. Did I catch you at a bad time? It's Phillip."

Munro stopped short. Phillip was a water druid, the only one of Frankie's friends who called him regularly after his cousin's death. "Nah, that's fine. I was on my way out, but I've been meaning to call you. I have some news." He carried the phone to the sofa and sat down. He'd been so busy, he hadn't given much thought to what the Higher Conclave asked him to do, but now was as good a time as any.

"Oh yeah? What's up?"

"The faeries on Skye want to meet you guys." Munro outlined the invitation and the stipulation he'd placed about none of them getting bonded against their will.

"Whoa. I guess I thought it was rare. I suppose I've wondered, but you know how they are." His tone was halting, as though he struggled to take in the news.

By *they*, Munro assumed Phillip meant the fae. After what had happened with Cridhe, their original mentor and the one who'd gathered the druids together in the first place, the group had been reluctant to meet Eilidh and distrustful at first.

They eventually warmed to her, but they always relaxed when she left.

“Are you interested?” Munro asked.

“I think so. It can’t hurt to meet them, right?”

“There’s more you should know.” Munro explained his and Eilidh’s experience with their magical bond. They’d talked about it before, but now he wanted to impress on Phillip the intimate and sometimes oppressive feeling of having someone else in your head all the time. But he also shared the newfound benefits: strength, seeing in the dark, speed and stamina. What he left out was that he hadn’t experienced any of that until he’d gone to the Otherworld. Nobody could know about that little jaunt.

“It’s a lot to think about,” Phillip said.

“You can always say no. They won’t force you.”

“The thing is, I dunno, it seems right somehow. Like that’s the way it’s meant to be. Like I’m not quite all here, if you know what I’m saying.”

Munro knew exactly what he meant. Once his own druidic powers were unlocked, he experienced a deep need. When he laid eyes on Eilidh, he knew she was the only one who could fill it. Fortunately for him, the two events happened close together. The other druids, though, had all been unlocked by Cridhe, who already had a bonded druid. So they were left feeling empty. Munro saw that now for the first time.

"Listen, I'm on my way to Skye now. I have to get there as soon as possible." He hesitated, but he couldn't think of a way to explain without talking about things he shouldn't. "Will you talk to the others? Anyone who wants to go ahead within the next couple of days should come to Skye. Go to Portree when you're ready and give me a call. There's no rush. Anyone who needs more time to think it over can have it. I doubt the conclave will give up asking, but one thing you can say for faeries is they're patient."

"Okay," Phillip said. "I'll have everyone around tonight."

After they said goodbye, Munro picked up his bag and slung it over his back. Turning his thoughts away from the druids, he got in his car and followed the internal compass that would lead him straight to Eilidh.

CHAPTER 9

BY THE TIME MUNRO REACHED the fae village centre, he felt tired. Sometime during his travel, he felt Eilidh's presence grow distant. She must have gone to the Otherworld. He headed straight for Oron's, hoping she'd left him a message.

Alyssa, Oron's granddaughter, was the only one at home. "Hello, Quinton Munro." She greeted him at the door.

He couldn't help but smile. "You can call me Quinton."

When she returned his smile, she shone with beauty. "You honour me, Quinton." She fidgeted with her braid, a most human-like gesture. Faeries rarely allowed themselves to appear impatient or restless, but he had to remind himself that she was, by their standards, quite young, being closer to his age than to Eilidh's and fifty years away from reaching adulthood. Although physically mature, she had a softness about her that the so-called adult fae didn't. "Eilidh will return soon from the Otherworld. The Higher Conclave sent a message to Queen Cadhla." She touched his arm and said softly, "Come in."

"Thanks. Nobody else home? I thought I might lay down in Eilidh's room for a bit, if nobody minds. I'm knackered."

Her eyes sparkled. "Would you like to join with me?"

Munro removed the bag he'd worn slung across his back during the night. "I'm sorry?" Even after spending so much time with Eilidh, he still experienced a slight language barrier. The fae all seemed to speak English well, along with a multitude of other languages, but many had trouble with modern idioms.

She stepped closer, lowering her gaze. "Would you like to lie naked with me and experience mutual pleasures." Her breath smelled sweet, and he felt a heady warmth that could only be magical. Before he could speak, her lips were on his. She rested her hands on his chest, then ran them lightly to his waist.

Heat rushed to his cheeks, and he took her hands and gently guided them away while taking a small step back. "I, uhh, that's quite an offer. I'm flattered, really, but I'm exhausted. I need to sleep." He couldn't deny the inexplicable temptation, but he was wary, knowing most of the fae would never consider bedding a human.

She smiled knowingly. "Another time, perhaps."

He hated himself for not giving a firm no. He was in love with Eilidh, he reminded himself as he took his bag to Eilidh's room, leaving Alyssa near the front door. As soon as he lay in Eilidh's swing bed, his head started to clear. Next time, he told himself, he'd make it plain he was a one-faerie kind of guy.

Sleep came quickly, and he didn't wake until he felt a small hand run up and down his arm. He knew it was Eilidh before he opened his eyes. "Come, Quinton," she said. "You must rise and eat. We need to go to the Otherworld. The queen wishes to meet you."

Munro breathed in the morning air and tried to clear the sleep from his mind. "She what?"

Eilidh smiled. "She wants to meet you."

"Now?"

"Not yet. It's still daytime. We will be expected to leave soon after nightfall. Oron is coming as well."

He tried to sit up, but the swing bed flung awkwardly to one side. "I hate this thing," he grumbled, then added, "That's good news about Oron. Isn't it?"

Eilidh nodded. "I think so. We shall see."

"Do you need to sleep?"

"No. I will rest for a few hours before we leave, but I'm not tired yet." Even though the fae were nocturnal, they seemed to get by on only three or four hours' rest during the day, and he'd seen Eilidh do with one or two. She crawled over to him and lay beside him, resting her head on his shoulder, an unusually intimate gesture for her, but he didn't mind.

"Alyssa said you rejected her offer."

Munro was suddenly glad she was lying with her head down, so she couldn't see the heat on his cheeks. Alyssa told Eilidh? What did that mean? The cultural differences between faeries and humans couldn't be larger if they came from different planets. "I have to say, she caught me by surprise." Treading carefully.

"She's very beautiful, and she's closer to your age."

"Yes, she is."

Eilidh tilted her head and looked him in the eye. "You were too tired?"

"I didn't want to offend her by telling her I wasn't interested." He touched Eilidh's cheek. "I'm in love with someone else." He'd promised himself he wouldn't pressure Eilidh. He constantly had to rein in his need for her. Her culture taught her faeries and humans didn't belong together. It seemed like the fae looked on the younger race as barely above animals on the evolutionary scale. Although she'd come to view him differently, and he could tell she felt close to him, he wasn't going to act like some kind of caveman.

Her silver eyes swirled with green filaments, and her emotions were unreadable. "What does *in love* mean to a human?"

He didn't hesitate. "To me, it means when you're gone, I miss you, and when you're near, the world is right. It means I'd never hurt you—I couldn't hurt you—and if someone else tried to, they'd have to kill me to get to you. When I hear something funny, you're the one I want to tell about it. And when another woman asks me to 'join with her,' I'll always say no." He paused, uncertain what she was thinking. "Remember the words we said to each other when we bonded?"

"*Dem'ontar-che*," she whispered.

"You told me it means loyalty, servitude, blind faith, and complete devotion. That's the word right there. Eilidh, I'm devoted to you, heart and soul."

Suddenly, Eilidh kissed him. She slipped her arms around him, and they were soon entangled in an intimate embrace. Her emotions released and rolled over him like molten lava. He couldn't hold back any longer, and it became clear she didn't want him to. He thought that when they did finally make love, they'd take it slow the first time. He had planned to be patient, tender, gentle. Instead, it was like being caught up in a storm, their passions completely devouring them. Their thoughts and instincts fused. For a short while, their minds and bodies were as one.

∞

At nightfall, Eilidh, Munro, and Oron travelled into the Otherworld by way of the gate at Fionn Lighe. The azuri fae still refused to unblock the Skye gate, because doing so would break the enchantments protecting them from earth magic. But with Munro's increased speed and stamina, the journey passed quickly enough.

As soon as they set foot on fae soil, Oron and Eilidh used their magic to create the illusion of appropriate clothing. He dressed in resplendent white robes, a style suitable for a conclave leader. Eilidh wore a gown of deep sky blue, and she created an illusion for Munro's clothing as well, replacing his jeans and rugby shirt with a set of robes the same colour as her gown.

"Hell, no," he said, looking down with dismay.

"You're a druid. It's appropriate."

"I don't care." He stared at her hard. "I'm not wearing this."

Eilidh sighed. He looked very handsome in the formal garb. The sight of him in faerie clothing gave her a pang of longing to touch him again. "What about this?" She changed the illusion to look more like what Griogair had worn at court when she first met the prince-consort. The new trousers and shirt were midnight blue, and the long cloak was the same shade as Eilidh's dress. The fur on the collar was white fox with an ornate silver clasp.

Munro still frowned. "Some better. Can we do without the fur?"

With a thought, the fur was gone, and she put her hands on her hips. "We must go, Quinton."

"All right," he replied. "Thank you." He kissed her cheek and squeezed her hand. If Oron noticed their affectionate display, he said nothing, but Eilidh flushed with embarrassment.

They left the gate behind, and as they ran, the three spoke very little, each seemingly consumed with private musings. Eilidh respected Oron's desire to keep his thoughts to himself. He had not discussed the business of the Higher Conclave with her any further, although she was aware meetings had been going on since she first delivered the queen's message. The issue of Munro's clothing aside, her druid's mind felt more focused and settled than she'd ever experienced. Of course, perhaps she only now allowed herself to touch it fully.

Lying with him had been more than she'd expected: more intense, more fulfilling, more than the passing pleasures she'd experienced in her youth. She never hoped to find that with anyone, much less with a human. Before, they both worried the magic bonding caused these feelings, but now they seemed to accept the magic was a part of them and cared little about which came first, love or magic. She suddenly wondered why she'd resisted so long.

When they passed through the gate into the Otherworld, Munro breathed deeply. His eyes had not only started to glow, but Eilidh could see the seed of magic in them, as though the Otherworld air ignited his power.

A silent tear slid down Oron's cheek. When Eilidh stared in disbelief at the emotional display, he said simply, "A thousand years, Eilidh. *A thousand years.*"

She suddenly understood. Her exile lasted only a quarter century, and by the end of that time, she was just starting to accept the finality of what she'd lost. She couldn't imagine going a millennium without hope of seeing the blue moon of her homeland again.

As agreed, they headed toward the portal that granted access to the Halls of Mist. Every kingdom had one such entry, leading to the place any faerie could walk in absolute safety, a neutral ground and a centre for politics and scholarship of every kind: religious, historical, and magical.

"Why did they want to meet in the Halls of Mist?" Eilidh asked as the three loped easily through the plains of the Otherworld. "Wouldn't that imply the queen acknowledged you may not be safe in her kingdom?"

"Or it could be seen as a magnanimous gesture of good faith," Oron said. "However, I think there is another reason."

"What is that, Elder?" Eilidh asked, but he did not answer. Instead, he looked back at Munro, who ran behind the pair. "Quinton?" she said quietly to Oron. "What advantage would there be in bringing him there?" Worry began to surface. "Will he be safe?" It hadn't occurred to her because they travelled at the queen's invitation, but now Eilidh wondered if the protection of the Halls of Mist would extend to a human. But why would the queen wish to harm Munro?

Her druid picked up speed to catch up. "What's wrong?" Munro must have sensed her disquiet.

She glanced at Oron, who looked at the sky, the grasses, the trees, as though seeing the landscape for the first time. "It's so beautiful here, isn't it? I tried to forget. Now, it will be like losing it all over again should we fail."

Eilidh shook her head at Munro, and her uneasiness became his.

By the time they approached the portal, her thoughts had become calmer. The queen would not invite them to the Halls of Mist just to hurt Munro. If she wanted to do that, she could have easily done it in her own territory, and the other kingdoms wouldn't even know. There must be some other reason the queen wanted Oron, and perhaps more specifically Munro, to be seen by fae of other nations.

Could she want the others to think she was allying with humans? They were considered the lesser race, but how much longer would this idea persist? Fae of every kingdom, even the sea kingdoms and those of the ice regions, had felt their territory encroached upon. None had been able to stop the incursion into their lands on earth. In some places, the fae had been all but completely driven into the Otherworld, and those kingdoms were dying out. They could not make the proper sacrifices to the Mother to ask for the blessing of fertility. One such kingdom had been swallowed into another, their queen marrying the son of another queen to cement the loyalties.

Ahead, Eilidh could see the platform, a perfectly round dais with a glowing sphere atop. Stairs approached from all directions. It was guarded by nearly a hundred Watchers, but they faced the dais, not the kingdom. Their job was to keep out an invasion from other kingdoms, not to prevent departure. Any faerie was free to visit the Halls of Mist.

"Come," Oron said. "The queen's delegation will be waiting."

∞

Munro was not disappointed in his first view of the Halls of Mist. He'd not yet even adjusted to the Otherworld and all its incredible sights. The simplest things were magnificent, like the way the stars looked so close. But when he stepped through that huge blue ball, his skin tingled almost to the point of pain. His system overloaded, and a wave of nausea flooded him.

"Breathe," Oron said quietly.

Breathe? Munro could hardly even think. Still, he tried to focus on inhaling and exhaling. When he opened his eyes, he saw a hundred faces staring at him from an immense round courtyard. Faeries of all descriptions, with skin colours varying from ebony to paper white to bluish tints and shades of pink and tan. Some appeared as old as the crypt-keeper himself, while others looked bright-faced, the way only the truly young could.

When he finally got his bearings, Munro saw that the courtyard, which was large enough to hold thousands, had dozens of bridges leading up and outward. If viewed from above, it would have looked like the rays of the sun. Each bridge floated over an expanse of opaque white mist and led to an immense dome in the distance. Each dome must have been the size of a sprawling hamlet at least.

"The Hall of Caledonia is this way," Eilidh said, nodding toward one of the pathways.

The eyes of all the fae in the courtyard followed them, but conversation resumed as soon as their backs were turned. The bridges were so narrow as to only allow walking single file. Oron led, followed by Eilidh, then Munro. He experienced a touch of vertigo, and he tried to keep his eyes on Eilidh's back, not looking down into the endless cloud that supported the bridge. He didn't want to think about what was below them, if there was anything at all.

When they arrived at the end of the path, the huge dome rose up, and an archway led inward, open and unguarded. Inside was a crescent-shaped entryway with many high-arched doorways leading deeper within. As they entered, Munro was surprised to see Prince Griogair standing among other faeries sedately going about their business. "Greetings, honoured guests," he said warmly, addressing Oron. The elder only slightly inclined his head, while Eilidh curtsied deeply.

Munro had no idea what to do, so he said, "Hello."

A look of amusement passed briefly over Griogair's face. "Elder Oron, the queen requests your presence as soon as you are ready. She awaits in Autumn Hall. I will escort you, if you will allow me."

"I would be most honoured, Your Highness," Oron replied.

"Eilidh, I will entertain you and your druid for now. The queen wishes to see you after she has conducted business with Oron."

"Of course, Your Highness." Eilidh followed behind as the prince led the three through one of the doors and down a corridor.

The translucent walls of the hallways went all the way to the glass-like domed city roof. Munro could see black granite floors above, and it gave the entire place a dizzying feel, like he was trapped in a maze. The angles felt sharp and strangely placed, as though the architect was high when he drew up the plans.

Griogair showed Oron to a huge wooden door, where a steward greeted them and showed the elder inside. When they were alone, Prince Griogair gestured to an archway across the hall. "We can wait in here."

"Sounds good," Munro said as they went inside. "Maybe then you can explain why you lied."

CHAPTER 10

"QUINTON!" EILIDH HISSED.

Munro hadn't realised they weren't alone, and the dozen or so faeries in the chamber froze. When he sensed the genuine fear in Eilidh's mind, he understood how stupid he'd been. He was a long way from home. Without Eilidh, he wouldn't make it to the portal, much less through the Otherworld and back to a gate. If by some miracle he did find a gate, the likelihood of finding the right one was remote. On the other hand, Griogair needed a little shaking up. He'd been blasé about the truth, at the very least. Quite possibly, he intentionally sent Munro and Eilidh blindly into a dangerous situation.

Griogair smiled at the others in the room. "They're so delightfully impetuous, don't you think?" The tension in the room dissipated. The others replied with subtle signs of agreement, a nod or tilt of the chin. Munro found the fae's indirect way of communicating both fascinating and exhausting.

He preferred plain speech, something he wasn't likely to hear any time soon.

The prince turned his eyes to Eilidh. "You look delicious." His tone was low and seductive, and the way his gaze roamed over Eilidh's gown made Munro's blood boil. He remembered Eilidh's warning that Griogair pretended Eilidh was his lover. But facing it like this, so soon after Munro had been in her bed, wasn't easy to swallow.

Eilidh blushed and cast a glance at Munro that he couldn't read. Turning to the prince, she said with an intimate smile, "It's always a pleasure to see you, Griogair. How unfortunate we won't have time to be alone." Her purring voice was barely above a whisper, but Munro had no doubt every ear in the chamber heard the soft seduction in her tone.

Griogair responded by taking her hand and kissing it. "What makes you think we won't have time?"

"My druid will not leave my side. We are at a point in our magical bonding that would make him reluctant to be parted from me."

Munro wanted to scream. Was she *actually* batting her eyelashes? This was not the Eilidh he knew.

"If you wish him to join us, I'm always open to new things." Griogair took his eyes away from Eilidh as though with difficulty and glanced to the others in the room. "The rest of you may go," he said.

They filed out silently, and the last one stayed in the doorway, facing the hall. Griogair released Eilidh's hand. "That is Reine. He will see we are not disturbed." Then with a glance at Munro he added with a sigh, "You're going to get us all killed." The prince gestured to a set of low, sloped chairs shaped out of cherry wood.

Eilidh sat, but Munro stood and looked Griogair in the eye. "You very nearly got us killed already. Why didn't you tell us about your son?"

"You found him?"

Munro glanced at Eilidh, whose gaze implored him to sit as she motioned to the chairs. "Your Highness," she began, "We can't be sure it was Tràth."

"It was him," Munro said as he sat next to Eilidh. "He looks a lot like you."

"Thank you," Griogair said, joining them. "You're right, of course. I didn't tell you everything. I had hoped no one would need to know."

"Know what?" Munro asked.

It was Eilidh, not the prince, who answered. "That the crown prince is gifted in the Path of Stars." She shook her head with disbelief. "He is azuri fae."

"But you said you didn't recognise his magic." Munro turned to her. "I thought that meant it was some kind of earth magic you hadn't learned, since you're weakest in the Ways of Earth."

"Where is he?" Griogair asked eagerly.

"We have no idea," Eilidh said. "He disappeared before our eyes. This is no magic I am familiar with. Your Highness, I *must* have your permission to speak to the Higher Conclave. Surely you can see this is the only way. Otherwise we are working with the glare of the sun in our eyes."

"No," the prince said firmly. "Things have gotten difficult enough already, and with your druid's display today, there will be even more rumours. At least now," he said with a wry chuckle, "the rumours will be about an intimate encounter for three. And with a human involved. That should increase my reputation as a licentious profligate."

"It seems to be a well-practised subterfuge," Munro said, having difficulty showing any respect, even knowing Griogair could have them both killed on the spot without even getting his hands dirty.

The prince ignored the comment. "I planned to tell you to stop looking for him. Soon after you left our last meeting, my retreat was swarmed with the queen's guard. They claimed to be there in advance of my wife's visit, and indeed she did come, but after a few hours, she left again. Never before have they been worried about *security* in my home. She grows more paranoid. Even still, I got the distinct impression she was disappointed to find me alone."

"Why?" Eilidh asked.

"If she'd caught me with a maiden in my bed, she would not have to suspect me of treason." He paused. "Things have gotten dangerous for all of us. You must stop looking for Tràth. It comforts me to know he is alive, and for now that has to be enough."

"I can't do that," Munro said. "I have an even bigger problem than your spat with your wife."

Griogair raised an elegant eyebrow.

"I have forty-five missing villagers. We don't know what happened, but my people know it's something strange. It's my job to get them back. Maybe Tràth took them. Maybe they saw him and ran off when he did some weird magic thing. I don't know yet, but I know they disappeared because of your son. Locating him is my concern, whether you want him found or not."

"You cannot do this," Griogair said, leaning forward in his seat. "Please. There is growing unrest in the kingdom."

"What happened?" Eilidh asked.

"This is the reason Cadhla asked to speak to Oron and why she wanted to do it here. As the word has spread of the colony, and of your actions to save Caledonia last summer, the kingdom has grown divided. Many want those who follow the Path of Stars found and stamped out." A sympathetic frown spread across his face. "Others, though, especially ones who have lost children or friends to execution or exile, not to mention some progressive thinkers, feel the fear is destroying us, and they want to see the azuri restored to the kingdom."

"Exile is one thing, but how could Queen Cadhla pursue stamping out those who follow the Path of Stars when her only child is gifted with that form of magic? We aren't dangerous to you." Sadness rolled off Eilidh as she implored the prince, and Munro felt the pang deeply in his own emotions.

Griogair turned to Munro. "Do what you must in your own world, but I can help you no further. The rift in my people is spreading, and quickly. There is unrest like I have never seen."

"You would abandon your son?" Munro asked.

A pained expression spread over the prince's face. "Not by choice and not forever. I will find him. I will restore him to his rightful place, but I need time. I'm holding the queen's council together with a thread. The conclave has crippled itself by allowing the usual divisions to splinter even further."

For the first time, Munro felt a certain respect for the prince. He was a lot more than he first appeared, but perhaps that was his plan all along. It was easy to dismiss him as a playboy, but he was willing to sacrifice his own desire to find his son for the sake of his people. That couldn't be easy. "It would help if I could speak to his friends, to the Watchers who helped him cross into the borderlands."

"No. I'm sorry. You have no idea how this pains me. Find him if you can, but you'll have to do it without my help." His violet eyes glowed in the dim light. "I wish you the best of fortunes, my friend. I need you to do this. You don't know me, and you probably don't even like me. I'm not your ruler..."

"Don't worry about that," Munro said. "I'll help any way I can." Ten minutes ago, Munro had hated the guy, but suddenly he understood the prince.

"Thank you," Griogair said. "I have said this to Eilidh, but I give you my pledge as well. I will give you anything you ask if you return my son to me."

Munro dismissed it with a wave of his hand. "It's my job, sir."

"You must do it quietly and without involving the azuri conclave. My son's abilities cannot be made public."

"Surely it would heal the kingdom if you came forward. If the queen herself could have an azuri child, everyone would realise it's not a curse but a gift," Eilidh said.

Griogair chuckled. "You'd have to convince Cadhla of that first. She cannot know of this. If the queen learned what has passed between us…"

"And just what," asked a voice from the doorway, "has passed between you three?"

The faerie striding toward them was tall, blonde, and magnificent. Every aspect of her was flawless, from her delicate skin, to the magnificent ivory gown she wore. Her eyes locked on Eilidh, who dipped into a deep curtsy.

"Your Majesty," Eilidh said, and Munro bowed low as well, not daring to show any sign of disrespect. It was one thing to mouth off to Griogair, but Munro could tell this woman wasn't someone he wanted to mess with.

Magic crackled in the air, causing the hairs on Munro's arms to stand on end. "Get up," the queen said to Eilidh before turning her attention to Griogair. "I asked you a question."

"I was entertaining our guests, Cadhla," the prince said, holding out a hand to encourage a frightened Eilidh to rise.

"And with your clothes on, for once." The queen seemed less than charmed. "I heard otherwise. I came to see the entertainments for myself." Sarcasm dripped from her voice.

"Alas," Griogair said, his features well-schooled and serious. "Eilidh's druid showed some reluctance. But then, we've always known his people are more restrained than ours in the pursuit of pleasure." He glanced at Munro, who felt a tug at his emotions, similar to what Alyssa had used when she invited him to bed her.

Munro realised the prince was trying to send him a message with this magic, but he didn't know how to respond, so he just looked down.

The prince touched Munro's face. "He blushes prettily though."

"You can cease this pointless charade, Griogair," the queen said, her red lips crinkled into a pucker of distaste. "Even you would not go so far."

"Cadhla, I assure you, I don't know what you mean."

"Your Majesty," she corrected him and then spat, "You have betrayed me. You and your worthless son. Return to Elmerick at once. I will deal with you when I arrive." She turned to Eilidh. "We are in the Halls of Mist, and you came at my request, so I cannot touch you for your treachery. Your elder waits at the portal. You have this night only to pass through and return to your exile. If you ever set foot in my kingdom again, or if anyone finds out what you know about the boy, it will be war, and you will pay with your life." With a cruel smile, she added,

"And that of your father. He won't, I think, be leaving his house again. His life will ensure your cooperation, I hope. As long as you remember your duty, he will live well."

Munro started to step forward and put himself between Eilidh and the queen, but the second Eilidh realised what he was doing, she grabbed his hand and pulled him back as though he were on a leash. She gave a quick curtsy. "By your leave, Your Majesty." Eilidh led Munro out of the room before anyone could say another word.

Outside the dome, they moved in silence. He followed her beyond the narrow bridge, looking over his shoulder occasionally, uncertain if they would be followed.

As promised, Oron was waiting. As soon as they came close, he motioned them toward the portal. "Come quickly," he said. "We must return to Skye at once."

"What happened?" Eilidh asked.

"Go, child," he said. "We must reach the gate before it closes at dawn."

CHAPTER 11

EILIDH'S MIND WHIRLED as they raced through the Otherworld. It was happening all over again. Exile. She had let her guard down, begun to feel safe. She'd had her father back. And now the dream had been snatched away. This time, it felt even worse. The queen herself had accused Eilidh of treason. Despite the queen's assurances, Eilidh worried for her father. He'd been through so much in the past century.

Astral magic roiled within her, and her control slipped. Her focus went hazy, and hers and Munro's clothing returned to the modern fashions of the human realm. Munro's presence was the only thing holding her together. He became the foundation beneath her feet. Determination carried him forward, and she followed his aura like a beacon.

When they arrived at the gate, they ran through without stopping. There wasn't time for a forlorn goodbye to her homeland. *It's happening again.*

Her nerves didn't settle until she breathed in the thinner air of the borderlands. When her newfound earth powers drained away as they travelled through the protective enchantments on Skye, she finally began to feel safe. She had a million questions for Oron, but the elder didn't pause to explain his meeting with the queen. He merely told Eilidh and Munro he'd called an emergency congregation of the Higher Conclave, and she was not to leave the safety of his house until he sent for her.

∞

Munro leaned against a wall, arms crossed, thinking, while Eilidh sat on the floor and meditated. After an hour of concerted effort, her mind had yet to relax. Her emotions whirled out of control after the encounter with the queen, so he suggested she try the mental exercises that had become part of her daily training program. When talking didn't help and resting proved impossible, this was the only thing he could think of to help her calm down. Even now, she wrestled with her own mind as though she were fighting dragons.

Quietly, he slipped out the door and went into the kitchen. He didn't feel comfortable making himself at home, even though Oron had said many times Munro should treat this like his own house. But hunger overwhelmed politeness, and he made himself a sandwich of sorts, or as close as he could approximate with the odd food choices Oron kept.

Munro hadn't eaten since just before their journey, and he'd run many miles that night. They'd made it back well before dawn, and the sun had only begun to rise. The lightening sky lifted his spirits for no reason he could explain. After washing the dishes he'd used, he turned toward a large east-facing window. He jumped when he saw a faerie he didn't recognise in the garden outside, then froze as realisation dawned. The build was familiar, the shape of the face, the hair, but the eyes were wrong. He lifted a hand in greeting to be sure, and the figure in the garden mirrored his movements.

Munro stepped forward and studied his reflection. It had been partly a trick of the light, but his eyes glowed strangely. His skin too had a shining quality, and his hair seemed to have gone a shade or two lighter. He thought of himself as an average-looking guy, so seeing his image now, he hardly recognised the strikingly handsome man. It was him, but better, stronger, more vibrant. He appeared older, which was strange considering how smooth and perfect his skin looked. Pushing back his hair, Munro looked at his ears. He hadn't even felt them change, but now each one had a subtle point at the top.

"Holy shit," he said to the man in the glass.

Light footsteps in the hall told him someone approached. He scrubbed his hair forward with his hand, not wanting anyone else to see the full extent of the changes.

Alyssa walked into the kitchen and took an apple from a wooden bowl. With a small paring knife, she began to peel it in one smooth motion, round and round the fruit, not acknowledging Munro's presence.

"Good morning," he said quietly. "Off to bed?"

She smiled without looking up. "Not yet. Why do you ask? Have you changed your mind about bedding me?"

"No. I mean, look, it isn't personal. It's just..."

Alyssa smiled. "It's all right. I told her you'd say no."

Munro stopped short. "You mean you and Eilidh talked about it *before* you propositioned me?"

"Of course. Do you think I would have suggested it if she hadn't asked me to? Not that you aren't growing more handsome by the day, young druid, but Eilidh is a guest in my grandfather's house. I would not risk offending her, considering how much she obviously cares for you."

"She asked you to seduce me?" His mind reeled. "Why would she do that?"

Alyssa shrugged. "Perhaps she thought you needed companionship? I don't know. I told her you would say no. Perhaps," she said in a tone that was almost too casual, "she wished to test your loyalty."

Anger rose in Munro's chest. *It was a bloody test?*

Alyssa's eyes widened as she watched his expression. "I've said something wrong. Forgive me, druid. I'm young and not as socially adept as a human my age would be."

"Don't try that bullshit on me," he said. "You knew exactly what you were doing. Just like she did." He strode toward the door.

"Forgive me, please," she said. "I meant no harm."

He turned back to respond to Alyssa, but just as he opened his mouth, Munro felt the connection between his mind and Eilidh's shut down. Completely. It wasn't like the vague distance he felt when she travelled into the Otherworld. It was as though she'd ceased to exist. Alyssa forgotten, Munro ran through the house, shouting Eilidh's name.

Returning to the meditation chamber where he'd left her, he was surprised to find she wasn't there. Without his internal sense of her, he felt like he was searching with his eyes closed. He took the public areas of the house first. After Oron's explicit instruction to stay put, he doubted she would leave. His heart wouldn't let him add the word *voluntarily*.

When she didn't seem to be in any public part of the property, including the gardens, he went to her bedroom. It was the last place he expected to find her, considering how wound up she had been, but he saw her as soon as he came to the doorway. She wasn't alone. She sat on the edge of the swing bed, one foot on the floor, slowly rocking the bed. Lying beside her was Griogair. Munro froze, his mind reeling, when he saw Eilidh stroke the prince's face. She whispered to him in a trilling language Munro couldn't understand.

"What the...?"

Eilidh cut Munro off with a glare and held her finger to her lips, motioning for silence. She stood and quietly walked to the door, closing it behind her and Munro.

"What the hell is going on?" Munro asked in a growling whisper. "And why can't I feel your thoughts anymore?"

"Outside," Eilidh said. She led Munro to the garden and turned to face him. "Griogair barely escaped. The queen tried to kill him."

Curious, Munro thought. He didn't *look* injured. "She wouldn't just order that done?"

"A faerie of Griogair's power? No, that would not be possible." Eilidh laughed bitterly. "You do not sound as though you even care, to speak so casually of whether she could order it done or do it herself. Does it matter?"

Munro sat on one of the cold stone benches, grateful his new druidic power meant the temperature didn't bother him. He couldn't even remember where his coat was. "Why can't I feel you, Eilidh?"

Her expression softened. "I don't know how I did it. I just found the right button to push, as you would say. Our bond is not broken, only our sharing of emotions."

"Can you un-push it?"

"Perhaps."

"But you don't want to," he said.

"The queen may come for him. He claims she's lost all grip on her reason," Eilidh said. "I can feel your anger. Isn't it good for us to have space for our own thoughts from time to time?"

"Was he hurt in the attack?"

"Not seriously, no. He was fortunate she had enough dignity not to chase him, while he didn't mind running for his life. It's the earth shield making him sick. He can't touch the Ways of Earth on the island, and one as powerful as he would find that more painful than most."

Munro didn't like her wistful tone when she described how powerful the prince was. "I talked to Alyssa just a minute ago," he said. If Eilidh could change the subject, he could too.

Eilidh stared at him blankly. "She lives here now. She came to care for her sister Flùranach while the child receives instruction from Oron. The girl is quite gifted."

"She told me you asked her to seduce me. Is that true?"

Eilidh looked at the sky. The sun had inched above the horizon, and the morning's red hues had faded to blue.

"Was it some kind of test? To see if I would be faithful to you? Or were you trying to deflect my attraction for you by passing me off to someone else?"

"Would it have worked?"

"Would you want it to?" Munro shot back. "Eilidh, what are you doing?" He couldn't understand her thinking, what she was trying to accomplish. "You keep running hot and cold with me. One minute you're getting other women to try to sleep with me, then you're jumping into bed with me yourself.

Next you're pawing Prince Lothario like he's God's gift."

"You're so angry," she said quietly.

"You're damned right I'm angry," he shouted, not caring that she probably didn't understand half the slang he'd just used.

Her silver eyes narrowed. "I have more important things to worry about than your trifling human outbursts."

"I wouldn't be having an outburst if you weren't intentionally screwing with my emotions." He wanted to shake her. He wasn't a violent person by nature, not even one to slam doors. But if there had been a solid wooden door between him and Eilidh right now, he would have slammed it with all the strength he had.

"I've been exiled. Again. My life threatened. My father's life. Now Griogair is under a death order, and we could be headed for civil war. The kingdom could very well fall apart over this rift in our people. Do you think I care about your feelings right now?"

"No," he said hotly. "You've made that abundantly clear. What I don't understand is why you're doing this. What did I do or say to make you want to hurt me?"

The anger slipped from her face, leaving only sadness. "Quinton," she said, "I need to be alone with Griogair right now."

If he hadn't been sitting already, he would have needed to sit. "You need to be alone with him? Or you need to speak with him alone? Because those are two totally different things."

"Go home," she said. "I have important things I must deal with."

He felt like he'd been punched in the gut. "You are my home, Eilidh. Push the button. Let me back in."

She breathed slowly and deliberately, then looked away, as though fighting tears. "If you won't go home, just leave. Griogair is waiting for me upstairs." Eilidh turned and walked away.

He sat in the winter morning for ten minutes, ignoring the cold, his mind spinning with confusion and anger.

"She does care for you. We fae, especially kingdom fae, aren't like you in so many ways. I have had a few human friends over the years, so I know."

He hadn't heard Alyssa come into the garden. "Did she send you out here?"

"No," Alyssa said. "I came because I could hear you shouting from the kitchen. Every faerie within ten miles probably heard you. You have a strong voice." She chuckled. "I thought you might need a friend."

Munro looked into her eyes. He did need a friend, and without Eilidh, he didn't have a soul in the world who understood what he was becoming. "Want to go into the city? I could use a drink."

"We have honeyed froth or fig juice," she said.

"I need a beer. By the time we get to Portree, we can find a pub that's open for lunch." They might have to wait an hour or two, but he didn't think he could stand being here one minute more. He couldn't return to Perth empty-handed either. He hadn't forgotten for one minute about those forty-five missing villagers. Without help from Eilidh or Griogair, he didn't have a hope in hell of finding them.

"Okay," she said. "I've never had beer before." Within a few moments, she'd used an illusion to round her ears and add freckles to her nose. "I'm ready."

CHAPTER 12

JUST AS GRIOGAIR STRUGGLED TO COPE with the loss of his connection to the Ways of Earth, Eilidh floundered without her connection to Munro. She could feel the thread that joined them, even though she could no longer sense his emotions or tell where he was. She hadn't figured out how to block the connection through meditations. Instead, it happened when she spoke to Griogair. His words had sent her into a panic, and the reaction was instinctual.

Now that she saw how selfishly angry and jealous Munro had become, not even caring what she was going through—her fears for her father, for the future of her people—she wasn't certain she wanted to open the connection. She sighed. How had everything gone wrong? Why had he become enraged when she needed comfort and shelter?

Griogair was preparing to meet with the azuri conclave, so she wandered the house, not realising at first she hoped to see Munro, sitting stubbornly somewhere, refusing to leave her side. But he had gone. Nightfall approached, and she hadn't slept all day.

"Where is your druid?" Oron said as he entered the room.

"I don't know, Elder." Eilidh explained what had happened, how Griogair's words shocked her into shutting off Munro. Oron pressed her, so she told him of Munro's inexplicable emotional outburst and that she'd sent him away.

"You must reopen the connection, Eilidh. You need him. We need *them*."

"I'm not certain I can cope with his emotions right now. He is wild with fury. I panicked." She added reluctantly, "He is right to be furious. I don't know why I said what I did." It shamed her to realise she had become as out of control as Munro. Her emotions heated purely because he had the temerity to get angry with her.

"Child, sit down." Oron's tone was stern, but his expression gentle. "You have neglected your practice lately. At the rate you're going, it will take you a century to master even the most basic astral incantations." Eilidh sat on the floor, and Oron joined her. "You are gifted, Eilidh. You have an enormous capacity. I can feel it within you. Yet, you spend much of your time in a human frame of mind. Too much of your youth was wasted, with elders and teachers trying to force you to become something you couldn't. A century of wrong teaching will take a long time to untangle, but even longer if you hide from it."

"Yes, Elder," she said.

"First, open your connection to your druid."

"I don't know how."

Oron reached over and touched Eilidh's hand. His powerful presence approached her thoughts. "Show me how you cut him off."

She shifted her focus to the thick vine that represented Munro's power, and showed Oron the glass wall separating them.

"Bring it down." Oron's thoughts pushed on her mind, prodding her forward. "You've created it, so unmake it."

"I'm afraid."

"Of what consequence is that?"

Eilidh opened her eyes and met Oron's for just a moment before delving back in. She didn't want to break the glass. The sharp edges might hurt them both. One thing she'd learned quickly was that when it came to the power of her mind, even symbolic barriers had real perils and should not be quickly dismissed. She could melt the glass, but the heat might burn the vine. "I don't see how," she said with frustration.

"How did you erect it?"

"It just appeared," she said.

Oron squeezed her hand, and she looked up. "Isn't it obvious?" he asked, his wrinkled face breaking into a smile. "You're thinking too hard. Life in the human world has taught you to think. Your training as a Watcher taught you to react. When you walk the Path of Stars, you do neither of those things. You must let yourself *feel*. Being fae does not mean not feeling. Being fae means not being ruled by feelings. You need this druid, because he will force you to learn this principle, and quickly."

Eilidh had spent the first part of her life with her father and others who tried to teach her the Ways of Earth, in which she was extremely weak. Then she spent twenty-five years in exile, trying to do as little magic as possible, doing only what she had to in order to survive. Now she was expected to forget all that. To start over. But being accepted back into the kingdom made her complacent. She hadn't put as much into her studies as she could have. In the Otherworld, she now had more access to earth magic than most faeries. Only on Skye did she have to work at her magic. "I've been lazy," she said. "I didn't realise it until today. I've spent as much time as possible in the Otherworld and not enough time here learning. Forgive me, Elder. I've not been a faithful student."

"The barrier. Bring it down." Oron sent a gentle wave of restful energy into her thoughts, bolstering her confidence.

Turning her attention again to the glass, she now looked past it, at the ropey tendril of her bond with Munro. As she drew closer to it, she reached out. The bond pulsed with power, like a strong, throbbing heartbeat. Suddenly he was with her again, and the glass disappeared.

"Well done. Now don't let anything come between you again. If you keep the barrier up, it will grow more and more difficult to deconstruct," Oron warned. "We must talk about Griogair." He stopped. "What is it?"

A sickening sludgy feeling overcame Eilidh. "Something's wrong with Quinton." She feared she might heave up what little was in her stomach. "I must go to him," she said.

Oron used his power to snap her attention to him. "This is a moment for you to learn. Acknowledge the feeling. Don't be ruled by it."

"It isn't mine, Elder. It's his."

"All the more reason."

"He's sick," she said, pleading. "Or hurt. Or something. I cannot do nothing."

"He's fine," Oron said. "Alyssa is with him. If he was in trouble, she would have called."

"Called? Alyssa can mind-speak?" *Alyssa was with him?* A pang of jealousy shot through her heart. She'd been foolish to try to pair them, shamed that she had tested him and was caught doing so, and relieved when it didn't work. But now she'd pushed him away. Perhaps he would find it better, easier, to be with someone else.

"No," Oron said. "But she has what they call a mobile telephone."

"What's wrong with him?" Eilidh said. What she'd wanted to ask was: *Where are they? What are they doing?* But she reined those thoughts in.

"He's fine," Oron said, firmer this time. "Let's take this opportunity to visualise the difference between his feelings and yours. This has been your difficulty. You take his pleasure, his pain, as your own. The bond is a tool, but it must not own you, or you will lose yourself. Both of you will. Although I suspect your druid is in less danger of that than you are."

"Because he is human?"

"Because he isn't confused about what he is. You've spent too much of your life wanting to please someone else or trying to hide. Now comes the hard work of growing up. Learn this lesson. If you control your thoughts, your emotions, and see your own potential, you will be the strongest astral fae in five thousand years."

Eilidh stared, searching Oron's eyes for some hint he was making a joke.

"Why do you think the queen fears you so, Eilidh? She brought you before her the first time because she heard of your potential, and people in her kingdom were talking about you as a hero."

"And the second?"

"She was curious about Munro and wanted to see him face to face, to convince herself he was truly just a human. But Griogair's deception about you being his lover, well, that went too far. A ruse that has likely worked for him in the past, but he misjudged her jealousy."

"Jealousy? Has he not had many such affairs?"

"He obviously would like others to think so. But it wasn't physical intimacy that would have worried her. She's felt for a very long time that Griogair has been plotting against her. She told me in our meeting. What she fears most is that you will ally with him."

"Me? But I'm her subject. I'm loyal to the crown."

"Why?"

Eilidh spluttered, "I am fae."

"Am I not?" Oron asked.

"That's different."

"I should remind you," he said with a laugh, "that you are an exile as well. Twice. And the queen has more reason to fear you—and to hate you. There is no going back, Eilidh. There will be no peace." Oron sighed. "I had not wanted it to happen this way."

"Can you not carry on as you have for the past thousand years?"

"Not anymore," Oron said. "Let us see to our guest. Griogair has much to tell us, I would wager."

∞

Pain hammered in Munro's head. He woke, not certain where he was. His perfect night vision showed him he was in a hotel room, and the sound of water running in the bathroom told him he wasn't alone. The glare of the digital alarm clock pierced his eyes like a knife. It was two in the morning. Sixteen hours since Eilidh told him to go away.

He had only fragmented memory of the previous day and night. Phillip had called, saying he and three of the others were in Portree. They wanted to meet with the azuri fae.

Munro agreed to catch up with him that afternoon at the hotel where they were staying. He knew he had to take them to Oron. He'd given his word, even if Eilidh didn't want to see him. And maybe, while he was there, he would give her a chance to change her mind. But first he'd wanted a beer. So he and Alyssa found a pub that served lunch, and he had a beer, then another, then another. That was the last thing he remembered. *Alyssa.* Holy crap. *What had he done?* That was when he realised he wasn't wearing a shirt. He still had on his jeans, thank god, but what had he done?

First things first, he told himself. He had to call Phillip. He didn't want to acknowledge that he planned to call the other druid mostly because he wasn't ready to think about Alyssa just yet.

The small hotel room had a double bed with a flower-print duvet, a small wooden table with two matching chairs, and artwork bolted to the wall. His phone rested on the table.

Munro moved to one of the chairs and picked up his phone, then scanned his received calls list to find Phillip's number. "Hey," he said when the other man answered.

"Look who survived," Phillip said groggily, sounding like the phone had woken him up. "Didn't Frankie ever tell you that alcohol and magic don't mix?"

The thought of his dead cousin jolted Munro. "Yeah," he said quietly, remembering the day he learned his cousin was a druid too. "I guess I wasn't paying attention."

"After last night, I doubt you'll forget again soon."

"About that," Munro said. "I can't remember entirely. Actually, I don't even remember seeing you yesterday. I mean, I hope I didn't do anything stupid." He winced at the brief silence that followed.

Finally Phillip said, "We've all been there. I don't think a single one of us gave up the drink without a fight. But one bad night, and you learn you aren't in charge anymore. I'm just glad I met you alone. I think the guys might have freaked out to see you raging like that."

"I'm sorry, Phillip. Eilidh and I had a fight. I guess I lost the plot a little."

"No worries, my friend. I've been *there* too. If you're up for it, we can meet in the morning. All of us."

"If you guys are sure about going ahead with this, it's better not to wait. There's some political shit going down with the fae, and nobody knows what's going to happen. So, better today than tomorrow or next week. Plus, the fae are nocturnal," he said. "If we wait 'til morning, we'll catch them off guard. They don't sleep that much, but they don't do official meetings and stuff during the day at all. The night is for work. The day is for sleep, rest, and friends." Only as he explained it did he really see how much he'd come to be part of their community, even if it was on a part-time basis while he juggled his time with Eilidh and his job.

"Okay," Phillip said. "I'll wake the guys. We can meet in the lobby in fifteen, if you're still at the hotel."

"Yeah," Munro said, casting his eyes toward the loo. The shower had just stopped running. She'd come out any minute, and he'd have to go through the humiliating ordeal of asking her what he did or didn't do. "I'm still here." They said goodbye and Munro looked around for his shirt. He couldn't find it anywhere. He started to panic a little. He couldn't go back to Eilidh half-dressed, and no shops would be open. Maybe he could get Alyssa to cast an illusion of a shirt long enough for him to get to his bag at Oron's house.

When Alyssa walked in, she was carrying his blue and red striped rugby shirt. "You're awake," she said with a smile. "I got the stains out, but it hasn't had time to dry yet. I wrung it out as best I could."

"You didn't have to do that," he said, embarrassed that the granddaughter of the conclave leader was doing his laundry. "Thank you."

She shrugged. "You needed a friend. We're not all like her, Quinton. I would never send you away if you loved me the way you do her."

"Don't," he said sharply, then instantly regretted it. "I'm sorry, Alyssa. My head is killing me." She sat on the edge of the bed, looking intently at him. He had to press on. "I don't remember what happened yesterday. The alcohol, I guess, doesn't agree with my magic. Did we...? Did I do something I should apologise for? Either way, I'm sorry."

"I like humans," she said. "I know the kingdom fae are dismissive, and even the azuri sometimes think humans are lesser beings, especially the elders who remember the old ways. But your passion is startling. It would be easy to believe in lasting love with someone like you." When he started to speak, she held up her hand. "Put your mind at ease. I find you attractive, I admit that. But I know my place. My grandfather would have my ears if I shamed him by dishonouring a guest."

He felt just as guilty at his relief as he did by the possibility of having slept with her but not remembering it. "Do I want to know why you had to wash my shirt?" he asked.

Her quiet laughter was delightful. "No," she said. "I'll tell you sometime, but perhaps on a better day. By then you'll laugh about the incident with me."

He couldn't help but smile. "Okay. It's a deal."

Suddenly, with a rush, he felt Eilidh's presence again. He looked west, feeling her like a warmth in his mind. She was worried, and he wondered what had happened with Griogair that made her so anxious. He steeled himself for the anger she would feel when she learned he hadn't left Skye as she'd told him to.

He explained to Alyssa his plan to return to Oron with the four druids, and she gently reminded him she'd met one of them yesterday.

“We should go now.” He hit redial on his phone and called Phillip back. “Hey, before we go downstairs, can I borrow a shirt?”

CHAPTER 13

TOO MANY HAD COME TO SEE Prince Griogair. Every room and corridor was packed with faeries. Most had grown up in exile and were naturally curious about the faerie queen and her mate, and they all wanted to hear the news of the kingdom rift. Rumours spun about Eilidh's communications with the queen, but the Higher Conclave kept the details to themselves. Hope and distrust ran in equal measure.

Eilidh negotiated her way through the crowd. She half expected to discover Griogair in a limp puddle in the centre of it all. Instead, she found him in the west hall, the largest and least-used room in Oron's large house, standing erect and looking every inch the royal. She recognised the weariness in his eyes but doubted anyone else would notice it.

When he saw her, he extended a hand and said, "Ah, Eilidh. Is it time?"

She didn't know what he meant but followed his lead. "Yes, Your Highness." The crowd turned to her, so she addressed them. "Prince Griogair is needed elsewhere. After he meets with the Higher Conclave, he will be available to speak with everyone again I'm sure."

The crowd quickly began to thin, and Griogair came to her side. She led him out, and people stepped aside as they approached. She took him to the garden, but found it full of faeries too, many she'd never seen before. Considering she had lived on Skye for six months, it surprised her. They walked toward the front of the house and continued down a path that led to the village. The way was lined with faeries who halted as the prince approached. They stared openly. Griogair said nothing beyond a wave and a casual word to a passer-by that gave him a slight nod of acknowledgement. He followed as though he knew exactly where they were going.

That was when she caught sight of Alyssa. Eilidh hesitated, confused because she thought Munro was with the young faerie. Her internal senses told her Munro was still miles away.

Eilidh stopped Alyssa, who was going in the opposite direction, back to the house. In a whisper, she said, "Please pass a message to your grandfather. I need to get Griogair to a place with fewer people. Tell him we'll be at the stream where Oron and I counted rocks. He'll know the place." That had been one of Eilidh's least favourite lessons. Thinking about it now, she couldn't help but chastise herself for not having worked harder to learn from Oron.

Alyssa's eyes were locked on Griogair. Her human illusion slipped and the twisting peaks of her ears emerged.

Eilidh shook her head. "I'm sorry. Your Highness, may I present Alyssa. She is Elder Oron's granddaughter. Alyssa, this is Griogair, prince-consort to the Caledonian queen."

He inclined his head to the young faerie. "A pleasure to meet you. Thank you for your kind assistance." He turned to Eilidh. "No longer consort to the queen. Just Griogair."

"I…of course…I…yes," Alyssa said and bolted toward the house.

Eilidh called after her, "You will tell your grandfather?" But Alyssa had gone too far away to hear, and Eilidh didn't want to shout, since they were not alone.

"I'm sorry. She's young," Eilidh said, but Griogair just smiled as though accustomed to that reaction.

To escape the crowd, Eilidh turned and cut through the trees at full speed, and Griogair followed. She couldn't help but wish she'd had the opportunity to ask Alyssa about Munro. So many things she wanted to know, but now wasn't the time. After a few miles, they approached the stream, and Eilidh slowed to a walk.

"Thank you," he said. "I hadn't expected the draining of my power. It's affected me badly. I was having difficulty keeping up appearances. Your numbers and the interest in me came as a surprise.

I half expected to be detained when I set foot on the island."

"What do you mean by no longer consort to the queen?" Eilidh asked, waving off his gratitude.

A pained expression crossed his face, and his violet eyes darkened in the moonlight. "Cadhla made her wishes clear. I suppose killing her own mate was not a legacy she wished to be remembered by, so she severed our relationship before ordering my death."

Eilidh watched him in silence for a moment. He gave away no clue as to his feelings about the more personal aspects of past days' incidents. "You're still a prince," Eilidh said, making herself comfortable on the grass near the stream. "I know you're the cousin of Queen Zdanye of Tvorskane. So you are royalty no matter what Cadhla did." She paused, thinking. "Will you go back there? To Tvorskane?"

He shook his head. "I wouldn't drag them into this. If they shelter me from Cadhla's death order, it could be war, and my family's kingdom is even smaller than Caledonia. It would cost them too dearly."

"Where will you go? You can't stay here." She quickly added, "I mean because of the enchantments. I can only access the Ways of Earth through my druid, so the loss is not keen. For you, it must be unbearable."

He sat beside her and sighed. "It's disorienting, and no, I won't stay here. I intend to go back to the Otherworld. To face Cadhla."

Eilidh stared in horror. "You can't. She'll kill you."

"You almost sound as though you care."

"Of course I care. The kingdom cannot be divided. We must find a way to heal the rift, to bring together those who follow the Father of the Azure and the Mother of the Earth. There must be a way."

"I have no specific plans," he said, watching her closely. "However, I should speak to your conclave to see what assistance they would be willing to offer."

"Of course," she said. "I didn't mean to suggest otherwise. I'm merely a student here." She laughed when she added, "And not a very good one at that."

"I know better," Griogair said. "Cadhla said you were more powerful than you pretended to be. I understand the subterfuge, but I'm afraid she saw through it."

"Subterfuge? I think the machinations of court have addled your thinking, Griogair," she joked.

"And there. We finally have it. You've called me by my name instead of my title. Who knew it would take being attacked and exiled before you thought me worthy of your friendship."

"Oh, be quiet," she said with a smile, then looked up when a presence tickled her senses. "Someone's coming."

"Your druid?"

"No." She stood to wait, and Griogair followed suit.

Alyssa came through the trees, keeping her eyes firmly on Eilidh, as though consciously avoiding the prince's gaze. "Grandfather wishes you to escort the prince, I mean our guest, to the village hall. The Higher Conclave has convened and is speaking with your druid and his companions now."

"Quinton?" she said. "What companions?" It embarrassed her that she didn't know what was going on with him. They'd been apart less than a day, but the divide felt like miles.

"When we went to Portree, we met with four other druids. He's brought them here to…"

"I know what they're here for," Eilidh snapped. She didn't like to be reminded that when she'd sent Munro away, he'd chosen to be with Alyssa. It was her own fault, of course, but she didn't like it. She turned to Griogair. "Your Highness?"

He rolled his eyes. "I should make you nobility and name you Lady Eilidh so you can appreciate what it feels like to be known as a title rather than as an individual. In fact, consider it done. I hereby decree it." He indicated the path. "After you, milady."

Eilidh replied tartly, "I'll have to count myself lucky that you can't do things like that anymore." But inwardly she was enjoying herself. It pleased her that Griogair wanted to be friends, and their banter seemed light and easy, a relief from the real concerns that weighed on them.

The trio headed for the village, and on the way, Eilidh noticed the larger than usual number of faeries, so she asked Alyssa quietly, "Who are all these fairies? I thought I knew all the azuri on Skye."

"I don't know," she said. "I heard they came through the kingdom gates all over and have been making their way here."

"They're kingdom fae?" Eilidh said, glancing at Griogair, wondering what his reaction would be.

"They came from the kingdoms, but not all from Caledonia. They've been travelling through the human realms as well, with more coming every hour since the prince arrived." The trio entered the village hall. "The rest you will need to hear from the conclave, milady," she said, her tone deferential.

"Don't you start," Eilidh snapped.

"But His Highness said..."

"Oh, never mind." She glared at Griogair, who laughed quietly to himself.

Alyssa led them to the back, where the Higher Conclave met. When she opened the door, she announced, "Prince Griogair and Lady Eilidh." She bowed her head slightly, and the room went silent. Eilidh wanted to pinch her.

Alyssa stepped aside and Eilidh and Griogair moved forward together. Eilidh suddenly realised she should have sent him in first, and alone. Arriving together implied they were on equal footing. She cursed under her breath, because she could see the message wasn't lost on the conclave, but rather than taking it to mean that Griogair was some average faerie, they now looked at her as though she *were* nobility. She wanted to explain the title was a joke, but she didn't dare show disrespect to the conclave. Instead, she gave the same bow of deference to the conclave any student would. It infuriated her when Griogair did the same. He waited for the elders to address him before he spoke, another sign of humility.

Oron broke the silence. "Prince Griogair, the conclave welcomes you to Skye. You will forgive the delay, but we have just learned that Quinton Munro has brought four more druids to us. Despite the difficult times, this has caused some excitement, as I'm sure you can imagine."

Only then did Eilidh allow herself to look to the place where Munro and the other druids sat. She saw the hurt and confusion in his deep blue eyes, but she couldn't address it now. Taking Oron's earlier lesson to heart, she worked on separating his hurt from her own, trying to see it as a distant thing. She smiled at the other druids: Douglas, Rory, Phillip and Aaron. She'd met them before, of course, but not often. They seemed relaxed and not as fearful as she might expect. It gave her hope to think they may want to stay and bond with her people.

Griogair also nodded to the five druids. "Your power is growing," he said, turning to Oron and the rest of the conclave members. "And your numbers." He gestured to the door.

"We are a peaceful colony," said Dalyna, one of the conclave members. "We are not now and never have been a threat to your kingdom."

"I have no kingdom," Griogair said. "I am merely a refugee, seeking temporary asylum, grateful for the faith you showed in taking me in."

Dalyna leaned forward, her black eyes narrowing. "This could be a ruse. Will you ask us to put down the enchantments so you will be more comfortable here? How do we know you're telling the truth?"

"He is," Munro interrupted.

The entire conclave looked at him, and even Eilidh and Griogair turned in surprise.

"How do you know this?" Dalyna asked.

"Because of his son." Munro nodded to Griogair. "You'd best tell them the truth," he said. "All of it."

Griogair turned to the conclave. "I couldn't agree more." He took his time and told them about Tràth, including the long-held secret that the heir to the throne was gifted in the Path of Stars.

CHAPTER 14

MUNRO WATCHED AS THE conclave questioned Griogair for hours, but he seemed relaxed and comfortable. The prince was uncommonly frank and open, revealing the extent of the queen's obsession. She planned to purge the Otherworld of all who followed the Path of Stars. She'd only pretended to consider the reunification of the kingdom because of the pressure caused by Eilidh's rising popularity, as stories of her saving the kingdom spread.

The meeting came to an abrupt halt when someone brought word to Oron. The messenger slipped in and whispered into the elder's ear.

Oron's brow wrinkled and his face creased into a deep frown. "Prince Griogair," he said. "Do you know a faerie named Mira?"

Griogair blinked in surprise. "Of course. My bodyguard and friend."

"She was brought here by one of our earthbound children. They just arrived." When the prince looked confused, Oron went on to explain. "Not all of our offspring are gifted in the Path of Stars. Our enchantments mean they would be impotent and miserable here. So we foster them with willing allies in the kingdom who raise them as their own. When they come of age, some patrol the borderlands nearest us, helping to protect our colony as they can, trading, sending messages, whatever is necessary."

Griogair nodded, his brow furrowed slightly. "May I see Mira?"

Oron nodded. "You should go quickly. She is severely injured."

Griogair stood, just as another faerie entered the room. She was taller than most and had fine, sculpted features. She looked shaken and ill, so Munro assumed she must be a kingdom faerie. "Forgive me, elders," she said, addressing the conclave. She turned her sad eyes to Griogair. "Your Highness," she said, bowing. "I am Sennera. Mira...Mira is dead."

The prince's features tightened. "Show me," he said.

Munro felt a wave of rolling earth power surge as the prince left the room. The rush of power fought for a moment against the enchantment. He turned to the other druids, but they hadn't noticed it. He had never been affected by the enchantment that prevented the faeries' connection to the Ways of Earth. He could sense something was different here on Skye, but because he could tap into his limited abilities the same here as anywhere else, he never thought much more of it.

"It is nearly sunrise," Oron said. "We should allow our guests to rest." He looked at the druids and smiled. "Thank you for coming. You have arrived, as you see, on a very busy night. But we have not forgotten you, and your presence brings joy in dark and uncertain times."

Munro felt his friends shifting uncomfortably beside him, unaccustomed to so much attention and praise. He'd had the chance to introduce them to the conclave before Eilidh and Griogair arrived and to reiterate his conditions that none be forced to bond if he didn't want to. Somehow, he became the official go-between, and they established that he would oversee the introductions. It seemed every faerie on Skye—several hundred even before the huge influx of faeries from abroad—wanted the chance to be considered for bonding with a druid.

"Munro," Oron said, "I'm afraid my home, while large, is not adequate to accommodate four such important guests, five, counting yourself, of course. As the leader of the Higher Conclave, I am obliged to host the prince."

Munro wanted to laugh. He didn't doubt for a minute that Oron would rather boot the prince in favour of the druids if he could get away with it.

Galen, a sour elder who had never liked Eilidh, and therefore by extension Munro, spoke up. "The house of my sister Beniss, may the Father of the Azure cradle her soul in his bosom, still stands empty. It should serve the druids well. I'm afraid it may need attention, but I can have it stocked and prepared within an hour."

At first Munro wasn't sure why she would make such an offer, considering she held Eilidh responsible for Beniss' death, but then he realised she, and most others, would do just about anything to get more of a chance with one of the druids. Such a bonding would allow them full access to the Ways of Earth, something they could never dream of touching beyond a faint trickle of power.

"That's very generous of you, Galen," Oron said. "Munro?"

Munro turned to the others, who nodded. "Sure," he said to Oron. "That sounds great."

"While you and your friends are getting settled for the day, I will have a word with *Lady* Eilidh." He gave Eilidh a meaningful look. To the room, he announced, "Thus concludes the conclave."

Eilidh went to the elder without even glancing back at Munro. Maybe, he thought, it was better if he stayed at Beniss' place after all. He didn't know what had happened between him and Eilidh all of a sudden. Things had blown up, gone wrong for no reason. At least he could sense her again, even if it was a more subdued connection than before. But if he knew anything about her, it was that pushing never did any good.

∞

True to her word, Galen had Beniss' house prepared, and everything the druids might need was provided: beds, food, and some privacy. The only additions they could wish for would be a telly and maybe a games console. The others were restless, and Munro thought they could use something to keep distracted while they processed their new situation. They'd learned a lot in just a few hours and been exposed to a world they only caught a glimpse of before.

"What now?" Phillip looked at Munro as they sat in the front room. Phillip seemed a quiet type, but he was the one the group trusted.

"To be honest," Munro began, "I'm not sure how all this should work. When I met Eilidh, I felt something right away. I could sense some spark between us, even before we bonded."

Aaron laughed. "Or it could be you noticed those legs of hers. Crikey, she's hot." When Munro shot him a look, Aaron added, "Sorry, mate, but she is."

The others joined in with a chuckle, nodding that they agreed with Aaron.

"Did you feel anything with one of the elders? Something tugging or..." Munro's voice trailed off. He didn't even know how this was supposed to work. They all shook their heads.

"That's okay," Munro said. "There are hundreds of faeries here, and you'll get a chance to meet them all eventually. It might take some time. I really don't know. But we'll figure it out."

"What if we don't ever feel it with any of them?" Rory was stocky, had flaming ginger hair and narrow eyes. He was the happy-go-lucky one of the group, but now his face furrowed with worry. "I mean, I don't have all that much keeping me in Perth, you know?"

"Afraid you'll be the last one without a date to the dance?" Aaron asked with a smirk.

Phillip grinned. "Wouldn't be the first time. Would it, Rors?"

The ribbing was good-natured, but Munro could tell they all felt some anxiety about the many unknowns. "I'll talk to Oron," he said, "but I'm sure we can all stay as long as we want, no matter what. I've heard there are lots of new faeries here, ones that follow the Path of Stars, and more will be coming all the time. I don't see them sending away anyone who wants to stay."

Douglas weighed in. "I could get used to this. Free food, free house, being treated like a rock star. Did you see some of those women? Yeah, I'm in." He was the youngest of the group, only just out of high school the year before. He talked big, but Douglas had taken the events of last summer the hardest. Munro was glad he'd come. The only one who hadn't shown up was Jay, and Munro couldn't say he was sorry about that. He suspected Jay had more than a small hand in the deaths last year, although he couldn't prove it.

"First thing," Munro said, "is you'll have to get used to being awake all night. They sleep at various times during the day, but some barely sleep at all. Anything official though, that's always at night. I think it'll get easier once you're bonded. I know it seems a lot more natural for me now."

"I didn't like to say anything," Phillip said slowly, "but how long before you started looking like that? Or is that one of Eilidh's illusions to hide your normal ugly mug?" The others chuckled at the joke.

Without thinking, Munro put his hand up to one ear, reassuring himself that he hadn't grown a full, spiralling twist. "Not until I visited the Otherworld." Now that Griogair had spilled the beans about his and Eilidh's involvement in finding his son, Munro could tell them about his venture beyond the human realm. "Everything changed: my speed, endurance, my eyesight. I don't really know what happened."

"When do we get to go there?" Rory asked.

"Not for a while," Munro said. "If ever. You heard them. There's a war brewing." He told the druids more about the political situation, about the Halls of Mist and his one and only encounter with the Caledonian queen. "Let's do one thing at a time. Today, get some rest. Sleep if you can. Eat if you want. Their food is different, but pretty good. You'll get used to it fast. I'll have to come and go. I've got to check in with work in the morning, and I promised Griogair I'd help him find his son."

"You mean you're still on with the polis?" Rory asked. "Looking like Link?"

"Who?" Munro asked, and the others laughed.

It was Phillip who explained. "Didn't you ever play Legend of Zelda as a kid? You know, Link? The elven guy who saves the princess?"

"He wasn't elven. Technically, Link was Hylian," Rory corrected him.

Aaron chuckled. "Only you would know that, Rors."

Munro laughed too, but he'd wondered about the changes, thinking he should ask one of the elders how far it would go and what to expect. It would get harder for him to keep up his normal life if he got more deeply involved here, not to mention that his eyes glowed in the dark. On the other hand, Eilidh didn't want him around, and the guys seemed fine with the new environment. He had every confidence they'd know if they met someone they could bond with. So it was really up to him what he should do next. Maybe he could go on as he had, splitting time between the two places. In some ways, it was good he had the job holding him in Perth. It provided him an excuse to get away and breathe from time to time.

"Munro," Phillip said.

When Munro looked up, he realised that while he'd been lost in thought, the others had stopped talking. They all stared at the wall behind him. He turned and saw Prince Griogair standing in the doorway, looking pale and drawn.

Munro scrambled to his feet. "Your Highness," he said. He didn't much like being formal, but he figured he'd better set a decent example for the others.

Griogair looked shaken. Hollow. "She's going to kill my son."

"Come sit down," Munro said, offering Griogair his own seat. "Rory, will you get the prince some water? There should be cups or something in the kitchen." He pointed toward an open doorway.

"Sure," Rory said.

Munro went into cop mode. "Let's start at the beginning. Did Mira bring a message?"

Rory came back with a wooden cup filled with water, and Munro handed it to the prince, who looked at the cup, slightly puzzled.

"Drink," Munro said. "It'll help." He didn't know why, but just the action of taking a sip of water was often enough to snap people out of a shock. It gave them something to do, something to concentrate on.

The prince did as instructed, and Phillip whispered, "Eilidh's here."

Munro turned for a second and saw her in the back of the room, looking on with a worried expression that matched the unrest Munro sensed in her emotional state. Focusing on the prince, Munro said, "Mira's message. What did she come to tell you?"

"She'd been bound," Griogair said.

Munro turned to Eilidh with a raised eyebrow. She explained. "Mira had been stripped of her magic. Severed from the Ways of Earth."

Munro could tell it pained her to think about it. His eyes back on the prince, he said, "Griogair, I need you to focus. For Tràth. What was Mira's message?"

"Cadhla has ordered a fifth of her personal guard, the *rafta*, to pass through the Ashdawn gate.

They're the best, and their orders are to find Tràth." Griogair stared at Munro, his violet eyes dark and unblinking. "To find him and kill him."

The other druids sat back, mystified. Munro frowned. "She would kill her own son?"

"She knows where I am, so she's smart enough to know I'd tell the Higher Conclave about Tràth. Yes, she'd rather see him dead than have people know she'd given birth to a child gifted with the Path of Stars. You don't understand the depth of the prejudice amongst my people."

"No," Munro said. "I do." He'd seen how Eilidh was condemned to death not because she'd done what they called casting the stars, but because she was merely able to. If she hadn't discovered this then-hidden colony on Skye, she would have lived her entire existence running from the kingdom, always feeling the executioner's axe hanging over her head. "Do they know where Tràth is?"

"If they don't, they soon will. Their talents in the Ways of Earth are unparalleled. The earth itself will tell them where his foot tread. The wind will carry his scent."

Munro grumbled to himself. Why couldn't they have talents like that on their side? Suddenly he realised they did. Griogair could help track his son. Munro wasn't wild about the unpredictability of counting on someone personally involved in an investigation, but he had little choice. He told Griogair what he was thinking.

"I will help in whatever way I can," the prince said. "Just show me the way."

"No," Eilidh said. "It's too dangerous. There are many gates between here and Ashdawn, and every inch of the borderlands could be filled with ten times the usual number of Watchers. Your Highness, she knows where you are and what you'll want to do. You cannot sacrifice yourself for Tràth. Think of the kingdom. It needs you to stay alive."

Munro stood his ground. "I don't know if I can find Tràth without his help. We don't even understand what happened to him."

"Too bad none of us is bonded to his son," Aaron said. "We could lead you right to him."

Munro stared for a moment.

"What?" Aaron said. "I was just thinking out loud." Then he muttered, "Sorry."

"No, he's right. All of you have to come with us," Munro said to the other druids. "If there's even a remote chance one of you can bond with him, it would be worth it. If you are compatible, you'd be able to feel it right away. It might induce him to trust us. We didn't have a lot of luck with that last time we encountered him." He paused. "What we need is a plan."

"What are his powers exactly?" Phillip asked. "It might help us figure out what he *would* do, if we understand what he *could* do."

Munro looked at Griogair. "What can you tell us about your son's abilities?"

"It's hard to explain, really. We always discouraged him from practising. His mother..." He hesitated. "I can barely bring myself to call her that after what she's done." His tone was tight and angry. "Cadhla sought help in restricting the forbidden flows. She called in a few experts, but only people she trusted implicitly, and that list is short."

"What were the signs?" Eilidh asked, stepping forward and sitting beside Griogair. "When I was a girl, I would cast illusions without thinking, influence my teachers to change their minds, let me off my lessons. Did Tràth do things like that?"

Griogair shook his head. "No, it was very different with him."

Eilidh sighed. "He must be of the blood then," she said.

Munro explained the distinction to the other druids. "There are only two remaining types of azuri or higher magic, astral, like Oron's people have, and blood."

"Like Cridhe," Douglas said quietly.

Munro nodded.

"And you think Tràth is like Cridhe?" The young druid's voice was tight with fear. Cridhe had nearly killed them all.

Munro looked at Eilidh. "What would be the early signs?"

"Oron says the simplest manifestations of the blood shadows would all have to do with control of the physical form. He might be able to stop an animal's heart if he had a dark nature, but he might also be able to heal it. He could possibly change his eye colour, his hair or skin colour, but unlike the illusions of the astral flows, they would be real, physical changes. His senses would be keener at the very least."

Griogair shook his head. "No, nothing like that. It's hard to explain. He was a difficult child." He seemed apologetic.

Phillip turned to Eilidh. "Munro said there were two *remaining* types of azuri magic. Were there others?"

"Yes," she said slowly. "Millenia ago, but the talents died out. They no longer exist."

"What were they?" he pressed.

"One was called spirit or soul magic. Like blood magic, it was often used for dark purposes. There were many practices that taint our history. The resurrection of the dead to a half-life, the enslavement of others. Even among the azuri, those who wielded those flows were feared and even shunned. The other lost art was temporal."

"Temporal?" Rory asked.

"Time," she said. "This form was the most rare. It was said that—"

"Time," Griogair interupted. "That's it."

"Your Highness," she said softly, "that's not possible. No one can wield temporal flows anymore. No one even remembers how the power worked. There are only the vaguest references to it in any of our surviving documents."

Griogair looked up, excited. "He would sometimes be reported in two places at once. He would claim he'd been away for days, when it had only been minutes. Other times he would disappear for a week, but insist he'd not gone anywhere at all. I always thought he was lying to annoy his mother, but now, looking back, it seems obvious."

Munro turned to Eilidh. "What does this mean?"

She stood. "It means that Tràth must be protected, no matter the cost." She looked down at Griogair, who still seemed shaken, although his expression at least now seemed determined and hopeful. "I'll get Oron. We need a plan."

CHAPTER 14

IT TOOK SOME CONVINCING for Oron and the others to agree the druids should follow Eilidh, Griogair, and Munro to Auchterarder. Every member of the Higher Conclave wanted the first shot at the druids, and none were crazy about the idea of a druid bonding with Griogair's son. He might be talented with azuri magic, but he was untrained, and more importantly, he wasn't *one of them*. Eilidh had given Oron the bad news that none of the druids felt a connection with any of the elders. He sighed, clearly disappointed, but agreed that one who could feel temporal flows must be saved.

The two faeries rode with Munro in his car. They wanted to run, but even with their incredible speed and strength, the journey would take too long on foot. The other druids rode together and would wait in Perth until Munro called them from his mobile, telling them it was safe to approach Auchterarder.

Munro insisted they play a part, but Eilidh wasn't so sure. To her, they seemed like any other human men. They were decent, she supposed, but they didn't seem special like Munro. She knew it was the bond talking, but perhaps something more as well.

They drove to Munro's house in Perth and ran from there to Auchterarder, thinking it best to make a cautious approach. It would also give the faeries time to recover from the drive. Neither had an easy time with the confinement in a vehicle, and their discomfort made Munro uneasy driving. Taking a few minutes to breathe the fresh air would do them all good.

As they closed the last couple of miles to Auchterarder, she felt Munro close behind, heard his heavy footsteps in the darkness. They'd had to take a slightly circuitous route to avoid the kingdom gates and patrolling Watchers. Yet between her use of mental misdirection and confusion when they did encounter a patrol, and Griogair's connection with water and stone telling him if any were near, they'd managed to carve a path that hadn't taken too much extra time.

They approached the village in a roundabout way, avoiding streets and shops Munro knew would have CCTV. Eilidh didn't quite understand how they created pictures of people and played them back later without using magic, but she did appreciate Munro's insistence on caution. The three climbed through back gardens. In one, they attracted the notice of a large black dog, who whined and eyed them curiously, clearly confused at their scent.

When they were at a house near the one where Tràth had disappeared, Munro made a call on his mobile. "We're here," he said quietly into the small black device. He disconnected and said to Eilidh and Griogair, "Wait here. I'll check the perimeter and confirm with Hallward, then you two climb up when it's clear."

Griogair nodded. "Thank you," he said.

Munro looked wary. "Don't thank me yet." With deft movements he could not have managed a few short weeks ago, he scaled the fence dividing the two gardens. Eilidh heard his feet hit the ground on the other side with a thud. "Sarge," Munro said.

Eilidh reached out and took Griogair's hand. He seemed surprised, but grateful. "He can do this," she whispered. "We'll find your son."

They listened as Munro talked to Sergeant Hallward. It had been at Munro's insistence that they allow the human policeman to help. The house would be watched, Munro explained, and it would be easier to work with the police than to try and hide from them or circumvent their investigation. Hallward could ensure they were not disturbed.

"We have a group of four others coming," Munro explained. "Humans. Druids, like me. We'll need them to help in the event we do see Prince Tràth. They'll arrive by car in a little while."

"You can have the property for an hour to do what you need. Have them pull up in a driveway two streets over," Hallward said quietly. "It'll look strange to see cars coming and going on this road.

With the disappearances, no one is home. We've managed to keep most of the area inside the cordon clear, but we aren't the only ones watching. With the press, well, you know how it is. Have you seen the reports on the news?" He paused, but Eilidh couldn't hear Munro's answer. "Count yourself lucky. We're getting hammered this time. One hour. That's what I can give you." Another pause. "You think this will work?" Eilidh recognised the scepticism in his voice.

"I think if it doesn't, we're never going to see any of those missing people again," Munro said. "Eilidh and another friend are here to help. I'll go signal them in."

"All right. I'll be out front. And Munro?"

"Yes, Sarge?"

"We need to talk. Find me when you're done here." Eilidh couldn't read what he meant by his tone, and she couldn't hear Munro's reply, but it was only a moment before Munro whispered through the fence that it was clear to come over.

The plan was simple. Griogair would use his earth magic to track Tràth, and Eilidh would use her limited psychic abilities as a second locator, the thinking being that she might be able to sense a mind out of sync. Everyone else was much more confident in her abilities than she was. People talked about her talents and *vast potential,* but she didn't see it. Her efforts were always stymied by a century of trying to stifle her forbidden abilities. She couldn't turn off those instincts overnight. But everyone was counting on her, so she had to try.

Munro had a part to play as well. If more natural means failed, he and Griogair would use the star talisman Munro had crafted. She had an intuition that it amplified Griogair's essence, and guessed that it could help attract Tràth's attention. No one knew if it would work, and Eilidh worried their combined power would only attract the attention of the *rafta*, who might be nearby. The other druids, once they arrived, were the line of last resort. If one of them was compatible with the crown prince, she knew from experience it would be a powerful inducement for him to reveal himself.

Munro sat in a white plastic chair on the patio. Eilidh still hadn't had a chance to speak to him alone since he'd come back from Portree with the others. His calm focus centred her, though. She didn't know if they would get back to the sweet, comfortable relationship they had before, but she drew strength from him now. As she thought about him, he looked up and smiled. She felt reassured, and had a new confidence that everything would be all right.

While Griogair paced around the back garden, speaking to the paving stones and touching individual blades of grass, she opened herself to the astral plane. Her vision shifted, and she saw them all from above. Her senses grew sharp, and she noticed what appeared to be a blue bubble that extended over several houses. Slowly and methodically, she investigated it. She couldn't help but wonder if all the humans within this area had been the ones who disappeared. It couldn't be a coincidence.

After some time, she opened her eyes to find Griogair standing in front of her, pacing back and forth. Munro was gone. "What happened?" she asked.

"The earth," Griogair said bitterly, "for the first time in my life, it's lying to me."

"What do you mean?"

"The stones, the earth, the drops of water. every natural voice in this place has told me Tràth is *here*. They say he never left this place."

Eilidh, although powerful in the Ways of Earth since she bonded with Munro, was inexperienced. She put her hand to the ground and listened. She shook her head with frustration. "The bubble won't let me hear him."

"Bubble?" Griogair stopped pacing and looked at her.

She opened her mouth to explain what she'd seen, but just then, Munro came through the front gate, leading the four druids. "Any luck?" he asked.

As best she could, she described what she'd seen.

Munro nodded. "It does sound like it covers the area where the people disappeared." He turned to Griogair, "So, you think none of them actually left?"

"How is that possible?" the prince asked with frustration. "Unless..." His face showed his concern.

"We can't assume the worst. Not yet," Munro said. "Rory had an idea, and I think we should give it a shot."

Rory stepped forward. "The guys and I are always messing about with our talismans, right?" When no one answered, he pressed on. "So, we talked on the way down. We're all water druids, except Munro, of course. That's not going to be much help, but we can sort of link. I don't know how to explain it. The effect isn't much, but maybe we can clear things out."

"Here," Aaron said, pulling a small wooden ship out of his pocket. "Let's just show them." The four water druids stood facing each other, all holding a talisman of wood.

Eilidh watched, fascinated. She and Munro had practised their connection with each other, but it never occurred to either of them that druids could unite without a faerie. As the four concentrated, she sensed a ripple in the astral plane. "By faith," she swore quietly. It grieved her how much druidic lore was lost because of her people's fear of humans. "Do you see it?" she asked Munro and Griogair.

"No," they both said at the same time.

She went to the druids and guided them each backward, touching their minds briefly to help solidify their concentration. As they stepped away from each other, the ripple grew. Eilidh had an idea. She motioned to Griogair. "Come stand in the centre."

He entered the circle and stood close to where Tràth had appeared.

"What does the earth tell you now?" she asked as she continued to guide the druids further apart, until they were standing at the furthest corners of the fenced-in garden.

He breathed in deeply, then his eyes snapped up. "The earth tells me he is here. Right here." He pointed to the exact location where she'd seen Tràth before.

Eilidh closed her eyes and again tapped into the astral flows. "Think of him. Give me his essence," she said to Griogair. He seemed not to understand at first, but he let down his defences and relaxed, letting her guide his thoughts until he focused completely on his son.

Then a shimmer appeared. The shimmer turned to a form, although it was indistinct. An echo sounded. "Time?" a voice said distantly, as though speaking to someone they couldn't see. "It's all I've got."

"Tràth!" Griogair shouted. "Son, where are you?"

The figure turned toward his father, and he smiled sadly. It was him. Eilidh could feel his presence clearly, but it faded in and out.

Griogair stepped forward, but Tràth seemed to dissolve before their eyes. "No!" his father shouted.

"Eilidh," Munro said, jogging over to her. "Use me. Take my strength."

Waving Munro off, she concentrated on Tràth, his mind, his thought patterns. This wasn't going to require Munro's earth powers, but rather her own astral training. With all of her abilities, she called to Tràth's awareness and made a connection. Elated, she fought to communicate with him. Words failed her in this state, where thought and abstraction held so much more power. "The star," she said to Griogair. She feared her communication was disjointed, but she had to work to hold this together. If she slipped, she knew they'd lose Tràth.

Griogair took the star out of his pouch and let it hover.

"Send it higher," Munro said.

Griogair obeyed, and the star lifted above their heads.

Eilidh reached for Munro's hand. "Touch your power to the star."

He reached toward the star as though caressing the air. She knew the instant he'd accomplished the connection. Through him, she could access the well of power within it, and through Griogair's mental image of his son's essence, she could create a beacon. Sending her voice through it, she whispered, "Tràth. Your father needs you." Using images and abstractions, she poured everything she had witnessed Griogair going through to find his son, the fear, the need, the unashamed emotion.

Tràth returned, his eyes focused upward on the blazing blue star. Eilidh was so connected to both of their emotions that she had to fight back tears.

Griogair reached out for his son, and the instant their hands touched, Tràth became solid and collapsed into his father's embrace.

A loud explosion sounded a few feet away, and everyone spun toward the house. A startled human woman in a housecoat stood in the darkness. A man, also in pyjamas, held the barrel of her shotgun as though he'd just redirected it into the air.

The woman looked dazed. "Who are you people?" She turned and blinked at the man in the doorway behind her.

Munro stepped forward, retrieved his ID card from his wallet, then showed it to her. "PC Munro, madam. Tayside Police. We got a call about a disturbance." He pulled out his mobile and dialled Sergeant Hallward. "I'm with Sarah and Hamish McBride. I could use some backup." He paused. "Everyone seems to be fine."

He turned to Eilidh and said quietly, "I'll stay and take care of this. You get them out of here before someone notices Griogair and Tràth aren't from around here."

The human couple stared upward at the floating blue star that lit their back garden. Their mouths were agape, and they leaned into one another for support. Eilidh signalled for Griogair to lower the star, and she motioned for the four druids to follow. They helped spirit Tràth over the fence, and they slipped quietly into the night, leaving Munro behind.

∞

Police swarmed the neighbourhood, checking in with each of the houses that had reported disappearances, while trying to keep reporters at bay. It was tightly controlled chaos. Munro did his best to stay in the shadows. He waited for Sergeant Hallward to come have a word with him. He had no idea how the police media office would explain the reappearances. It was probably going to turn into one of those Unexplained Mystery documentaries on the Discovery Channel. And no conspiracy theory would be as strange as the truth.

He felt Eilidh's progress back to Skye, and he worried that she might encounter the *rafta*. He'd have to remember to tell Hallward to be on the lookout, but he also knew even faerie assassins would stay away from a loud, busy group of humans like the ones here now. Safety in numbers.

After an hour or so, Hallward sought him out, striding with that authoritative walk, like always. "Munro," he said as he approached. He leaned with his back against a tree, and he breathed in the night air. After a moment, he looked up. "Jesus," he muttered. "What a clusterfuck." He motioned to the end of the street where several officers were keeping the press back. At least one helicopter hovered over the village. "Start at the beginning."

Trying not to spend too much time framing the story to sound less crazy, Munro detailed as much as he could about what had happened. In the end, it was an inexperienced kid messing around with time. Just a magical accident, he explained.

Hallward didn't ask any follow-up questions. Instead, he peered toward the street. "So they won't remember being gone."

Munro shook his head. "Seems like, in their minds, they *weren't* gone. They blinked, and suddenly here we all were. With perhaps a bit of overlap."

"That squares with what they're getting from the house-to-house. Most of the people who disappeared were sleeping. They didn't even notice having a nightmare, and one sod actually yelled at PC Janey for waking him up." Hallward chuckled.

"Sarge," Munro began, "I can't stay on with the police."

Hallward looked him in the eye. "When did you decide this?"

"Tonight. I know it seems sudden, but it's the only thing that makes sense. I just don't fit in here anymore. I could never imagine being anything other than a copper, but now, well…" He didn't want to bring up the obvious, that the subtle changes in his appearance and abilities might grow even less subtle, making him stand out in human society in a way that wouldn't be good for anyone.

He knew Hallward could see it plainly. It was written all over his expression as he stared at Munro's glowing eyes. "Going to Skye then?"

"For now," he said. "Eilidh and I both have a lot to learn from her people up there."

Hallward nodded. "You're a good copper."

"Thanks, Sarge. I feel like I'm cutting and running, but I can't see any other way."

With a wave toward the street, Hallward said, "Can we expect shit like this to happen more often? Is something going on with them?"

"I hope not. Believe it or not, last year's murders and this were unrelated. The fae have been executing their own people for having certain forbidden abilities for years. If the Skye conclave has anything to say about it, that will stop. If they succeed, you won't keep getting faeries who are running away from death orders or oppression. They'll always be around, the fae. They need to be a part of the human realm. But we're more of a threat to them than they are to us."

Hallward chuckled, obviously not quite agreeing with that statement. "I wish you and your friends good luck then," he said. "Let's put you on an indefinite leave of absence. Don't hang up your baton and handcuffs for good. If I see anything strange crop up, yours will be the first number I call." He stuck out his hand, and Munro clasped it firmly and shook it.

"I'm good at explaining strange events," Hallward continued. "Most were surprised you didn't take more time after being attacked by a serial killer last year, so a cover story wouldn't be difficult to sketch out. It won't even have to be too far from the truth."

"Thanks." Munro appreciated the offer, but he didn't think he'd be back. Of course, with everything on Skye being in such upheaval, it was good to have options. But he knew that one important order of business in the next few days was to call an estate agent to put his house in Perth on the market. He'd work things out with Eilidh. They needed each other, and he wasn't ready to give up. But even if that didn't happen the way he hoped, his place was with the fae.

CHAPTER 16

THERE WAS MUCH DEBATE about how to get Tràth to Skye, and the druids provided the best solution. Eilidh led Griogair, who carried Tràth to Perth, where the druids had driven and picked up another one of their cars. Although the two faeries could have carried Tràth all the way to Skye, and Griogair certainly had the will to do so, that journey would have taken days and been far too treacherous.

Griogair was even more uncomfortable safety-belted into the smelly machine than she had been her first time. He seemed not to trust the vehicle's movement, and he watched other cars on the road with a mixture of awe and horror.

Eilidh turned around from her position in the front passenger seat and looked at the crown prince, who rested his head on his father's shoulder. She smiled at Griogair, who mouthed the words, "Thank you."

When she faced forward again, she caught Douglas staring at the crown prince in the rear-view mirror. “What is it?” she asked him.

Douglas frowned. “I’m not sure exactly. I’m just worried about him. Is he going to be all right?”

Eilidh watched the druid closely. “I hope so.”

“It’s…well…I need to do something. Does he need a doctor?”

With a gentle touch to his wrist, Eilidh did her best to send calming energy to the druid’s mind. Influencing his mind wasn’t as easy with Douglas as it was with Munro, but his forehead relaxed, and his breathing became more even. Even still, he stole glances into the mirror frequently, and Eilidh knew he must have felt drawn to Tràth in more than just a casual way.

She considered what Douglas bonding with Tràth would mean. The other fae wouldn’t like it, but then, *anyone* not chosen would feel aggrieved. If Tràth had permanent problems with the stability of his mind and his magic, possibly he could force that instability onto Douglas. On the other hand, the druidic bond might soothe him and help him heal.

If Tràth didn’t survive, though, it would be better for everyone if Douglas didn’t bond with him. The bond could only be completed once in the lifetime of a druid or a faerie. It couldn’t be severed or transferred. She had no idea what the grief of losing a bonded faerie would do to a druid. As she pondered it, she considered what it would do to her to lose Munro. It was one thing to feel some friction, brought on by what she realised was mostly ego and misunderstandings. But the thought of losing him completely made her feel anxious and sick. If anything happened to him, she thought she might go mad.

The hours spent in the car made her queasy. She could have told Griogair she had to wait for her druid, then she and Munro could have run to Skye together. But when she had seen Tràth and his confused, helpless state, she'd worried about what might happen and acted without thinking.

Now, she sat in the rumbling machine and went through her focus exercises, practising breathing, mind expansion, touching the astral plane. As she let her mind go, her body relaxed. She lost awareness of the road and the smell of petrol and even of Griogair, Tràth, and Douglas. Her thoughts sought out Munro, and she caressed the connection between them, and felt the bond quiver in response. When she closed her eyes, she could see his dark blue eyes, glowing like the Otherworld moon. He was close, she realised, and moving faster than they were, and seemingly ahead of them. His car must have passed them either when they stopped so Douglas could buy more petrol, or another time, when Griogair insisted they pull over so he and Tràth could steady themselves. She understood the feeling. It did her good to stop moving for a little while as well.

When they finally crossed the road bridge to Skye, Eilidh began to shiver with anticipation. In the last few miles, she gave Douglas instructions to take them directly to Oron's house. The druid could, she suggested, go back to Beniss' house to get some sleep. Douglas nodded, but she could sense the agitation in his mind. Was this, she wondered, what Munro felt before they bonded? Their situation hadn't been normal, but then, nothing about those who followed the Path of Stars had been normal for a thousand years.

When they pulled up in the drive, she felt her door open almost the instant the wheels stopped turning. She struggled with her seatbelt, and Munro leaned in and reached around her, snapping the plastic button to release her. He helped her to her feet, and suddenly his lips were on hers. "Don't ever send me away again," he whispered fiercely. He put his hands on either side of her face and looked into her eyes. "I love you, Eilidh. Promise me."

She nodded and tried to look down, but he kept her face tilted up, forcing her to keep eye contact. "Say it!" Then with a softer tone he added, "please."

Every part of him, from his heartbeat to their bond, throbbed, and she felt it all. He enveloped her in his presence. "I'm afraid of losing myself," she said.

"I won't let that happen. I give you my word. I don't want you to be just a part of me, to get absorbed into some mind-meld thing. I want you to be a part of my life, every day. We're connected, no doubt about that, but you'll always be you, and I'll always be me. I want us to do that together. I'm not going anyway, even if you try to get rid of me. I quit my job. I'm selling my house." His mind raced.

She felt stronger in her power after their success in Auchterarder. Her confidence surged, so she wanted to try to send him a message. Delving into his mind, she thought, *I promise*.

His eyes opened wide, and he grinned. "Look at you," he said.

She had done it. Warmth surged through her when she returned his smile and his kiss. Only then did she realise they were alone in front of Oron's house. She wondered how much of their conversation had been overheard but didn't care.

"Can you mind-speak with anyone else?" Munro asked.

"I wasn't certain until just now I could do it with you. I've made attempts before, but I don't think it ever worked. Let me try." She focused her thoughts on Oron. It took a long moment of concentration, and she sweated with the effort of picking his out of the other minds she sensed in the astral plane. But once she recognised him, she knew without a doubt. *We have returned. The crown prince is with us. He lives.*

She couldn't be certain Oron heard her, but she would know soon enough. Taking Munro's hand, she led him into the house. The public areas of the house were silent, and no one seemed to be about. Eilidh tiptoed up to her room with Munro close behind, but they were intercepted outside the door by Alyssa, who was just exiting the bedroom.

"I'm sorry, Lady Eilidh," she said. "I didn't know what to do, so I gave Prince Tràth your room. His father said he needed to rest. And there are so many other guests with all those flooding in from the kingdom."

Munro stood behind Eilidh. He slipped his arm around her waist and whispered into her ear, "What's up with the *lady* stuff anyway?"

Eilidh gave him a playful elbow in the ribs. "It's fine," she said to Alyssa. "Is Prince Griogair with his son?"

"Yes, and the druid Douglas as well."

"Douglas?" Munro asked Eilidh.

"I'll explain later," She didn't want to discuss future bonding in front of anyone, much less Oron's granddaughter, who was eyeing Munro strangely.

"Do you think—" Munro began.

"Later, druid," Eilidh said in a mock-serious tone. "For now, we both need some food and rest too."

Without a second glance at Alyssa, Munro tugged Eilidh downstairs by the hand. "Let's find someplace we can be alone," he said, kissing her ear and leading her to the back of the house. "There's room at the druids' house. Come over there with me." He pulled her close.

"I should wait here for Oron," she said, not really wanting to do anything of the kind. Munro's kisses were so sensual, so passionate that it would have been easy for her to let herself go right there in the kitchen.

Munro swept her toward a wall and pushed her against it, his body pressing into hers. He kissed her neck roughly. "Then how about here?" He took her hands and pinned them over her head, leaving her defenceless. "I want you so much," he whispered.

He kissed her fiercely, and any pretence of resistance melted.

She savoured the feel of his body, his strength, even the rough stubble that scratched as he devoured her mouth. Then the front door of the house opened and shut several rooms away, and the moment was shattered.

Eilidh attempted to disentangle herself with some difficulty. "It's Oron," she said, breathless.

Munro sighed and let her go, but not before murmuring a low and husky, "Later, love."

"Later." She ran her fingers through her short white hair, then smoothed out her clothing. She quickly pulled down two cups and poured some cold berry juice for them both, and they sat at the table.

Oron walked in, his eyes gleaming. "Mind-speaking," he said. "You've done it."

Eilidh couldn't suppress her smile, both because of Oron's praise and her relief that he didn't notice the heaving tension in the air.

"I wanted to come as soon as I heard your voice, but there was so much commotion with the conclave that I couldn't break away. We have many things to discuss," he said. "First, how is the boy?"

That *boy* was a hundred and seventy-five years old, fifty years older than Eilidh herself, but she supposed to Oron, everyone seemed like a child. "I'm not sure," she said. "He is alive, and I've done what I can to stabilise his mind, but he needs someone more experienced. I think, but I'm not sure, that Douglas may bond with him. They seem to have formed a connection of sorts already, and he's up there now. I don't know if that's a good thing, if it will help the prince's recovery or hinder it."

Oron frowned. "Did you run into the *rafta*?"

"No." She outlined what had happened in Auchterarder.

"Lady Eilidh," Oron began, but Eilidh held up a hand and cut him off.

"Elder," she interrupted. "Forgive me, but I must tell you. That lady stuff, as Munro calls it, was all a joke. Griogair was making light. I'm *not* nobility."

"It's too late," Oron said. "The entire island is awash with the word that His Royal Highness has honoured you with a title of nobility. And it's a good thing he has too."

"What do you mean?" she asked, feeling slightly startled at the serious look on the conclave leader's face.

"It may be war." Oron's expression grew dark. "The queen sent *rafta* here, through the gate at Fionn Lighe."

"What?"

"Don't worry, child. They didn't make it through the enchantments."

Munro spoke up. "I wouldn't rely too heavily on them," he said. "I felt Prince Griogair's power struggling against them. I wondered if they might break."

Oron nodded. "Any enchantment can be broken by enough will and knowledge. The *rafta* are dangerous for many reasons."

Eilidh felt a chill. "But what does this have to do with me being nobility?" she asked.

"It was Munro who gave voice to the thought first, but the conclave is seriously considering making our own portal into the Halls of Mist."

"What? Our own kingdom?" Eilidh was astonished. "No," she said. "We must heal the rift, not make it deeper." Her mind reeled at the thought of an azuri kingdom. They would be tiny in comparison to the others, but their abilities with the Path of Stars and its greater power over the Ways of Earth would compensate some, in the eyes of any who might challenge them.

"Queen Cadhla sent taunting messages with her assassins. She has made it clear she will not let us be. She will come after us until we are destroyed. We have two choices. We either raise our own banner, or we claim hers."

"Remove Cadhla?" Eilidh struggled to take it all in.

"Either way, the Higher Conclave wants a queen. It is the only way we gain legitimacy in the Halls of Mist. Our people need that." He took her hand. "Someone powerful, someone noble." Then he added, "We need to talk to Prince Griogair. Call him, please milady."

"I..." She felt completely frozen, her mind blank. She wanted to argue, but words failed to form. Eilidh just stared.

Munro stood and gave a slight bow to Oron. "I'll get him."

CHAPTER 17

MUNRO SAT AND LISTENED as Oron told Griogair and Eilidh about the Higher Conclave's discussions while they were away saving Tràth. Soon they were joined by one, then two, then three more elders. Then others who heard about the discussions also came in and surrounded the large oak table. Munro gave up his seat to the elder Galen and stood behind Eilidh, who still said nothing. He could feel her mind working, her incredulity, and stubborn refusal to accept what she was being told.

Queen Cadhla had all but declared outright war. Oron explained the only reason she hadn't done it was that it would confer legitimacy on them. "Sennera brought other news," he said.

"Who?" Eilidh asked blankly.

Munro leaned forward and whispered, "The earth faerie who brought Mira, Griogair's bodyguard, to Skye."

She nodded.

"Milady, your father is missing."

Grief swelled in Eilidh's thoughts, and Munro squeezed her shoulders. "Is he dead?"

"We don't know, but we believe he's simply gone into hiding. He's not the only one. Many have been taken or disappeared. Families who sent their children into exile when they were discovered to have access to the Path of Stars have all been arrested. She's trying to break us."

"No," Griogair said. "She's trying to *kill* you, and every faerie who can cast the stars and every faerie who may have a drop of azuri talent in their family. Her obsession will lose her the support of the more tolerant and moderate members of the conclave and will worry even the nobles who once staunchly supported her. It was one thing to try and stifle magic most thought dangerous and corrupting. It's another to harm the innocent. There is a growing outrage in the kingdom."

"We have to stop her," Eilidh said, looking at Griogair. "Can you help us?"

"I'll do whatever I must." To Oron he said, "I am at your disposal."

"Thank you, Your Highness." Oron looked around the kitchen to the other elders who had arrived and set his gaze on Eilidh. "I know this is a lot to take in, but we need a queen."

"Me? But why me? I'm a student. I'm no one. Surely Galen or Juliesse or Qwe. They are all elders, more experienced, older, more regal." She barked a laugh. "Look at me!" When no one answered, she whispered, "Griogair."

The prince smiled sadly, as though he had sympathy for her confusion, but didn't agree with her self-deprecating comments. "Yes, milady?"

"No." Eilidh looked around the room. "I mean Griogair should be king. He's ruled the Caledonian kingdom with Cadhla for how many hundreds of years? He was here before it was even called that, hundreds of years before I was even born. He knows what he's doing. And most important, the kingdom fae would accept him. He could heal our people." She turned to Oron. "Don't you see?"

Oron rubbed his chin thoughtfully and looked at Griogair. "A king?"

"No," Griogair said. "That's not why I'm here. I didn't come to rule you."

One of the elder faeries Munro did not know said, "The Higher Conclave would not promote one of the Ways of Earth to rule those who follow the Path of Stars. As Lady Eilidh says, he has stood for hundreds of years beside Cadhla. We accept him on tolerance because of his son and because he is under threat from the same regime that cast each of us out. But how do we know he has not supported her all these years and only now joins us to save his own skin? We have compassion with his position, but it's not what we want in a ruler."

Griogair nodded. "I understand your scepticism."

"But Griogair," Eilidh said quietly. "The kingdom fae will never accept me as queen."

"You don't understand your own power. Why do you think Cadhla wanted to meet with you? Your popularity and influence were growing. Stories were being written about you. Songs and epic poems."

Eilidh sat back in her chair and lightly touched Munro's hand with her fingertips as she thought. "If I let them do this, if I let them create a throne for me or we take Cadhla's, there will always be those who consider me nothing but a traitor. You, they know. They trust you." She turned to the elder who had spoken up. "Please. There must be a way you can convince the conclave to accept Griogair as king."

The elder tilted his head. "Not as king, but perhaps as a prince. It is a role they would not find threatening."

Eilidh tapped the table in frustration. "He must be king, or we will not be able to claim our place in the Halls of Mist. A kingdom must have a ruling monarch. Even if we deposed Cadhla, with only a prince, we would quickly be consumed by one of the other larger kingdoms that sensed weakness. It's only a title. Surely a king is as good as a prince."

The elder chuckled. "Not only a prince, milady. A prince-consort."

Munro got the elder's meaning before Eilidh did, and he felt like he'd been punched in the gut.

She argued on. "That doesn't make any sense. Griogair can't possibly go back to Cadhla. She's planning to murder him."

"Eilidh, he doesn't mean as Cadhla's consort, but as yours."

She turned and rolled her eyes at Munro. "That's ridiculous. That would mean..."

Griogair's face was perfectly still, and Munro couldn't read him. He could read Eilidh clearly though. If she was in turmoil before, she was a hurricane of emotion now.

Oron's face brightened. "You're so right, Conwrey. It's the perfect solution. The azuri will accept her, and the kingdom fae will accept him. He will balance any question about her experience and nobility, and she will counter any argument about his loyalty to the exiles. The ceremony should take place as soon as possible. No, we must crown her first. She is queen first, then she takes a mate. This way there can be no question of his status." The room burst into conversation, each of the elders speaking over the others. Munro had never seen the fae in such a state. It was as though Eilidh herself had been completely forgotten.

She sat, shaking her head in disbelief. "No," she said quietly, but no one paid any attention. Munro could feel her anger rising, gurgling inside her. *No*, she thought, and the room froze, everyone having heard it. "I will not force Griogair into another loveless, political marriage because it is convenient for us. I will not..." Then she stopped whatever she was going to say and stood. "I will not," she repeated.

Relief washed over Munro. He exhaled a breath he hadn't realised he'd been holding.

"You would not have to force me," Griogair said, and every eye turned to him. He stood facing Eilidh, and he bowed to her. "It would be an honour."

Oron stood beside Eilidh and put his arm around her. "Of course no one would force anyone to do anything. It's a lot to take in. It's been a long day. Don't worry. We will take care of everything."

She started to argue, but Munro took her hand. "Eilidh, let's get some air. Oron is right. You need food and rest." His heart was pounding and his thoughts reeling, just like hers were, but he kept himself steady for her. To Oron he said, "I'll take her to the druids' house."

Oron barely seemed to notice their departure, but Prince Griogair slipped out after them. As they stepped hand-in-hand to the side gate, he said, "Milady, I would have a private word with you, if you will. These things should not be decided in committee, but sadly, they often are, when one is a head of state."

She glanced at Munro. "Where I go, my druid goes. Anything to be said to me can be said to him."

Griogair hesitated, then nodded. "As you wish." He followed them silently to the house. The other druids were nowhere about, so the three sat in the front room. When they got comfortable, he said, "This was not my plan."

Eilidh inclined her head. "I know. This seems very much an idea that was conceived at a moment's notice. It is not well considered. I don't know what the conclave is thinking, trying to raise me, of all the azuri fae, as their queen."

"No, that I understand. You are young, but powerful. You can mind-speak, which you demonstrated very nicely to all of us. You told Cadhla that was a rare talent only the most powerful can employ, did you not? Almost unheard of for one your age?"

"I don't have power. I have potential."

"That's the most we can ask for in a young queen. Cadhla was as young and inexperienced as you when she took the throne. But it's more than your potential power. Your popularity in the kingdom helps. They see you as self-sacrificing, where Cadhla has become a horror. Oh, she will try to contain the rumours as she always has, but with my whispers and those of my network of friends, she won't find it so easy this time."

"But—"

"I can, just with my word, make you noble. I can't, however, make you royal, give you legitimacy in the Halls of Mist. Only taking me as your mate, or someone like me, would accomplish that. Is there another you think would be more suitable? The queen of Prow has a son." Griogair sat back, thinking. "And they would be a powerful ally. They have restricted their azuri, but not been as harsh with them as Cadhla has. They may consider it. Then there's the queen of Saldire. She has an elder brother. Yes, that might work. I know him. I can get a message to him. It might take some time since we have to go down to the Andenan gates to contact my messengers. Or maybe the sea fae would carry our request for parley to the Halls of Mist."

"Sea...? Griogair. No. I won't take any of them. Yes, I would be accepted as a royal, but they couldn't bring me the hearts of the Caledonians the way you can."

Munro remained quiet, watching the two of them talk. *Was she actually considering this?*

"What about Tràth?" she asked gently.

"Tràth?" Griogair said thoughtfully. "Yes. It could work. He is younger, and perhaps not strong right now, but he will heal in time, and I would be on hand to advise you, if that's what you wanted. Although Cadhla disowned him when she sent the death order, many would accept him as the legitimate heir."

"What? No." She shook her head. "I don't mean I want to take Tràth as my mate. By faith, Griogair, he's been unconscious half the day, and even then, the kingdom might be nervous if both the queen and her consort had unprecedented talents in the Path of Stars. He needs guidance, teaching and care. What I meant was what about his feelings? Yes, fine, we can sketch out a plan, but we aren't the only ones we're affecting. Your son needs a father who can care for him, not one tied to an infant queen, a substitute mother even younger than he. I understand you would sacrifice your own desires for your people, and I admire that, but I love Quinton." She didn't look at Munro, but he could feel the swell of emotion as she kept her eyes on Griogair. "So, you see, I can't do this."

The prince met Eilidh's eyes. "You must. Yes, Tràth will need help, but he always has. With you on the throne, he would receive that help. I wouldn't have to fear for his life. You speak about the feelings of others, but what about your father? If you take me as your mate, you could ensure he was never harmed or threatened again. Him and hundreds of others. You could save others like Tràth, get them the training they need before they lose control."

"Hey," Munro interrupted. "That's not fair."

"No," Griogair agreed. "It isn't fair, but it is the truth."

Munro stood. "Eilidh is tired, and she needs to sleep. Can you find your way back to Oron's, or shall I walk you back?"

The prince looked from Munro to Eilidh. "Think about what I have said. I know you have endured a lot in your life. I share some of the responsibility for that. I didn't fight Cadhla to try and convince her to accept those who follow the Path of Stars."

Eilidh shook her head. "She wouldn't have listened. If she would kill her own son, she was beyond redemption."

Munro spoke up. "You said if I saved your son, you would do anything I asked in return."

Griogair's face froze. "I did. Is this what you ask? That I abandon my people in their most difficult hour? That I refuse the conclave's request to become Eilidh's consort? You are human." He waved away the protest building in Munro's chest that must have been evident on his face. "You are an important human, I see that, but I say this to remind you that you don't understand our people as well as you will in a few centuries. I can see the winds blowing, druid. Eilidh will be queen at nightfall. She doesn't belong to you. She belongs to her people. She will never be your housebound wife in a wee cottage in the heather. I gave you my word, and you gave me my son, but please don't ask me to abandon my honour."

Munro looked down. He had always known he and Eilidh would never be a typical couple, but he couldn't see how he could give her up to another man.

Eilidh stood. "Good day, Griogair. Thank you for your counsel. I value your thoughts and your experience. No matter what I decide, I hope I can count on your support." She smiled graciously, but Munro knew it to be a false smile.

"When you are crowned, my knee will be the first to bend. I made a promise to you as well. It's the least I can do for the life of my only child." He left without another word, closing the front door softly behind him.

Eilidh held out her hand to Munro, and he took it tentatively. "What are you going to do?" he asked.

"Ask me that at dusk. As Griogair said, I'll be queen tonight. The conclave has made up their minds about that much, and I know I have little choice if I want to remain part of this community. All that remains is to argue over the details. My only choice would be to go back into exile, to abandon them and my father forever. I can't do that." A tear slid down her cheek. "For now, can we hold one another? Can we forget our worries, the things that will come, and spend the last daylight hours pretending we're two young, carefree lovers?" She drew close and kissed him, but he could feel her sadness and desperation.

He returned her kiss, swept her into his arms, and carried her to bed. He did his best to distract her from her burdens and to ignore the weight he could sense in her mind.

CHAPTER 18

MUNRO LAY NEXT TO EILIDH and watched her sleep. Her pale eyelashes fluttered as she dreamed. She murmured once in a while, and he could sense her disquiet, so he brushed his hand softly along her bare arm and whispered, "It's all right. Shhh." He placed a small kiss on her forehead.

"*Te'drecht*," she muttered and nuzzled into his arms, but her thoughts grew calmer.

After a moment, Munro extricated himself from her embrace and stood, all the while trying not to swing the bed so much it would wake her. He paused briefly to take in the view of her perfect skin, the curve of her hips, the crooked smile that suddenly played across her lips. He tried to bury the grief he felt, knowing that if things went the way he feared and she married Griogair, this was likely the last time they would make love.

Sorting through the clothing they'd tossed on the floor, he found his jeans and slipped them on before making his way to the kitchen. He poured himself a cup of berry juice from the fridge and thought about how adaptable the fae on Skye had been, learning to cope with human technology while preserving their own culture. They combined the best of both worlds. He had hoped that he and Eilidh would be able to do the same. Now she was set to be a queen and was considering marrying someone he wasn't even sure he liked. He leaned against the counter and squeezed his eyes shut.

Could he go back to Perth? He hadn't yet put his house up for sale, and Hallward hadn't let him quit his job, so Munro didn't have to worry about looking for work. Since Eilidh learned to shut off their emotional connection, perhaps she could maintain that. He would always feel her presence, but at least he wouldn't have to endure feeling her so intimately within his mind. His chest got tighter as he thought about leaving her, but he didn't see how he could stay and watch her make her life with another man. Surely that would be too much to ask.

The front door opened, and Aaron, Phillip, and Rory's voices, lifted in good-natured banter, echoed through the house. They came into the kitchen, setting down bags from the supermarket. Apparently they'd decided to supplement the faerie cuisine with Jaffa Cakes and Irn Bru, an orange-coloured Scottish soft drink that was as much a part of the national identity as haggis and stovies.

"Douglas still with Tràth?" Aaron asked.

Munro nodded. "Last I saw, yeah. What happened? I wasn't really watching Douglas in Auchterarder, and then the next thing I know, nobody can budge him from Tràth's bedside."

"I'm not sure," Phillip replied. He gathered up the empty plastic bags from their shopping trip and, not finding a recycle bin, stuffed them into a drawer. "They drove with Eilidh and Prince Griogair. They got a bit ahead of us on the road though, and by the time we realised they'd gone to Oron's instead of coming here, we were told the prince couldn't be disturbed."

"If the prince is bonding with Douglas," Aaron said, "he's already disturbed." The others chuckled.

"So what's going on?" Phillip asked. "There was some big pow-wow at Oron's, but we couldn't get past the crowd."

"Looks like it might be war," Munro said. He explained that some of Queen Cadhla's people had attacked the island while their group was in Auchterarder. "They're thinking about whether to counter-attack and try to take on the kingdom, or to defend and stay independent but argue for recognition from the Halls of Mist. Either way, they're going to raise a queen. Eilidh."

The three other druids just stared at Munro for a moment. "Wow," Phillip said. "A queen?"

"Tonight, probably. So, their focus on getting you three bonded will take a back seat while they sort all of this out. But it might be a good thing. You can be around, meet more of them, and maybe it'll happen more naturally that way, you know? Without them trying to force pairings for political reasons." He couldn't keep the bitterness from his voice.

"Is that it? Do you think they coerced Douglas into bonding with Tràth because he's a prince?"

Munro chuckled. "Tràth is the last person they wanted any of you to bond with. And it still might not happen. Tràth seemed pretty unstable, according to Eilidh, and she doesn't know what the bonding might do. And if Tràth dies, well, Douglas could never bond with anyone else. So, nobody wants to say it, but they don't want Douglas wasted."

"That's pretty cheap," Rory muttered. "The kid didn't look that bad to me. Could he really die?"

"I don't know," Munro said.

"What aren't you telling us?" Phillip asked.

Munro set his cup on the counter. "It doesn't really have anything to do with you guys. It's Eilidh. After she's made queen, they want her to marry Griogair. It'll give her status with the Halls of Mist, and I think the elders are hoping it'll bring some support in the Caledonian kingdom. He's been the prince-consort there for hundreds of years."

"Crikey," Rory said. "He doesn't look that old."

"Shut up, you moron," Phillip muttered, shoving Rory lightly. To Munro he said, "But she's not going through with it, right? I mean, everybody knows Eilidh and you are an item."

"She might not have a choice." *Or none she could live with.*

Aaron clapped his hand on Munro's back. "I'm sorry, man. That really sucks. Want us to take him out? He's no big cheese here, where he can't touch his earth magic, right? We could take him," he assured Munro with a grin. "You probably know all kinds of ways to dispose of a body, being a cop and all."

Munro rolled his eyes. "Don't tempt me."

Phillip chuckled. "We could just break his knees then, or maybe that pretty nose of his. Nobody should be that good looking anyway."

Munro couldn't help but laugh, and he was grateful for the guys knowing just what he wanted to hear. "I think Eilidh might object, but I'll keep the offer in mind."

"That explains why he's loitering around then," Rory said.

"What?" Munro asked. "Where?"

"I saw him outside, kind of, when we came in."

"Kind of? Jesus, Rory. You might have mentioned it," Munro said. "He's probably waiting for Eilidh. She's sleeping in my room. I'll go talk to him."

"You sure you don't want us to come?" Aaron drew his finger across his own neck.

Munro grinned. "I got this. But thanks." His smile faded as he grabbed his shirt from the bedroom and slipped it over his head. Eilidh still slept, and this was possibly his last chance to talk to Griogair before the conclave made its final decisions.

The druids' house sat on a hill with trees and high grass all around. If Rory had seen Griogair, though, he must have been on the front side of the house. Munro didn't see the prince right away, so he walked down the road, not realising until he stepped on a sharp stone that he had come outside barefoot. In January. He wasn't even cold. Suddenly, his fantasies of returning to his old life didn't seem reasonable. With his glowing eyes and pointy ears, he'd have quite a time explaining himself. He could maybe take to wearing sunglasses at night to hide his eyes. It seemed ridiculous, but the idea of watching Eilidh marry this guy seemed that unbearable.

Half way down the long country driveway, Munro saw Griogair sitting in a small clearing under a large tree. "I was waiting for you," Griogair said. "I thought you would seek me out, demand a duel for your lady's hand. Isn't that what humans do?"

"Not for a couple hundred years." Munro sat on the grass across from the prince. "I really do love her."

"I know," Griogair said. "I saw the two of you together. I've had many lovers, but never love. I envy you."

"You are about to marry the woman I want, and *you* envy *me*?"

"She's agreed to it?" Griogair sat up straighter and looked Munro in the eye. "I saw the way she looked at you, and I thought she wouldn't have the strength."

"If she wasn't planning to go through with it, she wouldn't be so sad. You'd be surprised how strong she is." Munro toyed with a long blade of grass. "God dammit," he muttered. "There's no other way?" He realised how strange it was, asking Griogair if he could find a way not to marry Eilidh, but who else would listen?

Griogair shrugged. "She could try to stand on her own as queen, but even if the Halls of Mist accepted her, which I'm not sure they would, there would be difficulties. Nearly every kingdom has passed some form of law in the past millennia restricting the use of the Path of Stars, if not outright banning it. But you must understand, even if she does not take me as her mate, she will eventually have to make a political union. If she avoided that somehow, and I very much doubt she could find a way to do so, a queen could never have a human mate. Not even a druid. At least by creating a union with a faerie of royal lineage, it would take away concerns about her relationship with you. If she stood alone, many would question how much influence you had on the kingdom, and that would be a grave concern to either conclave."

Munro looked at the sky. The sun was getting low and just beginning to dip behind the trees. "So, you're saying even if you can't have her, I can't have her either."

"You must convince her to do this, to accept the crown, and to accept a royal mate. Myself, my son, someone else. Of course I want it to be me. Who would deny wanting to be a part of a change in our kingdom that would echo beyond centuries. And besides, I like Eilidh."

Munro sighed. "She likes you too."

"Then we would begin our relationship with a better personal foundation than I ever had with Cadhla."

"Then the promise you made me, to do whatever I asked if I saved your son, this is what I want: Take care of her. Support her always and protect her like I would, if I was there."

Griogair's eyes started to glow violet as the sky darkened. "I have no problem making such a promise, but why are you going away? She will need you. All of the fae on Skye need you, as leader of the druids. Those men look to you for guidance, and the faeries here respect you."

Munro suddenly wanted to punch the prince's smug, royal face. "Don't you get it? I love her."

"Then stay. Be her counsel, her bodyguard, her lover, her friend. She needs to be surrounded with people she can trust, those who know her and will keep her perspective honest and true, who won't be swayed by the political manoeuvrings she will soon encounter."

Munro blinked. "You're saying you have no objection? You want me to be some kind of concubine?"

Griogair shrugged. "People will expect her to behave a certain way in public. I will stand with her as her life mate. We will attend many functions, and we will have many obligations. There will come a day when we will be expected to try to have at least one child, but most fae women do not do this until they are in their second century at least, and many queens not until they are in their third. We have time," he said.

"You're not saying you won't sleep with her," Munro said, his mind turning.

"As her consort, I am required to do whatever my queen demands of me and whatever will most serve my people. The marriage will have to be consummated before witnesses, as is our tradition. It is the best I can promise you, and yet, I still envy you." The prince sighed and stood. "The night is coming. The conclave will send for her soon." He extended his hand.

Munro gripped the prince's outreached hand and got to his feet. He was stunned. Griogair was offering to *share* Eilidh. To Munro, the idea seemed unthinkable, and yet he was thinking about it. He looked at the prince. Munro hated him, but at the same time, he couldn't help but admire him. Griogair understood duty, and Munro knew it couldn't be easy for him to jump into another political marriage only days after his last wife divorced him and ordered him executed. "Give me a few minutes to talk to her alone, please," Munro said.

"You will stay then?"

"That depends on her response." He turned to walk away, not wanting to give Griogair another chance to speak. If there was one thing the prince was good at, it was talk. Munro couldn't help but wonder if by tomorrow, this would all seem ludicrous.

The dim light of dusk faded as Munro approached the house and went inside to find Eilidh. By the time he reached her bed, she was just waking. She smiled softly as he closed the door. "Come back to bed and hold me again," she purred.

"I wish I could, but it's nightfall, and they'll be here soon. I need to talk to you."

She pressed her eyes closed. "No, let me speak first." She reached out, took his hand, and pulled him to sit on the edge of the bed. "I will not take Griogair as my mate. Most of my people do not take life mates, we live freely, love freely. I have no desire to tie myself to someone when my heart belongs to another. It would be wrong for all of us. For me, to deny myself, for him, as I know I will never love him, and for you most of all."

"You must be the queen, Eilidh. Your people need you."

"Surely the queen can decide something so important and personal for herself."

Munro shook his head. "Look, I don't like it. I'm not going to pretend I do. I hate it more than anything. I'd do whatever it took if I could change the reality. But I have to step aside."

Eilidh sat up, her eyes welling with tears. "No, Quinton, please don't leave me. Our bond grows stronger, and I could not be parted from you like this."

He wrapped his arms around her and pulled her into a soft embrace. "I'm not going anywhere. Not as long as you want me with you." He pulled back and said, "But remember when I was talking about what happened last summer, how you drew from my life force because it was the only way to save hundreds if not thousands of lives?"

She nodded. "But—"

Touching his finger to her lips, he said. "Some things are more important than me. This is one of those things."

"You want me to take Griogair?"

"I want you to think like a queen. Save the azuri and, if you can, save the Caledonian kingdom. If marrying Griogair does that, how can I say my feelings are more important?"

Eilidh put her hand on his cheek and smiled. "Your feelings *are* more important to me."

He kissed her lightly. "You'll do what you have to do, though."

"I would have to lie with him, if I take him as my mate. It is our way."

"I know, and I hate it. Holy shit, Eilidh, the idea of you having sex with him makes me want to rip his arms off, but you do what you have to do. He and I had a chat, and I think we understand each other somewhat. He knows you love me, but I know you will have to play the part. Just, please, tonight or tomorrow night, or whenever you have to seal the deal, close the door to my mind like you did before. I can be as strong as I have to for you. I can let you marry him. But don't ask me to feel your thoughts when he touches you." Munro's chest tightened, and he hated that she would feel his anguish. But he wasn't sure which of those emotions were his and which were hers. Resigned sadness, gratitude, respect, but mostly deep, passionate love.

She kissed him gently, a tear sliding down her cheek. "As you wish."

Voices came from down the corridor, as though the house was suddenly filling with people.

"It's time," Munro said, and he stood to help her to her feet. "Your Majesty." He smiled, putting as much genuine feeling into it as he could.

Oron walked into the room without knocking. Eilidh seemed unselfconscious about her nudity, even though Munro was flustered by the intrusion. "Why are you still here?" the elder asked her.

"I was not summoned to the conclave," Eilidh said, standing and retrieving her jeans from the floor.

"You weren't?" Oron looked puzzled. "By faith, we forgot. Come now, milady. The Higher Conclave calls you to serve your people."

"Yes, Elder." Eilidh pulled her shirt over her head. "Oron," she began, "I want to ask a few questions before I am crowned. It won't take long, but I want to understand what—"

A huge groaning growl echoed from outside. The earth began to shake, and the bed swung hard, hitting Munro squarely on the thigh. "Away from the window," he shouted, pulling Eilidh to the ground, just as the glass shattered.

Eilidh's eyes went wide, and she shouted, "The protective enchantments have gone. I can feel the earth flows."

Oron opened the door and staggered to the corridor, even as the ground beneath them continued to heave. "Protect our future queen!" he shouted. "We are under attack!"

CHAPTER 19

A DARK-HAIRED FAERIE EILIDH RECOGNISED as Cane, a talented young teacher, came into the room. "Lady Eilidh, you must come with me. This house is not safe." He took a stunned Eilidh by the arm and guided her out, with Munro and the other druids following close behind.

"Where are we going?" Eilidh asked.

"Elder Oron's house has other protective enchantments that will shield you. The barriers on Beniss' house died with her," he said as they stepped outside.

In the night air, Eilidh could smell the familiar loamy scent of the Otherworld. "Faith," she swore. "They have opened the Skye gate?" Dread filled her. Skye could quickly be overrun with kingdom Watchers and the queen's elite guards if the gate remained open.

"Hurry, please," Cane said, trundling her toward the village. Faeries ran around them, some fleeing the earthquake, some shouting and calling out to others. Eilidh had never seen such chaos. They ran ahead, leaving the druids behind. Eilidh looked back, but Munro stayed with his friends rather than keep up. She hoped they would not be long and that he merely stayed back to protect them and make sure they arrived safely. That was his way. His words of self-sacrifice had pierced her heart. He would give up his claim to her for the sake of her people and to show his love. She doubted she would have made the same choice, if the Higher Conclave asked *him* to mate with another, with her watching from the shadows.

When they arrived at Oron's house a few minutes later, they passed guards stationed around the perimeter. They inclined their heads to Eilidh. It seemed sudden, so unreal. How could any of this be happening?

"The meditation room is the most protected," Cane said. "Prince Tràth and the druid Douglas are there already."

When they reached the bottom of the stairs, Eilidh stopped. "Go back. Make sure Quinton Munro and the other druids arrive. They must be kept safe."

Cane shook his head. "Oron ordered me to stay with you."

"I have fifty guards outside. Go. They are more important than I am."

He hesitated, as though not sure if he should obey the conclave leader or the future queen. Fortunately, the front door opened and saved him from having to decide. The four druids came in, looking harried and alarmed.

"This way," Eilidh said and led them upstairs.

She was intimately familiar with Oron's meditation chamber, having spent many hours there breathing, focusing, and exercising her mind. She felt suddenly grateful for the practice, because aside from Cane and Munro, the others were agitated and nervous. The room had no furniture except for floor pillows and kneeling benches. Someone had piled a few cushions together and Tràth reclined on them. Eilidh crossed the room to greet him. "Your Highness," she said with a tentative smile. She nodded to the druid who sat with him. "May I sit?"

A smile quirked across Tràth's lips. "A queen does not ask to sit down."

Eilidh returned his smile. "You can expect me to do a lot of things a queen doesn't do." She made herself comfortable beside him. "You look well. Your essence feels stronger to me."

"Douglas," Tràth said, "Could you give me a moment with the lady?"

The druid hesitated only a second before replying, "Sure. I'll say hello to the guys." He stood and went to the opposite side of the immense chamber. Eilidh heard him say, "Hey, I'm glad you all made it over. I was worried."

"What shall I call you?" Tràth asked. "Lady Eilidh? In a few hours, assuming we're all still here, it will be Your Majesty. Or perhaps Mother. I haven't called Cadhla that in years."

"So you've spoken to your father," she said, treading carefully. She could feel the unrest in his mind.

He answered merely by tilting his head.

"You can call me Eilidh, if you want," she said. "I think we'd both feel a little silly if you called me Mother, considering you're fifty years older than I am. Besides, I'm not queen yet, and Griogair and I aren't mated yet."

"Yet," he repeated. When she acknowledged with a half-nod, he said, "You'll make a good queen."

She smiled. "You've only just met me, but it's kind of you to say." She felt a wave of nausea as the earth shuddered, then suddenly stopped.

"You saved my life," he said seriously. "I was trapped. It's never happened like that before, not for so long." He frowned, and she was struck by how much he looked like his father, except his eyes were a startling shade of blue instead of deep violet, and while Griogair did not look old, he had a line or two beginning to crease his brow.

"It's going to be a difficult road," she said, putting her hand on his. "But I will help you as much as I can. It was hard for me too, but at least I found others with my same talent. You..."

"I stand alone," he said.

"As far as we know, but azuri have been flooding to Skye for days now. There may yet be others somewhere in the world. This colony was unknown except in a vague rumour until last year. Who's to say there aren't a hundred temporal fae tucked in a Romanian mountain hideaway? Don't give up hope."

"You are too kind," he said softly. "I haven't known a lot of kindness in my life."

Eilidh felt her resolve grow. "This is what we're fighting for. The right to exist. The right to survive. I want to end the prejudice against those who walk the Path of Stars." She was talking more to herself, understanding why she had to accept the crown and why she had to take Griogair as her mate, regardless of what it cost her personally.

Another round of fierce shaking made the house's foundation shudder.

"How many are out there?" he asked. "How many did she send to kill me?" He closed his eyes, looking weary.

"I don't know."

Tràth tapped his temple with a smile. "Well, find out."

With practised, smooth focus, Eilidh's vision went dark, and she dipped into the astral plane, feeling the flows all around her. She shifted her sight upward and scanned the village. She saw a fire spreading on the far side, and her heart clutched. Of all the azuri fae on the island, she was the only one with a bonded druid, and therefore the only one who could touch enough water magic to put it out. Unless… "Have you bonded with Douglas yet?"

Tràth seemed startled by the question. "Bonded? I don't know how. We do have some connection, like I'd found a long-lost brother, but I don't understand it."

"We'll talk about that later. For now, I have a fire to put out." Eilidh headed for the door, but Cane stopped her. "The village will burn if I don't do something," she said.

"You cannot put yourself in harm's way," Cane said. "You will be our queen tonight."

"I am the only one here with water magic," she pleaded with him.

The five druids also stood and came toward the door. "What's going on?" Munro asked.

"I'm sorry," Cane said. "You are safe in here. Someone else will have to tend to the fire."

"With what?" she shouted. "Buckets?"

"My father has some water magic," Tràth said, and Eilidh whipped around to look at him.

"Of course. I never even thought to ask…" Her voice trailed off as she focused again, this time finding Griogair, touching his mind. *Fire on the north side of the village. Please help.*

Suddenly Oron came in. "Thank the Father of the Azure you're all right," he said to Eilidh. "We have dispatched a dozen lookouts, and three elders are working to reseal the Skye gate. They can hold it for a while, but we all have to get off the island before they break through again and bring an army with them."

"And go where?" Eilidh asked. "She will know every escape route, and we will be pursued by five thousand Watchers with another five thousand waiting in the Highland forests, hoping to catch us in their net. She told me once she would use every Watcher in her forces to wipe us out if she had to."

"What choice do we have?" Oron said. "We can repel some, but while we are more powerful in some ways, they can outnumber us twenty to one. Not even I can stand against that. This first incursion came to test us, to see how quickly we could respond. They will be delighted to see how helpless we are against their numbers."

"We can hide," Eilidh said. "Tràth?" She rushed back to the prince. "Can you do again what you did before? In Auchterarder? You seem stronger now. Can you do it without hurting yourself?"

"I could make the shift easily, but the danger is in the return."

"I'll bring you back, just as I did before. I promise." Then she said to Oron. "How long can the gate seals hold?"

"A few hours at most, but more likely less than an hour. They are trying to break them even as we are working to set them."

"Elder, I'm calling everyone here. Tràth can hide you until they pass."

"Hide *you*?" he said. "You mean hide *us*."

She shook her head. "I have to stay outside the bubble, so I can bring you back. There isn't time to debate it. Are you ready?" she asked Tràth.

"Yes," he replied.

Eilidh closed her eyes, ignoring the protests of everyone around her. She sent the message out into the aether, projecting as far as she could. *All come to Elder Oron's immediately.*

"Who is working on the gates?" she asked.

"Galen, Qwe, and Dalyna."

Eilidh focused on those three minds and instructed them one by one to hold the gates closed by any means necessary until they heard from her again. It frustrated her, being unable to hear any reply, but she hoped they would obey her command. They had to, if her plan had even one chance in a hundred of working.

To Oron she said, "I must go outside the bubble with Griogair. Pull everyone in as tightly as you can, so we can be sure no one is left outside. They will be unable to defend themselves against the onslaught."

"I'm coming with you," Munro said. "No arguments."

Eilidh paused, then sensing his resolve, relented. "All right, but when I tell you to hide, go to the forest and hide. They won't be able to sense you because you're human, so stay unseen until it's time to bring Tràth back, and go when I order you to."

She could tell he didn't like it, but finally he nodded. "Agreed."

Aaron offered, “You’ll need us too. We did play our part in locating him last time.”

Eilidh shook her head. “I can’t spare you other druids. If you are caught, you’ll all be killed. Your lives are too important.”

“And if we get stuck in that bubble, don’t forget, you’ll be the only azuri left,” Aaron countered. “You’ll need our help.”

She sighed. “All right. Stay with Munro. Hide when he does.” To Tràth she said, “I’ll send you a message when we’re outside the bubble. How far do we need to go?”

Tràth shrugged. “I don’t know. It changes, but it seems to get larger every time.”

“Very well,” she said. “Far enough to be sure.”

She sent a quick thought to Griogair, telling him where to meet them. She opened the door, and the house filled with faeries. “Cane, please help us get through this crowd.”

“Yes, milady,” he said.

“Go,” Oron said. “I’ll get everyone as close to the house as possible.”

Cane led the way, gently asking people to step aside to let them pass. All eyes were on Eilidh, and she felt naked in a way she never had before. This *had* to work. She looked in their eyes and realised their lives were in her hands. If this plan failed, if she got trapped in the bubble, if she couldn’t retrieve Tràth, if he wasn’t strong enough to make another time shift, she would have made their entire population an easy target for Cadhla's forces to surround and pick off.

It frustrated her that the other druids couldn't run fast, and she wondered if she'd been wise to bring them. If Douglas was killed, the grief would distract Tràth. At least, she mused, they hadn't bonded yet.

They met Griogair at a roadside layby a mile south of the village with nothing around. No houses, no cars, not a soul. Just a few sheep dotting the distant landscape, with mountains rising up beyond.

She explained the plan to Griogair, whose face darkened more with every word. "You're risking the life of my son," he said. "He is not strong enough."

Eilidh took his hand. "If you are to be my mate and consort, you must trust me, Griogair. He is strong enough." She sent waves of calm toward him, but his will was like iron, and she found his thoughts difficult to subdue.

The druids remained awkwardly silent. She knew the humans, apart from Munro, wouldn't understand her choice to take Griogair as her mate, but she had to bear that disapproval in silence along with the other burdens that rested on her shoulders.

"I'm sending the signal to Tràth," she explained, then directed a short message to the crown prince that said simply, *Now*.

There was no sound, but as she looked north, she saw a blue flash in the sky. She breathed easier, praying the Mother of the Earth and the Father of the Azure would remember her people and look kindly on them.

"Now what?" Aaron asked.

"Now," she said, turning to the druids. "You hide. Make your way back toward Oron's house, but don't approach it. Their trackers may sense something, so they'll use every spell and enchantment they know to try to find our people. Locate a wooded area, a bridge to get under, a shed, whatever it takes, but stay unseen. Quinton, you most of all. You have been in the Otherworld and the queen knows your face, so we have to assume her people do too."

He drew her aside. "I don't want you to go alone. I can keep up."

She shook her head, her heart tightening. "I could disguise you, but you could not pass for fae up close; your aura would feel wrong to them. I need you to protect the other druids. Make sure they stay safe until I call for you, and then get back to Oron's together." She paused, hoping he didn't see her hands trembling. "No arguments."

She turned to Griogair, and as she looked at him, his face began to morph. She changed his clothing to look like the uniform of the queen's guard. Once she finished, she used the same illusion to change her own clothing, then gave herself straight brown hair, a long, hooked nose and a sharp chin. While she'd completed the illusion, Munro left. His presence grew more distant as the druids made their way back toward the village.

"What do you have in mind?" Griogair asked, touching his face in amazement. It seemed odd to hear his voice coming from a stranger's body.

"I send one last message, and then we wait." Touching the three fae holding the Skye gate closed, she sent the message: *Open the gates. Let them in. Confuse the minds of the first through, then disguise yourself among them. Hide.*

He watched her as they waited. Finally, she couldn't take his scrutiny any longer. "I will get him back, just as I did before."

"That wasn't what I was thinking," he said. "I believe you will."

"What then?"

"I was thinking that you will make a magnificent queen. I have decided what to give you as a gift on the day we make our pledge to one another."

"Help get the azuri back safely. That's all I ask." She felt uncomfortable out on the roadside alone with him. As the minutes stretched into an hour, the anticipation and feeling of pressing haste wore thin.

"What's taking so long?" she asked, but Griogair didn't answer. "What if we can't get them back?" Eilidh muttered to herself.

"We will," Griogair reassured her.

Long minutes of waiting made Eilidh's mind spin and whirl with thoughts of the future. "I worry you will regret becoming my mate when you see how truly incompetent, unqualified, irreverent, and unsuitable I am. You don't know me at all."

"I became Cadhla's mate the same day I met her. I've known you for what, a week? I consider this an improvement." Then he added with a smile, "In many ways."

"Quinton said you two talked about an understanding."

"Not to be indelicate, milady, but it was a conversation between gentlemen. I will say this much. I may not fully understand those who follow the Path of Stars. The faeries here are as different from the kingdom ways as I could imagine. But I do know this much. I would be a fool to try to sever a heart-bond created by ancient magic. He will be tethered to you, mind, body and soul as long as he lives, and I know my mere charm couldn't change that. Would I prefer that you loved me?" He shrugged. "What faerie wouldn't want love? Sometimes I wonder if we've bred that capacity out of ourselves." He tapped a rock, sending a tiny shiver into the earth. "I would consider it an honour just to have your respect."

Eilidh looked south, peering into the darkness, wondering when the queen's assassins and soldiers would finally come. "You have that," she said softly.

The gentle winter breeze turned bitterly cold without warning. The soldier's cloak whipped about his shoulders. "They're through the gates," he said.

"We stay away from them as much as possible," she said. "Do our best to blend in until they're gone." The kingdom fae would be able to sense hers and Griogair's presence. She just hoped they could pass for kingdom fae and fade into background when they left.

"We hide, yes. But if she's here, I won't let the opportunity pass."

"Cadhla?" The thought stunned Eilidh. "The queen won't come here. She would never leave the Otherworld."

Griogair chuckled. "Oh, she'll come for this."

"No," Eilidh said. "We stick to the plan. We lay low until they are forced to leave empty-handed. Then we slip out once they're gone and bring Tràth and the others back."

"Then what?"

"Then we have some room to breathe and plan while she's trying to figure out where we went. We will probably have to leave Skye as the elders suggested, but this way we go to a place of our choosing in the time of our choosing. It only gives us a slightly better chance, but consider this, how much will the confidence of the Watchers and *rafta* be shaken if we disappear under her nose? Some may wonder if we were ever here to begin with. Some may wonder if she is sane or if she's leading them in circles."

Griogair said, "If I get my chance with her, I'm going to take it."

"I said no. We have a plan. We stick to it."

He smiled. "You aren't my mate yet, so you can give me no commands, and I haven't yet bended the knee."

“Faith,” she muttered.

A smile broke out across his disguised face. “One of these days, I’ll have to break you of that. Queens don’t mutter oaths like Watchers on patrol.”

Eilidh heard the gentle footfalls of thousands of approaching fae. The wind carried their scent, and the earth trembled as their magic rolled ahead of them.

CHAPTER 20

GRIOGAIR CAUGHT EILIDH'S ATTENTION and gestured north. She immediately recognised Oron and four others walking toward her. "Sun in the blessed sky," she growled. "Does no one listen to me?" When she sensed Oron's astral power begin to pulse, she sent him a message. *It is Eilidh and Griogair. Do not attack.* Every mind-speak message she sent took a little less focus and effort. It still felt strange, as she had to locate and touch each mind, but she was learning the way of it quickly.

As the five approached, she watched them morph into *rafta*. Seeing the black uniforms made her shudder, even though they were friends behind their illusionary masks.

When they finally arrived, one spoke. Eilidh immediately recognised Oron's voice. "We will help spread a little confusion," he said.

“How many stayed outside the bubble?” she asked, not even trying to disguise the annoyance in her voice.

“A dozen,” Oron replied. “The entire Higher Conclave. The same as the number of *rafta* they sent through the first time.”

Griogair said, “Smart. Be careful, though. The *rafta* are a small, tightly knit group. They know each other well. Do not speak if you can avoid it and do not try to be too clever. I will help as I can, because I know them, so if you are near, watch me.”

“This is too dangerous,” Eilidh said. “We were to hide and wait. The more of us there are, the greater the chance we will be discovered. The kingdom fae know we can change our appearance, so we must be cautious. We are too far outnumbered.”

Oron tilted his head. She had trouble reading the unfamiliar face, so she wasn’t entirely sure he was agreeing to follow her command. It appeared being the future queen didn’t give her much influence.

“Attack no one,” she added, seeing a formation of figures approach quickly from the distance. “Remember, the three elders from the gate will be disguised among them.”

One of Oron’s company said, “We are not fools, milady.”

Feeling chastised, Eilidh inclined her head. “Of course not. I am just concerned.”

“We’re all concerned,” Oron said. To the others, he added, “Let them get close enough to see us, and then we fall back to the village and take the positions we agreed upon there."

"Where will you be?" Eilidh asked.

"Hidden," Oron said, "But this way they will see us and believe their *rafta* are alive. Report that we have not found what we came here for. We do not want to confront them, only confuse them. Our elemental weapons would not bear close scrutiny, since they are only illusions." When the approaching force, led by running foot soldiers came close enough to see their features, Oron said, "Salute me."

Eilidh and Griogair turned and offered sharp salutes, thumping their fists over their hearts. Decades spent as a kingdom Watcher made her feel confident that she could pass for a soldier. Oron acknowledged the salute stiffly, looking every inch the elite guard he pretended to be. Then he and the others turned and ran north toward the village with unhurried, even strides.

"I will have to be silent around the *rafta* and any of Cadhla's home guard, lest they recognise my voice," Griogair said.

Eilidh nodded, watching as one of the oncoming host pulled ahead, running directly for her and Griogair, while the others slowed. "What is his name?" she asked.

"Frene. He is *wen-lei* of the *rafta*. Be very careful."

When he got close enough to hear, Eilidh raised her voice. "*Wen-lei*," she said. "The other *rafta* ordered us to wait for you." She gestured ahead to Oron and the disguised elders' retreating backs. "They have not yet located the prince and ask you to follow."

The tall *rafta* leader stopped and held up a hand, ordering the many hundreds behind him to follow suit. Eilidh couldn't help but wonder how many more she could not yet see. The thought chilled her.

"Prove yourselves," he said, thrumming with power.

Without hesitation, Griogair lifted a hand to the sky, and a lightning bolt shot through the air, followed a few seconds later by a clap of thunder. She gestured to the ground, where a small cyclone just four or five feet high formed. She flung her hand away from the group, and the twister followed in a meandering path.

The *wen-lei* raised an eyebrow. "Not the agreed-upon signals, but sufficient to prove you are not tainted with the Path of Stars."

Eilidh shrugged, feigning indifference. "We were pulled off other duties and ordered here by the *rafta*. They did not inform us of the signs." She opened her thoughts to the astral plane, feeling the minds all around her. As subtly as she could, she pushed the *wen-lei* a sense of urgency. She was afraid to try for too much or to persuade him of anything he didn't already intend. The *rafta* were already suspicious of everyone.

Turning toward the village, the *wen-lei* signalled the host behind him. To Eilidh and Griogair, he said, "Fall in."

The pair saluted in unison and waited until more than a hundred kingdom fae had passed before doing their best to melt into the ranks.

They moved silently and with purpose, and Eilidh could not help but feel saddened that the kingdom was marching on the azuri. What could the queen have told them to make them believe this was right? Only weeks ago Eilidh had travelled the Otherworld freely, laughing with old friends, visiting her father. Her heart tightened as she thought of her father, and she worked to calm her feelings, to set them aside as Oron had taught her. This wasn't the time for worry or grief.

As they approached the village, she looked around for Griogair, but he'd faded into the crowd. She hoped he didn't go too far, because she wasn't sure how distance would affect his false appearance created by her illusion. It annoyed her that he refused to stick to the plan. If he cost them even one life, kingdom or azuri, she would hold him to account. He said he wanted her respect, but she wasn't certain she had his.

She followed along with a unit that went from house to house in the village, having been ordered to take a certain cluster as part of the search. She stayed silent, kept her head down, and did not even dare to cast one enchantment.

Finding every house abandoned, the various groups gathered at the village green, while others set up patrols. Eilidh spotted Griogair's disguised face. He talked with a small knot of senior soldiers. *What are you doing?* she sent to him. He glanced up and gave a subtle nod in her direction. Infuriated that he could not answer telepathically and that she could not walk up and demand a reply, she looked around, hoping to find Oron and the others who'd stayed outside the bubble or even the elders who'd held the gate, but she recognised no one. She tried to move between groups, not staying with any contingent too long, lest someone realise they didn't know her.

"How can they stand this?" she heard one elemental archer ask a companion.

"Faith, I do not know," replied the other, clearly feeling disturbed.

That's when she realised that even though the enchantment that would have sapped their earth powers had been lifted, they had spent little time outside the Otherworld. As time went on, they would grow more uncomfortable in the human realm. During her first exile, it had taken years to adjust to the thin air in this plane. It gave her hope that the *rafta* would not want to stay longer than necessary to verify that the azuri were nowhere to be found.

The stars swept across the sky as the night wore on. The kingdom fae waited restlessly. Patrols were sent out in a spiderweb pattern over the island, but Eilidh always managed to slip away and only once did she have to manipulate a commander into not questioning why she stayed behind.

She managed to work her way closer to Griogair, who had moved on to speaking with a different officer, and then another. As soon as she got near him, he turned from them and approached her, presumably so she couldn't overhear what he was saying to them. Surely he wouldn't betray her, she thought. But he had to ensure that she and the druids lived—if he wanted to get his son back. Her suspicions mounted, but she couldn't puzzle out what he hoped to accomplish. As she had predicted, Cadhla was nowhere near Skye.

He lowered his head and straightened his uniform, looking for all the world like he was flirting with her. She repeated her earlier question in a hushed tone. "What in the name of the rising sun are you doing?"

"I'm disguising myself as a soldier who is flirting with another, quite beautiful soldier."

Eilidh didn't smile, although it was difficult. "I know the face I created. It is not lovely," she said. "I thought it best not to attract any attention."

"Ah, but I know your inner beauty." He watched their surroundings carefully, and she realised, not for the first time, how practised he was at deception. It went against everything she'd believed about the core of her people, and again he made her question the philosophies of her youth.

"How long will they stay and search?" she asked, careful to keep her voice barely above a whisper.

"The *rafta* have already received the reports from the patrols that there are no azuri fae on the island. Their only concern is Oron's house."

"What?" Eilidh met his eyes, alarmed.

"Remember in Auchterarder, when I said the earth was lying to me? They have the best trackers with them. They will sense Tràth's trail and the other azuri hidden there as well. So many in one location."

"I will send a message to Oron. He and the elders can perhaps confuse the minds of those who search that area."

"No," Griogair said. "Not yet."

"What are you planning?" she asked, then understood. "By sun and stars, it's not that you expected Cadhla to lead the charge. You are plotting to lure her here. You want your revenge."

"Not revenge. Justice. An end to this once and for all."

Eilidh had to fight not to show her anger. "At what cost?" she hissed. "Your own life? If you touch her, they will cut you down before you can take one step."

"Maybe not," he said.

"And if you die, how will I get Tràth back?"

"I believe in you," he said. "You used my connection with him last time, but now you've forged your own. You can do it."

"My one hour with him is nothing compared to a father's love."

A soldier approached and glanced at Eilidh, then raised an eyebrow at Griogair.

"It's all right," Griogair said. "She knows me."

"Your Highness," the soldier said, his voice low. "Word has been sent through the gate. The queen comes."

Your Highness? Eilidh bit back the words she wanted to scream at Griogair. By telling them his true identity, he had risked everything—the fate of every soul hidden at Oron's and a rich vein of astral power. How many would die if the army turned on itself?

Patrols continued to arrive at the island, and some even travelled over the sound to the Scottish mainland and to the other nearby islands. Eilidh picked up enough conversations nearby to understand that the queen's forces surrounded the island before the assault, which was the reason for the long delay before the attack. She was grateful now they hadn't tried to escape as Oron suggested, or they would have been easily netted. Now she prayed to the Father of the Azure that Tràth's time bubble would hold.

Eilidh and Griogair managed to work their way toward Oron's house in the hour it took Cadhla's retinue to arrive. The queen shone magnificently, dressed for battle with an elemental sword that gleamed like ice, hanging from a sheath at her hip. She was surrounded by six *rafta*, who moved with her like a fluid barrier of protection. She approached the elder's house, and the vast crowd grew hushed behind her. "This hovel?" she said with disdain.

One of the commanders approached. "Yes, Your Majesty. We believe this to be the home of the renegade conclave leader Oron. It is where the trail is strongest."

"Could they be invisible? The filthy creatures can perform all kinds of tricks."

"My Watchers have covered every inch, swords swinging. It is as though they have turned to mist."

"Invisible mist?" the queen said, her ruby lips curling into a sneer.

Eilidh stood close to Griogair, hidden in the crowd. She leaned close and whispered to him, "Can she sense them?"

He subtly shook his head. "She is gifted with water and air, with the slightest touch of fire, but she cannot wield the stone flows. She will have to rely on others for that."

Cadhla scowled. "Bring me the trackers again."

The *rafta* gathered and brought twenty of her soldiers before her, and she questioned them relentlessly. But they described the scene much the same as Griogair had when he sensed Tràth in Auchterarder, insisting that the trail deceived them.

Griogair whispered to Eilidh, "Now would be a good time for Oron to confuse the issue, but delicately."

Eilidh hadn't been able to find Oron and the others again, but then she'd been carefully avoiding the *rafta*. She hoped they were safe, hiding as they'd agreed. She sent him the mind-speak message: *Muddle the queen's trackers. Be subtle.*

Eilidh wanted to aid them, but she left the work to Oron's people. She worried her unpractised skills would call more attention than they wanted.

The queen looked to the *rafta*. "Send out more patrols. This could be a ruse to keep us rooted to one place."

"Your Majesty," one of the trackers said. "The trail we sensed here. It's fading. I fear you may be right."

Cadhla waved the *wen-lei* over. "See, it is as I suspected. You have let your weak minds be fooled by enchantments, which likely broke as soon as the azuri got too far away." She growled. "They're probably in Andena by now. That bitch of a queen Vinye will no doubt give them refuge." She glared at the *rafta* leader. "Take your men and make one last sweep of the island to be certain, then return to the Otherworld to meet your replacement. You have disappointed me."

He bowed before the queen. "I hear and obey." He signalled to the other *rafta*. Most followed him, but Eilidh noticed a few did not. *Oron*, she thought with relief. It comforted her to know he was near.

The queen, unfortunately, noticed too. "You," she said, pointing across the crowd to one of the *rafta* who had not moved to follow his leader. "Come before your queen." She stepped forward, her voice quiet and menacing.

"It has to be now," the prince muttered. Griogair moved to intercept her, brushing off Eilidh's hands as she tried to hold him back. She couldn't help but notice his barely perceptible signals to others in the crowd. When he stood just a few feet in front of the queen, he bowed and said, "Show my face."

For a moment, Cadhla looked confused. "What?" she demanded.

He rose and looked the queen in the eye. "Show my face!" he shouted.

Eilidh hesitated out of pure fear. This could ruin everything. Two soldiers stepped to either side of Eilidh, and one whispered, "Please, do as he asks. We will protect you."

"Griogair?" the queen said, staring in disbelief. "You sound like my mate."

Eilidh concentrated on dropping his illusion, but maintaining her own. It took some care, and the result was that his false face melted away slowly, revealing the prince's identity. The crowd of soldiers gasped.

"I am not your mate," Griogair said. "Remember? You severed our relationship so you could order my death."

"Where is your little dog, Griogair?" she spat. "She must be near to have worked her twisted illusions on you."

Soldiers looked around uncomfortably, as though just realising any one of them could be an azuri in disguise.

"You mean the azuri queen? Her Royal Majesty, Eilidh of Skye?"

Cadhla laughed. "That exiled so-called conclave has raised a false queen? That insignificant commoner? They deserve her."

"They do," Griogair agreed, which caused her laughter to cut short. "And she is twice the queen you have ever been."

The queen looked to the nearest soldiers. "What are you doing gawping?" she shouted. "Arrest the traitor."

A few moved forward, but much to the queen's shock, the commanders shouted for them to stand down. A ring of senior soldiers formed around the queen and Griogair, swords raised and pointed at Cadhla. The air crackled with unspoken magic.

Eilidh heard rumbling in the crowd as word went back through the ranks.

Suddenly an elemental sword appeared in Griogair's hand. It gleamed like polished silver, but green light shimmered inside its core. He stepped up to the queen and before she could react, he held it to her throat. "Goodbye, Cadhla. This is for Tràth."

"No!" Eilidh shouted. She shoved her way through the ranks to the ring of soldiers. "Griogair, no!" She met Cadhla's eyes. "Surrender to me, and I will spare your life."

"So it is you," the queen said, her face tilted away to avoid the sharp blade at her neck.

Suddenly Eilidh's illusion began to shift, but it was not her doing. Her soldier's uniform turned to a long gown of deep blue, its bodice covered with diamonds. Long sleeves trailed the ground in points at the backs of her wrist, and she felt the weight of a crown on her temple. Shimmering wings sprouted from her back, sending a murmur of awe through the crowd.

Griogair glanced at Eilidh, staring, as though unable to take his eyes off her. "Cadhla must die for her crimes against our people. For the darkness and ignorance she has worked to spread. For the lives she took. For the lost fae children. For the execution of innocents. For the division in our people that never should have come to pass." With effort he looked back at Cadhla. "For our son."

"Your son," Cadhla spat. "Do it," she taunted him. "I've always known you wanted me dead, wanted my power for your own."

The prince brought back the sword to swing it, but Eilidh sent the shout *No* in her thoughts, the word echoing in the minds around them.

"Griogair, you made me a promise." Eilidh raised her voice to quiet the murmuring crowd. "To give me anything I asked in exchange for finding and restoring your son to you. I have done my part. This is what I ask. Release her to me, and I will accept her surrender and keep the kingdom whole. Let the kingdom's own conclave declare her crown broken. She will be allowed to live in exile in the Halls of Mist, or any other kingdom she chooses, but not Caledonia and not the realm of men."

"Eilidh," Griogair pleaded. "Not this."

"If you kill her, you are no better than she is. Show your people that you are merciful. Let them see you look for justice, not revenge." Then she added, "Or show me that your promise was empty." She hated to manipulate him, but he was too overwrought to see the consequences killing Cadhla would bring, how much that action would complicate their position.

The prince's inner struggle played out across his features, twisting his brow into a deep scowl. Cadhla closed her eyes, defeated. She clearly expected the sword to fall on her neck. But the prince withdrew the earth power that conjured the sword, and the weapon disappeared.

"Cadhla," Eilidh said. "Speak the words of surrender and I will spare your life. If you do not, I will not weep at your passing as Griogair takes your head."

Cadhla looked from her former mate to Eilidh, then to the commanders around her. "It was clever," she said to Griogair, "to trick me into sending my *rafta* away, the only ones with whom you have no influence. I'm shocked to see so many have fallen for your lies, that the corruption of our people runs so deep."

Eilidh pushed her fear aside with some effort, even though the queen had been surrounded. Eilidh knew Cadhla, with her centuries of experience, more than matched her own untrained abilities. "Your words of surrender and no others," she said. "I am tired of your speeches."

Cadhla shouted, "Remember your loyalty. This usurper cannot be trusted. She lies and changes her words as easily as she changes her face. She is twisting your minds, making you question your rightful queen. Resist. Be strong of mind and resist her deceits." Then the queen smiled at Eilidh, a gleam in her eye. "My *rafta* have returned."

A volley of blue-flamed arrows went up overhead. Eilidh was jostled to the ground as soldiers moved quickly and hands grabbed her roughly from all sides. The queen yelled, "Kill the traitors. Steel your minds against their illusions!"

Eilidh was dragged away from Griogair and the queen, but not before she heard him let out a long, anguished shout. She couldn't see for all the faeries around her, pulling her this way and that, or hear for all the shouting and chaos. Swords clashed, arrows flew, the earth shook, and lightning flashed in the sky. Monster dragons flew overhead, and Eilidh knew Oron and the other elders were taking part, trying their best to scatter any soldiers still loyal to Cadhla.

It broke her heart to hear the screams and sickening sounds as faeries fell to the ground dead. Although she had access to earth magic through Munro, Eilidh never learned combat with the elements. Still, even though bodies pressed in around her, some trying to defend her, some wishing to attack her, she had no desire to spill one drop of fae blood.

Suddenly the soldiers around her, who fought to protect her, melted away, and six *rafta* descended on her. She felt anguished. They would kill her, and she would never be able to save Tràth and the hundreds of others hidden with him. She only hoped Oron and the druids survived, praying they would be able to help him where she had failed.

The *rafta* grabbed her and one said, “Tell them the queen is dead. Quickly.”

“What?” she said, dazed. “Cadhla is—”

“Mind-speak, Eilidh. Tell them their queen has fallen, so we can save as many lives as possible.” The face in front of her changed to that of the elder Qwe.

Eilidh nearly wept with relief as she closed her eyes and sent the message to every mind within a hundred miles.

CHAPTER 21

THE BATTLE ENDED QUICKLY with word of Cadhla's death. The commanders loyal to Griogair took control, and he regained some semblance of order. Amnesty was given to all except the *rafta*, and Eilidh was pleased that Griogair proved to be even-handed and merciful.

Although many looked to her to give orders and take control immediately, Eilidh refused, saying the Caledonian conclave should raise a queen to replace Cadhla from among the Caledonian nobility, with no suggestion of who they should choose.

"They will choose you," Griogair said to her after she delivered the message to his commanders, asking them to convey her offer of peace to their conclave. A cheer went up around them, as hundreds of soldiers waited to hear her response.

The elders and Griogair had orchestrated this moment, as well as given her the proper response.

"If asked to serve my people, I will do so," she said, bowing slightly to the prince. "On one condition."

The cheers stopped, and a hush went through the crowd.

"What is that, Lady Eilidh?"

"That you become my prince-consort and rule by my side." She smiled at him, doing her best to hide how tired she felt. "If the conclave wills that I serve."

Griogair returned her smile and bowed deeply, but his answer was drowned out by further cheers. Eilidh knew the jubilant reaction wasn't universal, that many had yet to be won over. Some fears would take a long time to quiet, but it was a start.

Only then did she see Munro staring at her from the crowd. She wanted nothing more than to run to him, but she carefully maintained her bearing. Relief flooded over her when he smiled and began to push his way through the fae soldiers, followed by the other druids. She whispered to one of those who still guarded her to tell the others to let the humans pass.

When they approached, Munro bowed low. "My lady," he said, then rose, meeting her eyes boldly. She had to smile at the way he spoke the words so possessively, asserting that even though she'd just publicly proposed to another, she would always be *his* lady.

She tilted her head in formal acknowledgement, then leaned forward to whisper, "Now the hard part begins."

Munro nodded and whispered back, "Wings?"

She couldn't help but laugh and was pleased to see the surprised, yet happy expressions on the fae soldiers' faces. They would have to get used to a queen who laughed.

The pair gathered the druids and Griogair and repeated the ritual they had performed to bring Tràth back from the time-warped dimension where he'd hidden the azuri. The kingdom faeries stared at Eilidh in awe, even though it was Griogair's love for his son, the druid's connection and Munro's star talisman that allowed her to link to Tràth's magic and make the entire colony reappear in a stunning flash of blue light. Part of her wanted to insist she didn't deserve the accolades, but instead she stood and smiled serenely as the newly returned azuri all bowed before her upon their return.

∞

The ancient coronation ceremony was simple. A mere two weeks later, with only the two conclaves, Eilidh, Munro, Griogair, Tràth, and her father in attendance as her honoured guests and witnesses, she went to a sacred grove in the Caledonian Otherworld. This marked the beginning of a month of public ceremonies and appearances, orchestrated so every faerie would have the opportunity to see the new queen. There were also many pending meetings to negotiate how the azuri Higher Conclave and the recognised kingdom conclave would work together, but this moment marked private communion between Eilidh and the Mother of the Earth and the Father of the Azure. For the first time in a millennium, the Father had been recognised during a coronation, but Eilidh insisted, and none objected.

She stood nude in the centre of a circle of trees, with all witnesses standing outside the barriers looking in. She knelt before the largest tree and picked up a knife that lay on the ground inside the sacred circle. With one smooth movement, she cut her left palm and then her right, squeezing her hands together, blood dripping into the earth.

"I come before you humbly, Mother of the Earth and Father of the Azure, and swear with my blood to serve you and your people, to let no voice be louder than your own, to act with justice and with mercy, to remember always that my every breath belongs to my kingdom, from this day until the last of all days, in this realm and beyond."

Tears welled in Eilidh's eyes. When she'd memorised the ceremony, it seemed simple compared to the daunting public meetings she would face in the weeks ahead. But kneeling now, looking up at the full blue moon overhead, Eilidh wept, feeling unworthy of the titles she was about to receive, of the burdens and responsibilities she would soon bear.

She felt Munro, standing nearby, his presence filled with pride and love. It propped her up, and she inhaled the night air, drinking in his strength.

Standing, she turned and faced the highest of the kingdom conclave, Setir. He walked toward her, breaking the circle, followed by the other eleven of his assembly. He lifted a delicate diamond crown over her head. "In the name of the Mother and of the Father, we consecrate Lady Eilidh of Caledonia and Skye as their holy servant and lift her up as first among us."

He smiled, and she felt a cloak of fur being wrapped around her shoulders. "Queen Eilidh," he said. Then he and the entire company knelt.

She solemnly looked around. Every person she cared most about was in the glade. She promised herself not to let them down. "Rise, my friends," she said. She went to them one by one speaking ritual words of promise as the last part of the ceremony. First she approached the members of the kingdom conclave, then the azuri conclave, then Griogair and Tràth, then to her father, who embraced her. Although Munro was human, and many had argued against him witnessing the sacred ceremony, Eilidh spoke to him as well. As with all the others, she kept her voice low, because her promise to him was for him alone. "I will always honour the sacrifices you have made, druid," she said, then leaned forward and whispered. "I love my people, but you will always have my heart."

He nodded but didn't reply. Eilidh knew the changes were overwhelming, that he feared they would grow apart once she mated with Griogair the following night. Munro wasn't certain how he would fit into this new world, but she had faith. Despite the battles, death, destruction and heartbreak caused by Cadhla, as well as the confusion felt by many at the quick raising of an unknown outcast faerie to rule them, Eilidh believed they would make it through. The future would be better, she could make changes that mattered, and save lives.

∞

Munro hoped to have one last night with Eilidh, but after the coronation, elders shuttled her off to meetings that clearly did not include him. It felt good to be in the Otherworld again, and one of Eilidh's first decrees had been to invite the remaining azuri fae and the druids to the kingdom.

He went back to the Skye gate with Tràth to deliver the word and meet the druids. It turned out bringing Tràth back the second time was easier and more straightforward than the first. Tràth was getting stronger, and Munro wondered what else the temporal faerie could do. As they travelled from the Skye gate back to the azuri village, he asked the prince what he knew about temporal magic.

"I don't know anything about it," Tràth replied. "What does anyone know about it?"

Munro chuckled. He liked Tràth. He was like Griogair, but less hard, more open, and less subtle. "Nothing, as far as I understand."

"Will you teach me what you know about bonding? Queen Eilidh had said she would, but she is…"

"Yeah, occupied." Munro expected her distance. The coronation, the royal wedding, all the public appearances. knowing it was coming didn't make it less difficult. He sensed her tiredness, her inner conflict and how overwhelmed she felt. "Sure," he said to Tràth. "Creating the bond is easy. Living with it afterward is hard."

"You love her. I can see that," Tràth said. "It must be difficult, knowing she will take my father as her mate. Does it make things awkward between us? Should I not have asked for your help?"

"No," Munro said. "Eilidh has a duty. I understand duty." They ran in silence for a few minutes before he said, "When Eilidh and I bonded, we said the words *dem'ontar-che.*"

Tràth looked surprised. "Those are sacred words of extreme power, but of servitude. Even our mating ceremonies do not require such bondage."

Munro smiled. "Now you know why I'm not worried about Eilidh marrying your father."

"Yes, her vow to you would supersede all others, even perhaps her coronation vows."

"You don't have to worry about that. Eilidh will never choose me over her people." They slowed down as they neared the village. "I wouldn't let her, even if she wanted to."

Tràth inclined his head. "You do understand duty, Munro." They walked slowly toward the house. "How do we say the words? Do we need a priest or a ceremony?"

"Eilidh and I weren't even together when we said our words. I barely even knew what I was saying. I was so delirious and sick from the recent unlocking of my druidic powers. Eilidh said them with Beniss, an azuri elder, but she wasn't any kind of priest or anything. She only rushed to say them because a blood faerie was cutting out my heart at the time." Munro chuckled at the way Tràth went pale. "Look, there's no rush. Say them right now if you want. Douglas will say them when he's ready. Believe me, you'll know if it happens. Or take your time and say them next year, in five years. I'll be around. I'll tell you what happened with me, but I can't promise that's what'll happen for you. I don't think there are any experts alive on this subject. If there were, I certainly wouldn't be one."

Tràth nodded.

"The druids won't be able to run as fast or as long as you can, at least until we get to the Otherworld, if it works the same for them as it did for me. My abilities might have been due to the Otherworld air, or maybe it was my bond to Eilidh. Who knows? I get the feeling I'm the first human in a long time to visit the faerie realm. We'll talk as we travel. It'll give all of us, the azuri fae as well, a chance to discuss how bonding happens. They seem to think we just pick someone, but it doesn't work like that."

Tràth nodded. "When I first saw Douglas, I knew he felt different. I wondered if he was perhaps part fae. And the more time we spent together, the more it seemed as though I'd known him all my life, like a twin, or a part of me that had been missing."

Munro nodded. He knew that sensation well. He'd never thought of Eilidh as a sister, but then, he supposed it could work differently for everyone.

When they arrived at the druid house, they found it empty, so they headed for the village hall. Munro was surprised that every faerie from the azuri colony plus all the refugees from other kingdoms were there, ready and waiting to go. They buzzed with excitement, and he and Tràth were deluged with questions about the coronation.

The azuri were content to travel the forests at a slow enough pace to match the speed and strength of the human druids, just to give them more chances to hear the story over again. It made Munro proud, the way they spoke of Eilidh with such respect and reverence. The way she'd tried to spare Cadhla's life was already a thing of legend. When Tràth heard about his mother's death, he took it quietly, but nodded when he learned Eilidh had tried to show her mercy.

It was nearly daybreak when they arrived at the Skye gate hours later. Some fae passed through eagerly, others waited, staring up at its shining metal bars. All made it through before the gates closed at dawn.

Munro stayed close to the druids. As had happened to him, they each experienced a powerful reaction. Rory fell to his knees. Aaron became violently ill, but once his stomach had purged, he quickly recovered. Phillip's reaction was more sedate, but Munro could see the intense satisfaction as he breathed in the Otherworld air. Douglas wept openly as he stood beside Tràth.

"I feel great," Rory said suddenly as he got to his feet. He grinned at Munro, and his pale blue eyes started to shine.

They stood in a forest not too different from the one they'd left behind on Skye, surrounded by azuri fae who watched the process with fascination. As with the forest near the Ashdawn gate, Munro could tell it wasn't anywhere on earth with its glowing plants and deep, loamy air.

Soon, a host of kingdom faeries emerged from the forests around them, smiling and welcoming the azuri like long-lost brothers, which Munro supposed they were. What surprised him most, though, was that Griogair led the group. "Welcome home," he said. "We have made a place for you in the city of Canerecht. Your elders are there awaiting your arrival. If you have family and homes you remember, you may return, of course. If you do not, we will provide whatever you need while you find your place. Queen Eilidh has sworn that none of you will be persecuted and you can make your way as you please in the realm without fear."

The druids recovered from the shock of arrival into the Otherworld as Griogair made formal greetings to many of the azuri. The kingdom fae mingled among the newcomers, making them feel welcome and safe. After a short while, the prince made a beeline for Tràth and Munro. "The wedding is at nightfall. I expect you both to be there." He furrowed his brow at the pair.

Tràth tilted his head. "Of course, Father."

Griogair exhaled with relief. He must have worried his son would not welcome his new step-mother and might make a public spectacle. So far, Munro had no idea why everyone thought Tràth was such a problem. They spoke about him like he was a renegade, but Munro hadn't seen anything like that.

"And you, druid?" Griogair asked quietly.

"If it's all the same to you, *Your Highness*, I think I'll skip it."

"It isn't," Griogair said. "Please. This is something I need you to do. It is part of my wedding gift for Eilidh. If you will not watch the ceremony, then find Oron before it begins. He will show you where you can wait for me."

"Nothing sounds more torturous," Munro said. "But fine, I'll be there."

"Thank you," Griogair replied. He hurried away before Munro could object further.

"God, what an ass," he muttered. Realising who was standing nearby, he added, "Sorry, I forget he's your dad."

Tràth laughed. "No need to worry. I find your irreverence refreshing. It will do him good to have you around, I think."

"I suppose if we're going to the wedding, we can't go to Canerecht to see the new settlement yet."

"No, we should go to the Wayfinder Palace. It will be many hours before the ceremony starts, but I am sure there are seamstresses waiting to put me into some ridiculous formal clothing. I'm sure they'll want to put feathers on you too."

"No way," Munro said, then laughed when he realised Tràth had been joking. "I'm not going to the ceremony. I'll go find Oron, like Griogair said. If he's going to do something nice for Eilidh, what kind of sod would I be to not want to help? But I can't watch the wedding." The dread was building in his stomach already. "They can't ask me to watch."

∞

Eilidh sat stiffly in the anteroom in a daze. If the coronation had been simple and profound, her mating ceremony was like nothing she'd ever imagined. She knew millions of fae made up her new kingdom, but she hadn't expected hundreds of thousands would turn out to witness the ritual. Her handmaidens, none of whom she knew, giggled at her wide-eyed surprise.

She and Griogair met on a dais of sparkling crystals, lifted high above the open-air courtyard filled with fae nobles. She only vaguely remembered the vows they made to one another, the silk ribbons that bound their hands together as they spoke well-practised words. Griogair smiled at her kindly, whispering encouragements when she felt most overwhelmed. "Almost there," he said.

Voices, gentle hands, and guiding faces led her from one part of the ceremony to the other, until at last, her mind buzzing, barely able to take it all in, she and Griogair walked arm in arm down a mile-long promenade, the voices of thousands of their people cheering and shouting blessings and well-wishes. When they got to the end, he took her hand lightly and kissed it. "Don't be afraid," he said.

They parted and went into identical tents at the edge of the palace grounds. To call it a tent was perhaps an understatement. It was larger than Munro's home back in Perth. Her heart ached as she thought of her druid. She had anticipated he would stay in the human realm during her first night with Griogair, but she could feel Munro close. Throughout the entire evening, she'd thought of little besides him. Part of her wanted to run away, but somehow she managed to keep one foot moving in front of the other.

Her handmaidens removed her elaborate sky-blue wedding dress. She was grateful, because she didn't think she could take it off without them. She longed for her jeans and 'Visit Scotland' sweatshirt, her tennis shoes and slouchy socks. Her mind went to the day when Munro bought her those clothes. Back then she'd had no idea she would be sitting here. She sighed.

"What is it, Your Majesty?" one of the young faerie women asked her.

"Sasha, is it?" Eilidh said.

"Sharylia," the girl replied.

"I'm sorry," Eilidh said. "Sharylia." The girls all gasped. Queens don't apologise, Eilidh reminded herself.

"Is something wrong, Your Majesty?"

"No," Eilidh said. "I was just thinking of tonight. Of my mate."

The girls exchanged glances, working to help Eilidh remove the complicated undergarments that gave the extravagant dress its shape.

"You needn't worry," Sharylia said. "If I may be so bold as to say, His Highness seems a most kind faerie, noble in every sense. He will be gentle if, perhaps, you have not before..."

Eilidh stared. For a faerie of a hundred and twenty-five to have remained a virgin was ridiculous, but it was not the most ludicrous of the rumours she'd heard springing up about her already.

"I'm sure he will," she said softly. It was time. She stood before them naked, and they slipped a sheer robe around her.

"Are you ready, Your Majesty?" one of the girls asked.

No, she thought, but nodded. She let her thoughts caress the connection with Munro, then as she promised, she erected a wall between them. As much as she wanted to feel his love and strength, she would not make him endure her sorrow as she lay with Griogair.

One of the girls pulled a cord, and the back of the tent opened. Eilidh walked through, her head held high. Dozens of attendants beamed at her and guided her to the centre of the path behind the palace walls. She looked up to see a servant guiding Griogair forward. He wore a robe identical to her own, a tradition of the consummation ceremony.

He looked nervous, and that endeared her to him. She'd never seen him look anything but cocky and self-assured. She reminded herself that while she made personal sacrifices, he did too, and she must always honour that. When they met on the pebble walkway, he said nothing. He simply held his arm out to her, and she took it lightly.

They walked down the path, through the last remaining attendants, until finally they were alone, followed at a distance by four priests who would discretely witness their completion. They didn't speak as they walked the flower-strewn path to the immense bed, suspended between four towering trees. Faint blue lights danced in the clearing. It was everything Eilidh could have wanted, if only she could have been there with Munro. A tear slid down her cheek, and Griogair saw it. He frowned and looked sad as well. With a tender swipe of the back of his finger, he wiped the tear away, leaned close and whispered, "Don't cry."

She pulled away from him. "I can't do this," she said softly. "Please. Tell them I was too afraid. Tell them anything. Tell them I'm like ice with no passion in me, but I can't do this."

A smile quirked across Griogair's face unexpectedly.

"What?" she hissed. "Is this funny to you?"

"Eilidh, it's me. Open the bond. It's me."

Eilidh stared. "Quinton?" She stepped closer, glancing around to make sure the witnessing priests were too far to hear. Fearful she would find it to be a lie when she opened the bond, she did it anyway. As soon as she did, she felt Munro's presence right in front of her, ringing with amusement. "Griogair agreed to this?" she asked, stunned.

"It was his idea. His gift to you."

"The ceremony..."

"That was him," Munro said. "He explained that an illusion would have disguised my appearance, but not fooled the laws of magic. I'm not sure what that means, but he said you would understand."

Eilidh nodded. "The mating rite is a magical ceremony, not just a formality or for appearances. Illusion can deceive the mind of human and fae but not the Source. For our union to be legitimate, it had to be Griogair saying the words with his own lips."

"But this part, Griogair said, was more tradition than law, and he wouldn't force you." Munro lowered his head. "Not after everything you've done and been through. I have to say, it was decent of him."

"When did you switch?"

"Oron cast the illusion in the tent. He took both me and Griogair aside, much to the consternation of those attendant guys. A little confusion, a little illusion, and we exchanged faces. Unfortunately for him, he gets to spend the evening with Oron. They can't go too far away or the illusions drop," Munro explained. "Oron is the only one who knows, but Griogair trusts him to keep our secret. So do I."

Eilidh nodded and smiled, wrapping her arms around Munro's neck. When he leaned forward and kissed her, she melted into his arms, only two thin layers of sheer material separating them. "It is peculiar, hearing your voice from his mouth, seeing you in his body."

"Yeah, it feels strange. I can't even bring myself to look down."

Eilidh laughed. "Will you think me unfaithful if I do?"

With a tender stroke of her cheek, Munro said, "I wouldn't have thought that even if this really was Griogair standing here. Your body is yours. I have your heart, and I remember the sacred words you said to me. I would never think you unfaithful." He paused and peered into the forest. "Are they really going to watch?" he asked.

With a mischievous grin Eilidh replied, "Only the first time. After that they leave us until daybreak."

Munro reached down and swept her into his arms, laying her gently on the bed. "Griogair warned me I'd better live up to his reputation. I think we can give them something to talk about."

Eilidh let her worries float away as she and Munro had one night of happiness. They didn't think about the conflicts, the burdens, the sacrifices to come, or the difficult road ahead. Despite her coronation and the magnificent ceremony where she took Prince Griogair as her mate, her people were divided, with a young queen who didn't yet know how to rule. The Halls of Mist would never be the same, now that Caledonia had an azuri queen.

A NOTE FROM THE AUTHOR

Thank you so much for reading Azuri Fae, the second book in the Caledonia Fae series. If you enjoyed it, please take a moment to leave a review at your favourite online retailer.

I welcome contact from readers. At my website, you can contact me, sign up for my newsletter to be notified of new releases, read my blog, and find me on social networking.

—India Drummond

Author website: http://www.indiadrummond.com
Reader email: author@indiadrummond.com

The Caledonia Fae Series

Book 1: Blood Faerie

Unjustly sentenced to death, Eilidh ran—away from faerie lands, to the streets of Perth, Scotland. Just as she has grown accustomed to exile, local police discover a mutilated body outside the abandoned church where she lives. Recognising the murder as the work of one of her own kind, Eilidh must choose: flee, or learn to tap into the forbidden magic that cost her everything.

Book 2: Azuri Fae

A faerie prince disappears in the borderlands, and his father enlists the help of outcast Eilidh and her bonded druid, Quinton Munro. Tantalised with hints of a lost and ancient magic, they learn that time is working against them every step of the way. Is the prince's disappearance related to the vanishing of an entire Scottish village?

Faced with deception, assassination attempts, and a mad queen who would sacrifice her own child to keep a dreaded secret, Eilidh struggles with an impossible situation. Her people demand she commit treason and betray the man she loves. Will she do what duty requires, or throw away the chance to reunite the kingdom in exchange for the life she hadn't dared hope for?

Book 3: Enemy of the Fae

With a young, inexperienced monarch on the Caledonian throne and traitorous plots implicating those nearest Queen Eilidh, unrest is rife in the kingdom. She must sift through the intrigues and lies to survive, all while trying to discover which of her trusted companions hates her enough to commit mass murder.

Pressures threaten to overcome the young ruler, and to protect Quinton Munro, her bonded druid, she must send him away. His journey becomes a mission when he stumbles on an ancient truth that will shake the foundations of the entire faerie realm. Confronted by infinite danger and the promise of limitless power, Munro faces the most difficult choices of his life. Will he hide the truth to preserve stability in the faerie kingdoms or embrace the promise of his true druid heritage?

One friend will die because of that truth, one friend's betrayal will cause irreparable scars, and the once tightly-knit band of druids will learn that not all magic is benevolent.

Book 4: Druid Lords

The druids of Caledonia have taken their place in the Halls of Mist, only to learn that their path is fraught with many dangers. When their newest member, Huck Webster, finds a woman of magical talents in Amsterdam, their troubles multiply. Lying between them and a peaceful existence are a dead prince, a furious queen, and a druid accused of murder. Each druid must search his soul and discover where his talents, and his loyalties, lie.

Book 5: Elder Druid

As the Druid Hall celebrates the completion of the Mistgate, their leader Munro is abducted, leaving them in disarray. Queen Eilidh declares Munro dead, which threatens the fragile balance of power in the Halls of Mist. With the druids crippled by grief and uncertainty, no one notices the insidious force influencing them from a dark mirror realm.

That force has a voice, a sinister whisper in Lord Druid Douglas' ear, compelling him to feed the Source Stone and driving a wedge between him and his companions. Trath's magic could protect the druid lord, but the prince has fled heartbreak in search of a different life. But will his quest bring redemption or ruin?

Book 6: Age of Druids

Imprisoned by the demons of The Bleak, two lost druids fight to survive while Munro pushes himself to the brink to find them. In his search, he discovers a mysterious gate even the oldest and wisest of the Otherworld fear.

The Halls of Mists are in ruin, and people scheme, grasping at power as a new kingdom emerges and an ancient one reappears. Tragedy pits druid against queen, testing friendship, loyalty, and love once more.

Who will survive and who will be lost forever as desperation drives some to unthinkable ends?

Printed in Great Britain
by Amazon.co.uk, Ltd.,
Marston Gate.